Rude Awakening

Jacqueline James

SilverWood

Published in 2021 by SilverWood Books

SilverWood Books Ltd
14 Small Street, Bristol, BS1 1DE, United Kingdom
www.silverwoodbooks.co.uk

ISBN 978-1-80042-029-8 (paperback)
ISBN 978-1-80042-030-4 (ebook)

British Library Cataloguing in Publication Data
A CIP catalogue record for this book is
available from the British Library

Page design and typesetting by SilverWood Books

Rude Awakening

For my mother and father – Joyce and Viv

Chapter One

New Year's Eve Party

New Year's Eve. Barwell, a small town. Prosperous…safe…boring. A place where the residents are more likely to tut than take up arms, more likely to be seen weighing a parcel than waving a placard. A place where news is to be read and discussed, not made. A frustrating nightmare of a place for tumultuous teenagers, but a haven for women of a certain age, with pleasant places to shop and lunch. The women wear stylish clothes, hair carefully coiffed, with children in fancy buggies, the car parks full of four-by-fours and well polished hatchbacks. Driving around the town, a newcomer might be pleasantly surprised by its cleanliness and sense of order. The roads are swept, the houses look well cared for, hedges clipped, lawns mown, borders weeded, and cars cleaned and parked neatly on block-paving drives.

As a nurse, living and working in the town, Suzanne knew that some of the pristine net curtains hid terrible secrets. She knew how drugs and alcohol could wreak havoc on lives, however neat it all looked from the outside. But, like the neatly lined-up lidded wheelie bins, all the dirt and rubbish was safely hidden from view.

Suzanne surveyed her kitchen. The black gloss of the cupboard doors reflected the food prepared, ready to be cooked, and trays of canapés awaiting a finishing touch. She could hear the rattle of bottles as David checked the wine fridge in the dining room. It was almost time for their friends to arrive for what had now become an annual New Year's Eve party at their large, rather ungainly, mock Tudor house overlooking the golf course. The house was set back from the road, shielded by majestic chestnut trees, higher than the house and protected by the law, their massive roots pushing up the pavements in unwieldy lumps. The ever-expanding town meant that the once quiet tree-lined road was now a busy thoroughfare linking the town and the retail park. Suzanne still had to pinch herself sometimes to believe that she lived in this huge house with a garden measured in parts of an acre, beech hedges and herbaceous borders gently sloping down to the golf course. She loved the view from her kitchen, the sense of space it gave her. She revelled in being set apart from her neighbours. She remembered David laughing when she had walked all the way around the outside of the house when she first moved in. How privileged she had felt.

They had invited four couples to the party, friends they enjoyed spending time with, loosely connected, good company. Earlier in the week, Suzanne had bumped into Hilary, who lived in the bungalow opposite, running an errand with her mother. Hilary had seemed a little fraught, so Suzanne, out of pity, had invited both of them to the party. She half regretted the invitation, but David was uncharacteristically delighted. He admitted that he needed to get on Hilary's mother's good side as she had some sway with the planning committee and he was still having problems getting planning permission for a new build on the edge of town. Hilary knew everyone who was coming to the party and they all knew Hilary. In the end, Hilary phoned to say her mother wouldn't be attending, leaving an odd number for dinner.

Across the road, in her sprawling bungalow, Hilary was getting ready. "Does this look all right, Mum?"

Phyllis looked up from her crossword, her feet raised on her velveteen recliner, the soles of her red plush slippers at attention, repelling all boarders. She put her pen down, removed her reading glasses from her nose and studied Hilary, who stood apprehensively in the doorway.

"Very nice dear. I've always liked that frock. Black is so forgiving. Your hair looks nice and neat – you've got a lovely shine on it. But can I see a few grey hairs?" She chuckled. "My little girl with grey hair. Whatever next? Will those shoes be comfortable? It'll be a late night."

Hilary looked down at the black patent kitten-heel shoes she kept for special occasions. They weren't especially comfortable, but she liked the look of them and she'd be sitting down for most of the evening anyway.

"If I were you, I'd put on those flat velvet pumps with the bow that you got last year. You'd feel much better in them."

Hilary returned to her bedroom and did as she was bidden without a second thought. She returned her best shoes to their tissue-lined box and looked in the mirror on her dark wood wardrobe. Her mousy reflection stared back at her, face matt with pale powder, lips slightly pinker than normal, a suggestion of mascara on her lashes.

She returned to the living room for her mother's approval and was reassured by the positive response.

"I wish you were coming too. I hate leaving you on New Year's Eve."

"You know I never do anything for New Year – can't see the attraction. Your father and I never did anything, did we? Christmas was our thing, wasn't it? It's so nice of Suzanne and David to invite you to their posh do, though."

"It's not posh and you know all the people who are going. You'd enjoy it if you came, but I know you prefer to get to bed early. I'll come and say happy New Year if you are still awake when I get in. I shouldn't be late. It'll finish after the fireworks at the golf club… They have a great view of the display from their conservatory. I expect the noise will keep you awake anyway. Do you need anything before I go?"

"No. Stop fussing. I can get what I need and you're only across the road. There's a James Bond film on that I don't think I've seen. I'll watch that if I get this crossword finished in time. So, you get off. Have a nice time. Give my love to them if they remember me."

Of course, they'll remember you, what a silly thing to say, thought Hilary as she kissed her mum on the cheek.

She checked the kitchen to make sure that everything her mother might need was to hand. She half-filled the kettle in case Phyllis wanted a cup of coffee, and put the chocolate biscuits and bottle of Baileys within easy reach. Then, collecting her coat from the cloakroom by the front door, she stepped out, calling "Bye" over her shoulder.

The cold hit her as she hurried across the road and up the drive to Suzanne's imposing house. She could see through the brightly lit windows that everyone else was already there. She rang the bell, feeling a little nervous. The door was immediately opened by David and her muttered apology was swamped in a bear-like hug. Releasing her, he boomed, "Nearest one always last to arrive." He took her coat, put a glass of Prosecco in her hand in one smooth movement and half pushed her into the middle of the living room, abandoning her to a chorus of "Hello" and "How are you?", and air kisses from all directions. Then, just as suddenly, they went back to their conversations, leaving her marooned.

Suzanne rescued her, saying, "You've arrived just in time to give me a hand, if you don't mind."

Gratefully, she followed Suzanne into the immaculate kitchen, putting her glass on a sparkly counter already laden with all manner of dishes in various stages of readiness.

"Right, what would you like me to do?"

Her New Year's Eve had begun.

In the living room, the noise level rose, as David made sure the glasses stayed topped up.

"Any more, ladies?" He bent towards the three women comfortably ensconced on the settee, grinning as they eagerly lifted their glasses towards him.

"Should we be doing anything?"

"Can we help?"

Janet and Carol spoke at the same time.

"No. Hilary's in the kitchen helping Suzanne and I think I can manage in here. Just relax." David topped up their glasses and headed for the other side of the lavish sitting room.

Liz sighed, "It's lovely to do nothing for a change, isn't it? Christmas was so hectic." She rested her head against the settee, taking a big gulp from her glass before launching into a description of her 'terrible' Christmas. Liz had Jan's attention, but Carol's mind was wandering. She took a sip of her drink, remembering when she and Liz had first got to know each other. They had been to the same school and she had admired Liz from a distance, marvelled at her confidence, her ability to charm the other girls and the teachers, and how well she did, seemingly without effort. Carol kept her head down and worked, never quite seeming to please the teachers or her parents. Later, they met at the school gates with their own children, but they didn't really get to know each other until one evening, after a rugby club do they'd both been persuaded to attend, when they'd ended up doing the washing up together. Even then, Carol had told Liz that she could manage, thinking that Liz ought to be socialising and not up to her elbows in greasy soapsuds. With a flourish, Liz had removed her numerous gold bangles, hooked them over a milk bottle on the windowsill, rolled up her sleeves, waved aside the proffered rubber gloves and taken over, saying, "I used to really envy you at school and then watching you with your immaculate children."

"You envied *me*?" Carol dropped the tea towel in shock. "But you were a star wherever you were. I longed to be in your set."

Liz replied, "You seemed to just sail through school, never asking questions or badgering the teachers. You just seemed to get everything. I always wanted to be like you, not having to question everything. You seemed to understand straight away. I thought you were so clever, consistently good, not coming to the attention of the teachers. You even had hair that behaved."

Carol laughed, remembering the envy she had felt for Liz's auburn curls. At school, her own straight hair had always been scraped back into a pony tail.

"I was too frightened to ask questions. I just plodded through. Kept my head down, desperately wanting to be exciting, even naughty. And as for immaculate children, I think you must have been looking at someone else's."

The intimacy of the warm, cramped steamy kitchen had invited more confidences, as they revealed that they had both battled the same fears and uncertainties over the years.

A deep belly laugh from the other side of the room brought Carol back to the present.

"I was just thinking of all the things we were going to do when the children left home. What happened?" Liz was saying.

"I remember longing for them to go so that I would have time for myself. I don't know what I've done wrong, but I have less time now than when I was working full-time and bringing up three children." Carol took another long sip of her drink, looking thoughtful.

"I know. You always seem to be dashing somewhere."

"It's just as well Jonathan has cut back on work. He's great with the grandchildren. With my mum and his dad in homes, it's a nightmare."

"At least my parents seem to be coping at the moment. Mum is a bit vague but Dad's still great," Janet said, absently rubbing at the lipstick smudge on the rim of her glass. "I envy you your grandchildren, but work keeps me occupied and I can't see Claire blessing us with any in the foreseeable future."

"What's she doing now?" Liz turned towards Jan.

"Still the same. I wish she didn't have such a long commute. It worries me her getting home so late, but she thrives on it."

Suzanne appeared from the kitchen, managing to look elegant in an apron, her hair breaking loose from its complicated pleat. She perched on the arm of the settee and raised her glass to them.

"All sorted?" Carol asked.

"I think so." She paused to take a smoked salmon blini from the plate offered by Hilary as she made the rounds with the canapés. "You can rest, Hilary. It's all under control."

"I'll just take these around and then find my glass."

"I can't believe I heard her almost moaning about her mother just now," Suzanne confided, as Hilary took the plate to the other side of the room.

"I can't imagine how she puts up with living with her mother."

"She's never known anything different. She didn't even go to university, did she?"

"I struggle when I have to spend more than an hour with Mum. We just about managed Christmas Day without killing each other," said Liz. "She knows she'll have to go into a home if it comes to it. We couldn't have her at home and I certainly wouldn't move in with her."

"We usually spend Christmas with Mum and Dad, but this year, for some reason, Dad wanted us to have time to ourselves. It was lovely, but a bit strange. I think the last time it just the three of us was just after Claire was born."

"Oh, I wouldn't like that, Jan. I need lots of people to make Christmas real," said Carol. "And we certainly had lots of people this year. Our little house was bursting at the seams."

"I do love being at my parents' for Christmas, but whenever I go back, I feel like a fourteen-year-old again. My sister and I start bickering, just like we did when we had to share a bedroom. Didn't you move back in with your mum when she was ill, Suzanne?" asked Jan.

"Yes, I had to. Not an easy time, but there wasn't an alternative."

Hilary chose that moment to return with a bowl of nuts and her still full glass.

Suzanne rose and said, "Come and sit down. I just need to get a couple of things done in the kitchen." She smoothed her apron over her velvet skirt and headed towards the kitchen door, pausing briefly to whisper in David's ear.

The talk of moving back home had unsettled her.

Her father had died in his early forties, suddenly, of a heart attack. Suzanne remembered the anguish she had felt when she had been called to the headmistress's office in the middle of double chemistry. She'd passed the tongs holding the test tube of sulphuric acid over the Bunsen burner to Amelia. Amelia had taken them reluctantly; she hated chemistry experiments and Suzanne always partnered her, covering for her ineptitude. Suzanne had even asked Mrs Beattie if she could stay until the end of the experiment. She could imagine nothing so urgent that it couldn't wait for a few more minutes. That was before she heard the news that her father had collapsed on the golf course, that they hadn't been able to save him, and that her mother needed her at home.

Suzanne was fourteen, just thinking about which O-levels to take. The all-consuming grief following her father's death brought a lump to her throat even now. She had lost her way for some time.

It was her biology teacher, Mr Harcourt, who had put her on the path towards nursing. In front of the whole class, he told her that he wanted to discuss her low marks. She had been embarrassed and had to stay behind when everyone went to lunch. When she burst into tears, he had taken a crumpled tartan hanky from his trouser pocket and let her cry for a few minutes. Then, as if she were any other pupil, he had asked why she thought she had done so badly. He refused to accept her excuse that she couldn't concentrate and that she couldn't see the point of studying.

"You're bright – with a bit of reading you could have done this last test blindfold."

"I don't have time. There's too much else I have to read."

And that was when it all came out – her obsession with the details of the heart and its workings, her need to know why her beloved dad had died. Mr Harcourt said, "Well, if you want to do something useful with all that knowledge, you'd better go into nursing or something." It was like a light coming on in her head. That was it. She could prevent other people's dads from dying too soon.

Later, she realised that he had probably said the first thing that popped into his head so that he could get to the common room to smoke his pipe, but it had somehow shaken her and stopped her wallowing in grief.

She developed a closeness and understanding with her mother that saw her through the rest of school, nursing training and leaving home. She could feel her father's presence at her graduation ceremony, mirroring the pride that showed on her mother's face. As had been destined, she worked in coronary care, relishing the work and the challenges it brought. She had a job she loved, her own little home, good friends and her mother nearby.

But just when her life felt ordered and steady, her mother developed Parkinson's disease. At seventy-two, Jean was devastated by the diagnosis and, as the disease progressed, became depressed and anxious and less willing to go out alone. She was embarrassed by her inability to carry a cup of coffee or a tray in a café. The first time her legs stopped working, mother and daughter were at the supermarket together. Suzanne found Jean bent over her trolley, marooned in the centre of the aisle, other customers trying to manoeuvre around the obstacle she had become.

Suzanne took the lamb from the oven and left it to rest on the countertop. As she stirred the gravy, her thoughts returned to those difficult years.

As her mother's disease had progressed, Suzanne had no time for herself, helping her mother on her days off with shopping, hospital appointments, washing and ironing, cleaning; the list was endless. She knew that by doing everything for her, Jean would be less able to do things herself and would become more dependent, but Suzanne's time was so limited that it was quicker to do everything herself than wait for a mother who moved ever more slowly.

A series of events took place that eventually changed both of their lives for the better. When Jean had a fall at home and was unable to get up, she lay on the bathroom floor for several hours before eventually alerting the neighbours by banging on the wall. The police came and broke into the house, paramedics checked her over, and an ambulance was called.

On hearing that her mother had been brought into the hospital, Suzanne had rushed to be at her side, leaving others to do her work. She recalled the interminable wait for the lift from coronary care, dodging between visitors and slow trolleys in the dash to get to her mother. She had catapulted into the A&E department only to find her mother sitting, uninjured, on a trolley, enjoying a cup of tea and a joke with one of the porters.

Suzanne had taken her home in the car, still feeling annoyed at the disruption to her day. Jean seemed oddly unfazed by the whole episode, talking about it as if it had been a welcome day out, sending Suzanne home and insisting that she would cope.

Standing in her kitchen all these years later, Suzanne suddenly realised that perhaps she hadn't hidden her displeasure as well as she had thought, and perhaps her mother had been trying to protect her. She pushed this uncomfortable thought aside, remembering how, in the weeks after the fall, she had been forced to accept that Jean could no longer live alone. Exasperation at wasted food, missed appointments, minor falls and frantic phone calls turned to pity for the woman her mother had become.

She remembered sitting in her tiny kitchen, looking through the local paper during a rare moment of peace. The sunlight had found its way between the houses crammed onto the estate, and shone onto her scrub-top table. As she idly looked through the local paper, an advertisement for a practice nurse at her mother's GP surgery jumped out at her. Could that be the answer? She knew she could not give up work to care for her mother. Mentally, she would shrivel and, much as she loved Jean, she could not devote her life to her. With this job, however, she could move in with Jean and care for her while working normal hours. All she needed to do was get the job and persuade her mother that it was a good idea.

The next few weeks were a whirl of CV-writing, references, interviews, and difficult conversations with doctors, senior nurses and her mother, all of whom tried to persuade her that she was doing the wrong thing. On the day of the interview she had nearly backed out, fearing her knowledge of general medicine was too narrow. But Dr Jag Patel, an elegant Indian man with a soothing voice, had allayed her fears. In the months and years that followed, he had become a good friend, supported her training, and helped with the care of her mother at the end.

She moved back into her childhood home – back to the same room, with the same wallpaper and the same narrow single bed. The posters had been taken down long ago and the walls repainted, but it was the same room that had been her place of safety and solace in the terrible months after her father's death. The books that she had retreated into were still on the shelves: HE Bates, Lynne Reid Banks, Agatha Christie and many others – escapism or tales of people overcoming adversity. Suzanne gradually replaced the furniture with some from her own house. Taking her old bed to the tip had been heart-wrenching but necessary; sleeping on a single bed was a backward step too far.

The house was the same but felt different. The stair-lift made the narrow stairs difficult to negotiate, there were grab handles everywhere and, although her mother wasn't old, it felt like an old person's house. The smell of the house had changed to a pervasive smell of disinfectant combined with baby powder. An old person's smell. Her mother looked the same, but subtle changes had taken place. It wasn't only her abilities that had had deteriorated; she had become dependent. Suzanne found it hard to come to terms with the loss of Jean as a mother. Now she passively deferred to everything that Suzanne said, pitifully grateful but always making Suzanne feel humbled by her stoicism.

The last three years of Jean's life were a struggle for both women but they coped, finding things to laugh or smile about, making the most of tiny victories, just getting on with it. The Parkinson's disease affected Jean's mobility and her ability to care for herself but, after Suzanne moved in, Jean's mental state improved for a time. She was less anxious, her memory seemed to improve – or maybe they both simply adapted to the parts of her that were missing.

Suzanne's thoughts of her mother were interrupted by David bursting into the kitchen, bottle held aloft. "Any more in here?"

"No, I think we're ready. You get everyone seated and then you can help me serve."

"OK boss," he said, winking at Hilary as she came in with empty dishes. She blushed crimson.

Doing as he had been told, he went back to the living room and his loud voice boomed, "Right, dinner everyone." It caused a temporary lull in the conversation, but the noise swelled again as he chivvied everyone through to the panelled dining room where the beautiful oak table was fully extended and laid for eleven.

"Come on, Hilary, you've done enough now. You're here next to me. OK?" David gallantly took Hilary's arm and led her to the seat next to his at the head of the table.

What a sad old thing she is, he thought as she sat down. The black dress that she was wearing was smart but dated and her flat comfortable velvet shoes looked more like slippers than party wear, her greying hair framing her face like a helmet. She needs someone to take her in hand, he thought.

"Oh dear, I've messed up your boy-girl pattern," said Hilary, settling herself against the back of the chair.

"There's no pattern about any of us lot," countered Liz, taking the wine bottle from David and filling her glass before topping up Hilary's.

"Water anyone?" John held up the jug of iced water, filling Chahna's glass opposite before, hopefully, sending it around the table towards Liz.

As glasses were filled and napkins placed on laps, David and Suzanne pushed between their guests to place dishes piled with prawn cocktail in front of everyone. Suzanne touched David on the shoulder as he sat down at the head of the table. She glanced around the room to check that everyone had everything they needed, before squeezing between the sideboard and the backs of the chairs, everyone moving in a little to let her pass. Hilary watched David's eyes as they followed his wife around the room.

"How did you two meet?" she asked, the question bursting into a sudden silence in the room.

David laughed loudly and said, "I went to Suzanne for help and she's been helping me ever since."

"He came to a stop-smoking session and the rest, as they say, is history."

"Yes, and I stopped smoking, didn't I? Still don't."

Feats of self-control were batted across the table as Suzanne thought back to that fateful day.

It had been neither auspicious nor romantic. She had been running a smoking cessation clinic, her least favourite task. As a lifelong non-smoker, she simply couldn't understand the appeal. The day had started badly. She'd slept poorly the night before, as her mother had woken her several times, demanding that she put the telly on to watch *Deal or No Deal*. They'd both been tired and irritable at breakfast. The last thing

Suzanne needed was a florid-faced, bumptious, overweight man arriving late for his appointment and then demanding inappropriate treatment for his self-inflicted addiction.

Embarrassingly, rather than standing up to him, she'd burst into tears. She was furious with herself for giving this rude man the satisfaction of making her cry. He was distraught. "Oh God, I'm so sorry, everything is going wrong. Dad's been diagnosed with lung cancer and it's spread. Inoperable. He's dying. Aw. Come on, don't cry, for heaven's sake. It's just Mum, she isn't coping. She keeps going round saying, 'What is going to happen to me?' Doesn't seem to care what dad is going through. Dad's breathless, in pain, frightened. I don't know how to help them. I am so stupid. I came here to get help. I'm like a bull in a china shop, shouting the odds, upsetting people. I must stop smoking so that I don't end up like him. I am so sorry, please forgive me. I came to you because you've helped before. I chose you specially because you are the best nurse here and then I go and upset you."

His ranting apology gave Suzanne time to gather herself and, looking at him, she thought she saw genuine concern and distress in his eyes. But she wasn't quite ready to forgive him for upsetting her and replied, "I'm really sorry about your father. Sit down again… I don't think now is the time to stop smoking. You seem stressed enough." Holding up her hand to stop him interrupting, she said, "I could take a look at your dad's notes and have a word with his GP, if that would help."

Suzanne concentrated on her prawn cocktail as she remembered that meeting with embarrassment. They had both been at their lowest ebb. Perhaps that had been a good starting point, seeing each other at their worst.

"Mmm…delicious as ever." Jag put his spoon down and turned to Suzanne.

"Yes, gorgeous, isn't she?" shouted David from the other end of the table. Raucous laughter, the wine bottle passed around the table again. David had been a bit unsure when Suzanne had said that she wanted to invite Jag and Chahna to the party. He didn't have a chip on his shoulder but he was only a builder and Jag was a doctor, and

Suzanne's boss, and Chahna was some sort of high-flying executive, jetting off here, there and everywhere. But after all that worrying, they seemed really nice, getting on with everyone, having a good time and even having a drink.

Suzanne stood up to collect the plates. Hilary, mirroring her move, started to collect the plates from the other end of the table.

"What's your mum doing while we're enjoying ourselves?" Carol asked, as Hilary reached over her shoulder to pick up her plate.

"Oh, just watching telly. She's never really celebrated New Year. We used to have some lovely Christmases, but New Year just passed us by. It's lovely that you lot include me in your New Year celebrations, otherwise I'd be at home in front of the telly with cottage pie and prunes and custard."

"What is it about old people and their obsession with prunes?"

"It's not prunes they are obsessed with, it's their bowels," Suzanne countered. "If I ever get like that, shoot me," she said pleadingly to David as she squeezed past past again with the plates.

"I don't know how you and Jag put up with listening to other people's moans day in and day out."

"My mum does nothing but moan," put in Liz. "The only time she seems happy is when she's got a funeral to go to. If crematoriums were on Tripadvisor, she'd be their number one contributor. What a life, when the height of your social calendar is someone's funeral. Although it's something to celebrate if it's someone else's," Liz laughed at her own wit.

"It's different really," replied Jag. "I'm terrible. I have much more sympathy with my patients than I do with my mum. I get really irritated with her. She worries about everything and she never used to."

"I think the older we get the more cowardly we become. I used to revel in all the possibilities – now I can't cope with choice. I want everything to be simple," added Carol.

"Choice is vastly overrated. I've given up trying to get a coffee in town any longer. If I can decide which coffee shop to go into, I can't decide what to have off the menu, and on the rare occasions that I get that

22

far, I lose the will to live in the time it takes to make it!" Janet's views on coffee shops were well known to everyone at the table and this led to yet another heated debate about the coffee shops in town and the decline of the independents. Wine glasses were topped up, and the talk got louder, more animated and more illogical.

In the kitchen, Suzanne and Hilary started putting together the dishes to take in for the main course. The roast lamb reminded Suzanne of Sunday dinners as a child, the smell warm and comforting, the fat just slightly crispy, the green beans a bit softer than was fashionable and the crushed new potatoes shining with olive oil. Suzanne realised that it was all a bit retro, but she knew that they all liked it and it was easy.

When they returned to the dining room, the talk had, somehow, turned to cars.

"My mum and dad used to have a Morris Marina," said Hilary, as she reached between Carol and John to place the beans in the centre of the table. "Dad thought it was great. I just remember being really embarrassed when they came to pick me up from school. Mum got really cross with me one time and threatened to make me take the train. She had no idea how I wished she'd carried out her threat." Hilary shuddered, remembering the awful sensation of being ashamed of her parents, sitting in the back of the car on the unbearably hot, plastic seats.

"How is your mum, Hilary?" asked Janet, bringing her back to the present.

"She's really well. She thinks she needs to look after all the elderly in the neighbourhood. She's forever on the phone or the internet complaining about or campaigning for something or other. She's just given up driving though, you know."

"Oh, thank goodness for that," said Suzanne, squeezing past with the leg of lamb to place it in front of David. "I know she needed her independence, but I had to check before going out to avoid backing out of the drive at the same time as her."

Hilary laughed. She knew that her mum's driving had been erratic and possibly not safe of late. The car acquired new dents every time she went out but the thought of taking away her mum's independence had horrified her.

It had been a relief when, at her last check-up, the optician concluded that her eyes had deteriorated to such an extent that driving was no longer possible. Hilary had dreaded her mother's reaction, but it seemed a relief to Phyllis that she no longer had to try; she knew that her driving was poor but had wanted to carry on as long as possible to avoid being even more of a burden on Hilary.

"Is it me or is it hot in here?"

"That ought to be the rallying cry for you lot," said Jonathan as he fanned Liz with his napkin. "Carol and I have a constant battle at night. The bedclothes are thrown off, pulled back. I'm sure we'd be better with a fridge not a radiator at the end of the bed."

The men bemoaned their lot, the women compared symptoms and solutions. Everyone roared with laughter at the thought of towelling pyjamas.

The talk drifted on, the wine flowed, and the evening passed. Dessert and cheese were served, followed by port and dessert wine. Everyone was feeling very mellow, when, all of a sudden, it was quarter to twelve. Time to move through to the conservatory to see in the New Year and watch the fireworks at the golf club.

Suzanne chivvied them along as they scraped their chairs back, getting up with moans and groans, leaning on each other, a bit giggly. David picked up a couple of bottles of Champagne from the wine fridge behind his chair. He moved quickly to the front of the wobbly procession and started to fill the crystal flutes set out on a tray placed on the fashionably distressed iron table.

When everyone was holding a glass, they all turned expectantly towards the slightly steamy windows, and the lit-up golf club, which looked nearer than in the daytime.

David sat down heavily in the battered wing chair, the indentation in the tweed covering fitting him perfectly.

"If I was a piece of furniture, this is what I'd want to be. Expensive and well loved."

"Of course, you are well loved," said Suzanne coming to sit on the arm of the chair, "but you are more like a Barcelona chair – sleek, stylish and, of course, expensive."

(And a bit impractical and uncomfortable, Liz thought, uncharitably.)

"You, my darling, are an Edwardian tallboy. Elegant, useful and beautiful." David pulled Suzanne onto his lap and they merged together as if they were one being.

With a flash and a bang, the fireworks started and the grand-father clock in the hall started to chime. Suzanne, giving herself a mental pat on the back for remembering to check that the clock was keeping time, pulled David to his feet, saying, "Happy New Year". They all toasted and hugged and kissed each other. Putting their glasses to one side, they joined hands in a circle and sang Auld Lang Syne. Nobody knew the words after the first phrases, but they hummed along, gripping hands as they fell over each other's feet and got tangled up in the furniture. Retrieving their glasses from the window ledge, the table, under the chairs, they sat down to watch the rest of the fireworks.

Conversations became circular, speech became louder and a bit slurred, and they had heated discussions about nothing important, and raucous laughter rang out. Everyone was relaxed, problems and difficulties forgotten for a time.

Hilary was the first to make a move. "Thank you for a wonderful party. It was lovely. I'd better go and check on Mum. I'll wish her a happy New Year if she's still awake." Taking a deep breath, emboldened by the Champagne, she continued. "It's my birthday in February. What about us girls getting together for lunch or something, give us something to look forward to? I can email some ideas."

"Oh. How old are you Hilary?"

"Are you thinking of retiring?"

"What about that new bistro for lunch?"

The questions flew from all directions as the others followed Hilary's lead and dragged themselves up from the comfy chairs.

"I'm only fifty-five, certainly not retiring yet. If I was at home more, Mum would find more for me to do and if she didn't, I'd find things to do for her whether she wanted me to or not. We'd drive each other mad."

The group gradually moved into the big square hall. Collecting coats, hats, boots, they said their goodbyes, with hugs and kisses, see you soons and don't forgets…and slowly moved onto the step, as if reluctant to make that final move into the damp cold night.

Finally, Suzanne and David shut the door and turned back into the house, listening to the shouts and laughter of their friends as they headed home.

They collected bottles and glasses as they made their way through to the kitchen. Surveying the chaos, they made a joint but unspoken decision to get on with the clearing up. They told each other to go to bed but neither listened and they worked separately but in tandem, moving though the rooms clearing the detritus of another successful party, marvelling, as always, at so many empty bottles, but rejoicing in the fact that all of their friends had given up smoking and there was no longer the horror of clearing empty ashtrays and cigarette ends from unexpected places, sometimes months after a party.

When the house looked more like their own, with the dishwasher full, roasting tins soaking in the sink and the surfaces cleaned, they sat down on the cream leather sofa and toasted each other with a tiny limoncello straight from the freezer.

"Here's to us. A year for us. When we put *us* first," announced David. "Let's get on the internet before we go back to work and plan a few breaks. We don't have to consider anyone else any more. Mum is so busy she won't even notice we've gone."

"I'd love to, but I'll have to check with work and Hilary might need some help with her mum, and what about your business?" Suzanne paused. "Oh, why can't I just do things, be spontaneous, do things without guilt? Perhaps I should…could try."

"We'll both try. Together, we might succeed." He kissed her shoulder. "Right, that's enough pontificating. Bed," said David.

And with a final check around, she followed him upstairs.

Across the road, Hilary lay awake, her mind going over the details of the evening.

She'd put her head around her mother's door when she got in. Phyllis's bulk was covered in her treasured candlewick bedspread. She lay tidily on her back in the centre of the bed, her soft snuffling snores reassuringly regular. Hilary had silently wished her mother happy New Year before going into her own room across the hall.

She had had such a lovely time; they were all so kind. She would enjoy reliving it all with her mother over breakfast.

Gradually, she relaxed. Suzanne and David describing each other as pieces of furniture floated into her mind. Hilary found herself seeing her mother as an antique eighteenth century bureau. Polished oak, a shell pattern inlaid on the front, heavy, its feet planted four-square on the floor, tooled leather on the writing desk, compartments, shelves and drawers to keep everything neatly filed. Everything in its place, no secret compartments.

As her mind became quiet, she could still hear her mother's snores but knew that, in the morning, Phyllis would say that she had heard Hilary come in and, uncannily, she would probably know what time it had been.

Chapter Two

A Quiet Drink

"Quiet in here tonight." David leaned on the bar talking to Sheila as she polished the glasses.

"I long for peace and quiet during Christmas and New Year. It's non-stop for six weeks. Then when the quiet comes, I hate it. Ben gets all stressed because the takings are down and he spends hours looking at the spreadsheets as if that's going to bring money in or the figures will change if he looks at them for long enough. No-one wants to come out for a drink when the weather's like this, and drink is so cheap in the supermarkets, why would you bother. I don't know," she tailed off.

"Richard and Jonathan are calling in after work. We'll try and improve your takings to cheer Ben up! OK?" laughed David. As he finished speaking, a group of bedraggled students came through the door, letting a blast of icy wind whirl its way around the bar. David picked up his drink and swiftly moved towards the chairs by the fire before the youngsters could think of claiming them. They peeled off layers of wet clothing, shaking themselves like dogs, and proceeded to order their drinks individually, paying separately on cards or counting out small change. David was glad that it was Sheila behind the bar; Ben would have been very grumpy and he was never very good at hiding his displeasure.

Richard and Jonathan arrived together soon after he sat down and David was pleased to see that they had persuaded John to join them. They came and warmed themselves by the fire while waiting for the students to be served.

"I can't believe it's almost the end of January and this is the first time we've got in here," said Richard. "Life just takes over. I was just telling Jonathan on the way that Janet is having a terrible time with her parents at the moment. I think she is going to have to go up and stay. Her dad has broken his leg and I don't think her mum can manage on her own. I'm just keeping my head down and being as helpful as I can. Which isn't very. Claire offered to take time off work and come home or go up there to help out, but Jan wouldn't hear of it. It's all a bit of a nightmare."

"Are they far away?" asked David.

"Leckhampton." Richard named a town nearly a hundred miles away.

"That's a horrible journey. Poor Janet."

"I know, and she hates driving."

"OK. What does everyone want?" asked David, seeing the bar was now clearing.

"I'll get them, mate," said John. "You and Suzanne put on that fantastic spread at New Year."

Sheila had finally served the last of the students, who were now sitting around the big table at the other side of the pub, surrounded by wet clothes and the obligatory rucksacks that all youngsters carried around with the same possessiveness shown by toddlers for their comfort blankets.

Jonathan was extolling Carol's virtues as John returned to the table with four beers and packets of nuts on a tray.

"Carol is an angel about visiting Dad now he's in the nursing home. I hate it, can't bear to see him like that. You know what I mean? If it was left to me, I'd struggle to go once a month. She goes every week, even though half the time he doesn't know who anyone is. She has her own mum to visit too, and the grandchildren to look after. Although if I'm honest, I probably do more of the grandchildren bit. I love it and now I'm working less, I can really get involved."

"How's it going now you've cut down?" asked David, who struggled to take a holiday, never mind consider early retirement or working part-time.

"It's great. My job is OK but it's not as all-consuming as yours. I don't think I was designed to be as successful and powerful as you."

David wasn't sure if that was a compliment or a dig at his lifestyle. Jonathan never seemed to have any ambition; he and Carol lived in a small three-bedroomed terrace house on the other side of town, just the two of them now that their three children had left home. They plodded through life, always doing the bare minimum to maintain a house that was homely but not stylish. David thought that Carol would have done more if she'd been on her own or with someone else, but Jonathan just wanted to be comfortable. He earned enough to look after his family but would never look for ways to earn more. His motto seemed to be 'anything for a quiet life'. David realised that it would not even have occurred to Jonathan to be jealous of him, as he simply let life wash over him.

While David had been thinking, the conversation turned to John and Liz. John was distressed that Liz spent so many hours looking after their granddaughter, Siobhan.

"Lisa is a hopeless judge of character. Every boyfriend she's had has been a waster, and Siobhan's father is a nightmare. At least he's back in Ireland now."

"He seemed all right when we met him at the rugby last year," interjected Richard.

"Oh, he's very sociable, fun, lively, would have spoilt Lisa rotten if he'd ever managed to hold a job down long enough to earn any money. He just didn't take anything seriously," said John with an exasperated sigh.

"Anyway, talking of rugby, is anyone going to the match on Saturday?" John asked, changing the subject from uncomfortable family matters. "I can take my car if you like."

A discussion followed about timings, plans, chances of winning, before Richard piped up, "Will you be allowed to come, Jonathan? No parents or grandchildren taking precedence?"

"I hope not. It being Monday, if I get my request in now for an afternoon off on Saturday, I'm sure we can work something out between us," he replied, laughing. "I'll offer to be on grandchildren duty all week if Carol does the oldies. She's going out with the others for Hilary's birthday lunch in a couple of weeks on a day we usually have the children for Lucy, so I'll have to stand in then. It's all fair in the end."

"Right, I'm having one more before I go. Any more for any more?" asked David, getting up and collecting the empties and orders as he pushed past the others. A few more people had come into the pub. Sheila looked a bit more relaxed as he went to give his order.

"Not bad for a Tuesday night before pay day in January," she said, as she started to pull David's pint. He gave the order for the other three and took a note from his wallet.

"Everyone thinks we are really well off but I'm always juggling money," replied David. "Just as I think there's a bit spare, another bill comes along to take it away. I probably get as wound up as Ben when it comes to the VAT. I remember when I was a student," he said, looking towards the table of students that was now more crowded and noisy. "I could make half a bitter last a whole evening. It was warmer in the pub than in my room and a group of us would go in most evenings. It must have driven the landlord mad because we never had any money. They seem to have loads now, but I think I preferred scrimping as a student rather than starting my working life with a massive debt."

"It was like that in the pub we used to have in Yorkshire. You can imagine how Ben reacted to that. It's annoying enough that these lot all pay separately with plastic, but at least they put money over the counter."

Sheila put the last of the pints on the counter and took David's money, putting it in the till while he took the first two pints to the table and holding his change out for him as he came back to the bar.

"Just talking to Sheila about being a student and making half a pint last all evening," he said, as he sat back down.

31

"I don't know how we managed on the student grant. At least we didn't have course fees to pay."

"I got round it by working in the student union bar," put in Richard. "I got paid for drinking and got into all the concerts. I've no idea how I got a degree at the end of it. I must have just absorbed it all by osmosis."

The others laughed and chipped in with their 'when I was a student' stories until the drinks were finished and they decided it was time to brave the cold and the walk home. They parted at the door, David turning left and Jonathan, Richard and John turning right.

Jonathan had the longest walk, his home predating by a hundred years the 'new' estate where the others lived. After he said goodbye to Richard and John, he continued on his own for the last ten minutes of his walk home. He thought about the others and, although he knew they all had more money, bigger houses and better holidays, he wouldn't swap his life for any of theirs. He'd always been happy to meander through life, taking things as they came, making decisions only when he had to. He realised that he probably drove Carol mad sometimes but she seemed happy enough to muddle along without the stress that the others seemed to live with.

When he arrived home, his hands were so cold that he struggled to get his key in the lock. As he fumbled with the key, Carol opened the door.

"Gosh, you're frozen. Why didn't you take your gloves?"

"I forgot," he muttered, like a naughty school boy, happy to be ushered into the warmth and familiarity of his own home.

Chapter Three

Birthday Lunch

The last week of January was bitterly cold, with snow on the ground and icy roads. February started the same way, and then the snow stopped being a novelty. It lost its sparkling whiteness and the mounds left by the snow plough looked like piles of soiled sheets dripping into slushy puddles in the gutters.

Trudging damply home from work, Hilary was glad that she had suggested going out for a meal for her birthday. She had booked a table at the new bistro and hoped it wouldn't be a disappointment. She always worried about trying new things.

A lunchtime meal meant that, with a bit of organisation, her mum could go too. She had taken the day off and it wasn't her Sunday to work, so she had plenty of time to prepare.

Hilary loved working in the department store; she felt as though she was part of a great big family. She knew everyone by sight and she knew that people liked her. She had never been the sort of person to spend time gossiping over coffee and she avoided becoming involved with any of the cliques that formed and reformed like the blobs of mercury pushed around the petri dish in the distant chemistry lessons of her school days. She shrank as she thought of those days, never quite fitting in, always on the edge, hopeless at sport so always last to be chosen for teams, working hard so that at least her parents were pleased. Perhaps as an only child she'd never quite got the hang of friendship; long-term relationships had always seemed to elude her.

Hilary had been pleased but surprised to be included in the New Year celebration at Suzanne's. They were a nice crowd and had included her in a few of their events over the years. She knew they thought she was too quiet and a bit of an oddity, still at home looking after mother. She had got to know them all through Suzanne, who, for all her confidence and exuberance, had been a bit lost when she first moved in with David. She thought it was probably gratitude on Suzanne's part and, let's face it, she was really useful at parties because she cleared up without being asked. She liked to be useful.

Of all of the group, she related most to Janet. They shared some of the same anxieties and she felt that she could talk to her. Unfortunately, Janet had emailed to say that she didn't think she would be able to attend the birthday lunch. There had been several long rambling emails that didn't sound like Janet at all, usually so organised and precise.

The first email to Hilary read:

Dad's been admitted with a broken leg, I shall have to go up and stay with mum. Jan

This was followed by:

Hi,

How has he coped all this time? I knew her memory wasn't very good and she got a bit muddled and Dad was doing the cooking and washing but she's impossible, so annoying, keeps repeating everything, wanders round all the time or just won't move. She gets her clothes in a muddle, tights on top of trousers, then a skirt and an inside-out cardigan over the lot. I had no idea – she always looked so smart when we visited. Dad must have spent hours. She forgets to wash, asks for her lunch when we've just had it, and then, worst of all, the first night I was here, she wandered off in her nightie in January!

I find myself getting cross with her and then cross with Dad for shielding us all from this. He didn't want us to know how bad she was. If we had been a family that lived nearer to each other or who dropped in unannounced this couldn't have gone on for so long. But we're not, and we were brought up to be independent and live our own lives, so that is what we've done. I feel so guilty, but he didn't tell us.

Sorry I'm rambling. Sorry, I don't think I can come to your lunch do. Sorry.

Janet xxx

Hilary replied:

I'm so sorry to hear your news but how lucky you are to have such a fantastic dad. He must love your mum so much. He's broken at the moment but he's mending fast and, by the sound of it, he's keen to get back on his feet and take up the reins again. Mum sends her best wishes. Please let me know if there is anything I can do to help. Hilary xx

A day or two later, Janet wrote:

Hi Hilary,

Thank you so much for understanding.

Mum and I have sorted out a bit of a routine. Richard comes across to see me when he can and Claire phones frequently (my salvation).

Dad is still in hospital. We thought it would be a week, then he got an infection in his stitches and that slowed his recovery, so he's still there. Ten days and counting.

If Mum has stayed in bed all night (perhaps she's getting up because Dad isn't there next to her, because he says she hasn't wandered at night before), we get up at about seven. I help her wash, put out her clothes and then help her get into them. Some days she can do it on her own, then she gets annoyed with me for trying to help or 'rush her' as she says. Then we have breakfast. I sit her in front of the TV while I clean up and put the washing on, then we either go to the shops or watch the telly till it's time to go to see Dad in the hospital. I daren't leave her.

The trip to the hospital is an experience in itself and most days we go twice, to both afternoon and evening visiting, if only because it gives us something to do and adds some structure to the day. I never thought I'd miss work. I almost wish they hadn't been so good about giving me compassionate leave, but even their patience will wear thin soon. They haven't phoned yet…

I have started taking Mum to the shops or the hospital in a wheelchair, otherwise it's like trying to control a drunk toddler (a large one at that). I'll be choosing yogurts and realise she's left my side and is either talking rubbish to one of the staff or some unsuspecting customer or picking up things, sticking her finger in them and putting them back. On one occasion she literally disappeared and we had to make an announcement over the tannoy – how embarrassing! She was brought back by a young mum who recognised her from the description on the tannoy. Fortunately, she has always worn brightly coloured clothes, much easier to describe. She'd found Mum with her head in one of the freezers, 'cooling off'.

Dad and I had a good laugh about that one – if we didn't laugh, we'd cry. He must be made of sterner stuff than I am or he loves her an awful lot. I am exhausted!

Sorry, rambling again, wish I could be with you on Monday. Give my love to everyone.

Janet xxx

Hilary sat at her laptop contemplating these emails. How lucky she was with her relationship with her mum. How lucky she was that her mum still had all her faculties, even if it did mean being bossed around a bit. Perhaps I'm one of those people who is born without any ambition, she thought. Perhaps I was born to do as I'm told. It would be much easier if mum just wanted to stay at home and watch day-time TV. But she is very keen to keep going and she is well aware of the sacrifices I make and I've made, and the effort I put into making things happen. She certainly doesn't take me for granted. I can't imagine what it must be like for Janet. She has had to swap roles from daughter to mother, learning to know this new person her mother has become. Her dad must be grateful for what Janet is doing. Her mum has no idea that she has anything to be grateful for. What a terrible way to be.

On Hilary's birthday, Janet wrote:

Happy birthday, Hilary.

I hope all goes well. I'm sorry I won't make it. Pass my regrets on to the others.

I am so tired; I don't know which way is up. I don't know what to do with myself. I'm carrying on because I have to. I can't remember what happened yesterday (just like mum) but I have this ever-growing list of things to do tomorrow. If I don't write things down, they flit in and out of my mind before I have time to record them. They stop in there briefly like a train at a station but then they are gone, like a train disappearing into a tunnel. You know what it looked like but it lacks definition and you certainly didn't get the number. As you can tell, I've been tidying up a bit here and Dad asked me to sort out his railway books. All my thoughts now seem to be in railway metaphors. I must be going mad.

I'm so tired that I feel sick. I can't concentrate and I'm becoming irritable, not with Mum or Dad – I can keep up the pretence for them – but with Richard and Claire, and they don't deserve it. I managed to upset the cleaner who comes to the house once a fortnight. I didn't mean to. I'm not even sure what I said that upset her but she flounced off... Something else on my list of things to do: apologise to Tracy!

To top it all, work have been on to me (I can't say I'm surprised). Still, Julia will be back from Spain soon, so at least I won't be coping on my own.

Have a lovely lunch. Have a glass of wine for me (no don't, I'm drinking too much as it is – it's the only way I can relax). I can't believe what I have become in such a short time. I hope the real me is back soon.

Have fun.

Love Janet xx

P.S. Dad is doing well, hoping to be home at the end of the week, then decisions have to be made about Mum.

Hilary sent a quick reply, printed off all the emails and got her mother's walker from the garage. Phyllis used the electric riser chair to stand herself up and then Hilary helped her on with her coat and scarf. They made slow progress up the hall, down the ramp to the drive and into the car. When Phyllis was safely strapped in, Hilary returned to lock the front door. She loved to take her mum out but everything took so long. Spontaneity was out of the question, as planning and extra time were needed to check entrances and exits, toilets and seating. She'd made a point of visiting the bistro for a coffee, so that she could check all these things out and make sure there was disabled parking close enough to the door. She missed the days when she and Phyllis used to meet at the railway station and nip into London for the day, but at least her mum could still come for a birthday lunch. The thought of taking someone like Janet's mother filled her with dread. Phyllis's widespread arthritis caused considerable disability and pain, but at least they could still have a conversation, enjoy a drama or a quiz together and discuss clues in the crossword.

They arrived in good time and parked in front of the entrance. Hilary took the walker from the boot, unstrapped Phyllis and, after a few tries, she was out of the car. "I wish someone would invent an ejector seat for cars," she said.

The table Hilary had reserved was in a different part of the building to where she had had coffee the Sunday before, and the corridor was a bit of an uneven trek, but they made it to the dining area to see Carol and Liz already seated. There was a bit of shuffling around so that Phyllis had the seat with armrests, and then Hilary had to ask a member of staff for a cushion for her mother to sit on. When had she shrunk? Hilary made a note in her phone to put a cushion in the car for future forays. Suzanne arrived soon afterwards. They'd known for some time that Chahna wouldn't make it; she rarely got time off in the day.

They all greeted each other, wished Hilary a happy birthday, and passed cards across the table to her. They pored over their menus for a time and then gave their order to the young waitress, who seemed very nervous. Had they caught her on her first day on the job?

"What a sweet girl, just like Lisa used to be before she got all 'worldly wise'," observed Liz, thinking of her daughter, who had been so loving until she'd met Sean.

"Are you still looking after Siobhan, Liz?"

"Yes," she replied. "Fortunately, Lisa doesn't work at the hospital on a Thursday so today's my free day. Otherwise, we'd have had a very lively three-year-old to contend with."

"Instead you all just have me to look after," countered Phyllis.

A chorus of, oh no, you're not a bother, we love seeing you, followed, and when the drinks arrived, they all toasted Hilary with another round of happy birthdays.

Their meals arrived and as Hilary discreetly cut up her mother's steak, talk turned to Janet.

Hilary had brought all the emails but discovered that the others had received similar missives over the past week. They'd all experienced the same dilemmas in trying to find the right words to reply. For Suzanne, it brought back many of the feelings that she'd had but never expressed when she looked after her own mother. She'd responded to Janet with lots of practical help: contact details for the Alzheimer's Society, carers' associations and groups. Until David, Suzanne had never had any emotional support. She coped by doing things, keeping busy, and not allowing herself to think. She had found it difficult to read what Janet had to say about caring for her mother and found it a little self-indulgent.

Liz said, "We all have disasters to deal with – when that awful man, Sean, got Lisa pregnant, and then he abandoned her with a young baby, I thought I'd never sleep again. At least I'm really lucky with *my* mum. She has a more active social life than I do. She's at a tea dance today. But I suppose none of us know what is around the corner. I feel really sorry for Jan and I suppose she was just using us as a sounding board because she's been left in the lurch. Her sister's lovely, but she's a bit hopeless when it comes to practical matters or putting herself out, even just a bit."

Suzanne was relieved that Liz had thought the same as she did about Janet's emails but she couldn't bring herself to admit it.

"I'm afraid I sent a rather jokey email back," continued Liz, "telling her about the time when John's aunty – who is long dead – turned up at church one evening in her nightie and Easter bonnet and had to be escorted home by the choir master, much to the amusement of all the little choir boys in the middle of their practice. She was the talk of her village for some time. The whole family made light of it, hiding their embarrassment, as they were unable to hide their relative away. Villages tend to be more forgiving of eccentric behaviour and it went down in folk history rather than being something to be ashamed of. I heard about it the first Christmas I spent with John's family. Funny in retrospect, but I suppose it would have been sad and degrading at the time. I suppose I should have been a bit kinder to Jan but she does take everything so seriously. I was trying to lighten the mood and tell her she isn't on her own. I feel a bit ashamed about replying that way but I didn't know what else to say. I'm not much good at this sort of thing."

They all smiled at the image of the old lady in her nightie and Easter bonnet, reassuring Liz that letting Janet know she wasn't alone was the most important thing and perhaps it was the act of replying, not necessarily the words, that sent the right message.

"I didn't actually reply to them all," Carol admitted, "but I did tell her that I could perhaps help if it came to the point of needing residential care."

Hilary picked up her copies of the emails and put them back in her bag. "I just wrote back saying how lucky she was to have such a fantastic dad, caring for his wife and protecting them all."

"Also, her mum is probably a lot harder work than usual because George isn't there," put in Suzanne. "Her routine's gone. At some level, she will understand that he is not well, she will be anxious, and because of all the changes and all of these factors, her behaviour will be worse and more chaotic."

"Yes, it's like with children," said Carol. "You can 'ignore' your own children for long periods of time if you have given them boundaries and know what they are capable of. Whereas, if you're looking after someone else's child, those definitions are lost, the responsibility is greater. Isn't this exactly what is happening here? Janet is looking after someone else's 'child' so she can't relax for a second."

"I know. Nothing that we can say or do at the moment will be any help, but at least she knows we are all here," said Hilary.

Phyllis was chewing carefully on the steak Hilary had cut for her. She refused to give in to her disabilities. She was willing even to risk losing her false teeth chewing in order to taste this beautiful ribeye steak.

At the end of her mouthful, she put down her fork and said, "You girls try to do too much, working, looking after your men, your grandchildren, your parents. I had my mother living with us for her last years but I don't remember it being the trauma that you are going through. She occupied our front room, lying in her high bed, propped up on pillows. The district

41

nurse came regularly, although I'm not sure what she did – dressings somewhere. We washed her and fed her, she made very few demands. Perhaps I was lucky. Mothers of friends had to go into geriatric wards. I think one of the differences was that she knew that she was just waiting to die. There was not the expectation that if she became ill, her life would be saved by some miracle of medical science. If the doctor came, it was a painkiller, linctus for a cough, laxatives for her bowels. I suppose what I am saying is that mother was just another of my duties. I accepted it and got on with it, but I wasn't trying to be a superwoman like you. I keep telling Hilary not to fuss, to get herself away for a break. She looks after me wonderfully. I know how lucky I am. But I've had my life. I want her to have hers."

"I have a wonderful life, thank you. And I'm having a great birthday. How is everyone's food?"

The food had been as good as the write-up so far. The waitress had looked after them well.

They were all feeling a bit sombre and heavy when the dessert menu arrived. With a feeling of relief, talk turned to choosing between chocolate and fruit, healthy or not, hot or cold. Hilary hoped Phyllis wouldn't choose the meringue; it would go everywhere. But she said nothing.

The rest of the meal passed happily. Only Liz had a drink; the others had come in their own cars. Liz was making the most of her day off from child care and was still feeling a little guilty about her less-than-thoughtful email to Janet.

As they sorted out the bill, Carol said, "I hope you will all be able to come to our pearl wedding anniversary party. We didn't have a do for our silver. Neither of us can remember why. It will have been a child or parent crisis, obviously so awful that we daren't recall it." She laughed. "Anyway, we've booked a room at the St John's Hotel, so I hope you can all make it. Invites will be in the post very soon."

"Oh, lovely."

"Is it a posh do?"

"Can we dress up?"

"Who else is coming?"

The questions came thick and fast, all the women talking at once. As they put on their coats and scarves and found their car keys they made a general move towards the door. Arrangements for more minor meetings were confirmed, mooted, discussed. The birthday lunch was over.

Hilary helped Phyllis settle into the car, put the heater on full and set off on the short journey home in comfortable silence, full, tired and happy.

Chapter Four

A Shock

Since coming back from her parents at the end of February, Janet had got into the habit of dropping around to Hilary's for a chat. She found it reassuring to see Hilary and her mum interacting and living together. She knew she had to find ways to deal with her own parents, without going under herself. Hilary's common sense and calm demeanour made her feel better, slowed her down, and stopped her trying to do everything and be everything to everyone.

So when she called round on Wednesday to find the doctor's car in the drive, she was surprised but not too worried. Phyllis had had a bit of a cold on Monday; perhaps she'd developed a chest infection. A smartly dressed, slightly flustered young woman opened the door. "Come in...umm.... Are you a friend or a relative? Hilary is very distressed and...umm... I think it would be better if there was someone with her. Oh, I'm Dr Logan," she added as an afterthought. Seeing the puzzled look on Janet's face, the young doctor told her in an exaggerated whisper that Phyllis had died suddenly that morning.

Janet didn't have time for the information to register or to ask what had happened before Dr Logan ushered her into the living room. Hilary was sitting on the settee, her face red and blotchy, swollen and tear-stained, her hair a mess. There were screwed up tissues on the floor and cushions. She glanced up but didn't even manage a smile. Janet sat down beside her and put her arm across her friend's shoulder. Hilary didn't shrug her off but made it clear that she didn't want to be touched.

Dr Logan stood awkwardly over the two women and hurriedly wrote a prescription. She seemed to be relieved that someone had come to take over. She muttered that she was sorry she couldn't do more. With that, she turned and left. The wind caught the front door and slammed it behind her.

Hilary jumped at the noise and then slumped back to her torpor. Janet touched her arm and asked if it was all right if she went and made some coffee. Receiving no reply, she went into the kitchen and assembled a tray with a cafetière, cups, hot milk and a packet of bourbon biscuits (Phyllis's favourites – Janet wasn't sure if Hilary liked them, but she couldn't find anything else). Taking a deep breath, she returned to the living room with the tray. Hilary hadn't moved.

Janet pushed the plunger down on the coffee and poured a cup, adding milk and putting a biscuit in the saucer. She put the cup and saucer on the coffee table at Hilary's elbow. Taking her own cup, she asked gently, "Can you tell me what happened?"

Hilary started to sob again. "It's all my fault. If we hadn't gone to Tesco, mum would still be here. She didn't want to go. I persuaded her." Through sobs, Hilary described what had happened that morning. The minor disagreement over going to Tesco, the argument over whether to take the walker or the wheelchair, the unpleasant atmosphere in the car, the silence as they walked slowly round the store and then, in the freezer aisle, the sudden chest pain and collapse. "I should have made her go in the wheelchair. I didn't notice what was happening straight away. I was leaning into the freezer, trying to decide between crinkle or straight cut chips. It was all chaos and fuss and cold. The three things mum hated most in life. Before I knew what was happening, the first aider had come. The paramedics were called. At first, they thought she was on her own. As if I would let her go round on her own. I was pushed out of the way. They *cut* her clothes off her to try to shock her back to life. It was all so undignified. If they'd bothered to ask, I'd have told them that she didn't want all that. She'd often said she would just like to go when her time came. I felt helpless, pushed aside. I wanted to just sit by her side and tell her I was there. I wasn't allowed to until she was in the ambulance, and then it was too late." Hilary paused to blow her nose. "Why couldn't I have held her as she fell to the floor? Why did we go? Perhaps she knew something was wrong. I was cross with her for being 'awkward' about going. I wasn't there when she needed me. I failed."

Janet didn't know what to say. She muttered, "You didn't fail." She had never seen Hilary out of control like this. Hilary was always there with the right thing to say or do to smooth over a situation. They sat for several minutes in silence. Janet persuaded Hilary to have a drink of the now cold coffee. She went to the kitchen to put the kettle on, exhausted by all the emotion. When she returned, Hilary started again on the same sobbing tirade, as if beating herself with it. Janet became worried and told Hilary that she was going to phone Suzanne. Surely she would know what to do. Having spoken briefly to Suzanne, she phoned Liz to ask if she could collect the prescription, for what she presumed were sleeping tablets. Whether she wanted them or not, Janet thought that Hilary would need something to help her feel calmer. Sleep was probably out of the question. She asked Liz to phone their other friends, as she couldn't bear to be the one to spread the news.

Liz and Suzanne arrived at the same time, Suzanne still in her nurse's uniform, which in itself brought some calm to the proceedings. Liz went straight out again, to get to the chemist before it closed. Suzanne bravely sat on the settee next to Hilary, put her arms around her, ignoring the shrug of the shoulders trying to throw her off, and simply held her and stroked her hair, shushing her, like a child. Although at first she sobbed and tried to repeat the story, Suzanne quietened her, telling her she could tell her about it tomorrow. Hilary relaxed against her, exhausted, and between them they helped her into her bed. Covering her with the duvet and switching off the light, Suzanne reassured her, as you would a child, "We'll be just in the other room."

Back in the living room, Janet burst into tears. "I tried to calm her but she kept going over and over the same things."

"If I'd arrived first, I'd have been faced with the same thing. She had to say all that and she'll have to go over it again and again until she can tidy up the chaos, deal with the guilt and put it away so that she can properly mourn for her mum. The poor locum couldn't cope. She came back to surgery quite distressed and had put Hilary down for a visit tomorrow. She felt guilty for leaving you to it but she had other patients to see."

Like a child afraid of the dark, Hilary soon came back. She stood at the door of the living room for a moment, as if lost, and then sat back down on the settee.

Janet and Suzanne pottered about, tidying up around Hilary, who, by turn, cried quietly or stared at her mum's chair. Liz returned with the prescription.

In the end, they all left with the promise of returning soon, feeling at a loss and helpless, having failed to comfort their friend.

The next day was bright and sunny. Hilary had slept on the settee, lost without her routine, not knowing when to go to bed. For years, her life had followed the same pattern. Tidying the house and then warming milk for both of them while her mother got ready for bed, adding a tot of Baileys to her mother's mug and taking it through to her, making sure she had everything she needed for the night.

She felt numb and couldn't get herself out of the cycle of sadness and reproach. The last years of caring for her mother were all wasted because she had failed her at the end.

She found a note from Janet by the kettle, saying that Dr Patel would be calling to see her today. She'd put 'Dr Patel' instead of Jag, as if to signify that this was an official visit, not just a friend popping by. Hilary knew she ought to phone Janet, who had been so good, but she couldn't face it – another thing to feel guilty about. She hadn't even asked yesterday how Janet's parents were getting on.

She made a drink, automatically taking two cups out of the cupboard before putting one away again. She shut the door on her mother's bedroom, without looking in, and wondered how she had become this weak helpless person in such a short time. Two days ago, she had been strong capable Hilary, calm in a crisis, a comfort to her mother, a stalwart at work, calm and sensible. "Now look at me," she said to her haggard, dishevelled reflection.

Jag Patel arrived just after midday, knocking briefly before walking in through the front door that Hilary had forgotten to lock the night before.

"It's only me," he called as he walked through to the living room, where he found her sitting and looking exactly as Suzanne had described the night before when she had phoned to fill him in on the details.

On seeing Jag, Hilary burst into tears and repeated her description of her mother's last hours, expressing all the guilt and agony she felt at letting Phyllis down. Jag listened quietly, sometimes touching her hand if she was particularly distressed, neither agreeing nor disagreeing with anything Hilary said. Finally, when she had finished, she rested her head against the back of the settee, exhausted.

"There is nothing I can say to make up for your loss, but a life is not just about the final moments. You and Phyllis had a good relationship, envied by others. You cared for her when she needed it, but you both continued to be individual people. Phyllis knew what you had sacrificed to look after her. Wasn't she always trying to encourage you to go away or out with friends? This may not be a comfort to you now, but one thing you ought to know is that had Phyllis survived the heart attack or stroke that took her…" He raised his hand as Hilary tried to interject. "I know she didn't survive, but had she done, it is highly likely that she would have had absolutely no memory of the events leading up to it, probably not even the daft, insignificant disagreement over whether to go to Tesco or not!"

He sat back and allowed Hilary a moment to take this in. "Soon you will be able to mourn her as you would have done if she had died peacefully in her sleep. Shock plays havoc with our nervous systems. Add a bit of guilt and we don't know where we are."

After a few moments of silence, Jag stood up. "Right. I have to get back to the surgery now. I'll leave you the phone number for Cruse. They have excellent counsellors who you might find helpful in the future. I've done you a sick note for this week. Come and see me in the surgery next week." With that, he left, leaving Hilary in a more thoughtful frame of mind.

Carol was in the middle of organising her pearl wedding anniversary party when she heard the news. She immediately popped out to the shop to buy a card for Hilary. She couldn't believe Phyllis was gone. She had seemed so well when they met up for lunch and she'd seen her out and about with Hilary a few times since, as bright as ever. But then, once she reached eighty, Phyllis always said she was on borrowed time, just grateful that she woke each morning, half-jokingly replying, "Well, I'm still here," whenever anyone asked how she was.

Carol had invited Hilary and her mother to the party and now neither of them would be able to attend. Selfishly, she hoped it wouldn't put a dampener on the party. She knocked on Hilary's door but was relieved when there was no answer, and slipped the card through the letter box.

Chapter Five

Goodbye Phyllis

Hilary shut the door as the few remaining guests made their way down
the drive. Offers had been made to stay with her and help her clear up,
but she didn't want them. She wanted to be on her own in the house.
She didn't want to be controlled and polite. She wanted to get everything
back to the way her mother would have liked it. Her mother would have
been a bit disappointed that so few people had gone to the house after the
crematorium, but Hilary hadn't encouraged them. She hardly knew most
of the people who had turned up at the funeral. She hadn't felt able to cry.
She hadn't wanted to show herself up. Now they were probably all saying
how hard and unfeeling she was.

She wasn't sure how the funeral had been arranged. She must have
talked to the funeral director and the vicar, but it was all hazy. The funeral
director had been very kind, suitably respectful, but very business-like.
Money up front.

Her mother, bless her, had left few decisions for her anyway. A note
with her will detailed the hymns and the readings. At least the hymns

had been well known, but even then, their voices had not been enough to drown out the tinny quality of the recorded organ music, distorted by the poor-quality speakers.

The vicar had a terrible cold. Her nose, bright red and shiny, dripped throughout the service. Hilary had been transfixed by it, worried that she would end up wiping her nose on her red sash as she absentmindedly dabbed at it while hurrying through the prayers.

Hilary had very little experience of funerals. Her father's funeral had passed in a dream. She had never realised what a production line the crematorium was; a look of apprehension on the faces of those going in, replaced by something close to relief on the faces of those coming out; the pews hardly cleared of one grieving family before the next was led in. She had wondered if they ever made a mistake. The thought had gone through her mind that it might not be her mother's coffin on the rollers up there, that the flowers looked like the ones she had chosen, but perhaps they weren't. She hadn't checked the name plate. Was that the vicar's job?

She seemed to remember the vicar saying some words about her mother: what a good, kind person she was, details of her charity work and local good deeds. One of her committee friends must have spoken to the vicar, given her all the details. Hilary couldn't have done. Just as well there were busybodies about, otherwise the eulogy would have been very short.

Born, married, had a child, widowed, died.

There had been quite a few in attendance at the crematorium. She and Phyllis had once discussed whether it was better to have lots of people at your funeral or to just have the vicar. Realising that the former was likely to mean that you'd died young and the latter that you'd outlived everyone, neither was a good option, they'd concluded. So they had ended up deciding that there must be a critical number to make a funeral just right.

Hilary was reassured and comforted when Suzanne, Jag and Liz joined her in the front pew. Turning, she saw Janet and Carol with their husbands further back. Even her boss and Doris from work had come to support her. There were huddles of her mother's friends, overlapping groups of do-gooders. Nearly all women, all respectfully in dark colours.

They were politely hustled out after the service, only allowed to go out through the front door, so that they didn't get muddled up with the next family. Perhaps the next group actually was a family, not the rag tag collection at her mother's funeral. Perhaps it would have been nice to have an annoying aunt or an embarrassing uncle or even an unreliable sibling. But Hilary had no-one.

As if to shield her, her friends huddled around her as they got outside. Everyone else shook her hand and tried to explain who they were. She was surprised when a smart elderly man took her hand and said that he had worked with her father. He had seen the notice in the paper. She wanted to talk to him, ask him about her parents, but he slipped away before she had a chance.

It was over now.

She wandered around the living room, collecting cups and saucers and sherry glasses, piling them up next to the sink. There were a few dried-up ham sandwiches, the mustard leaking out onto the lacy doily. She absentmindedly put the last chocolate mini roll in her mouth. She screwed up serviettes decorated with purple pansies, her mother's choice, threw them in the bin and ran hot water into the bowl to start washing up. Orange tea stained her mother's china. One of the cups had a dark lipstick smile on the rim, and sticky sherry clung to the bottom of the tiny crystal glasses.

Washing up, looking out over the bare winter garden, she thought of the garden of remembrance beside the crematorium. It was crammed with rose bushes, laid out like an overcrowded graveyard, each bush with its plaque, all jostling for position like shoppers on market day. The standard roses looked like umbrellas raised high above the heads, the stems and thorns black against the pale blue sky. She had wondered what would happen if one of the bushes died. Would it be surreptitiously replaced? Might your loved one's memorial change colour overnight?

Interspersed with the sleeping roses, there were plastic flowers stuck in the ground and neatly arranged silk bouquets. And to make the place seem even busier, there were lots of bossy notices:

KEEP OFF THE GRASS

NO DOGS

NO ENTRY

KEEP LEFT

ALL CHRISTMAS WREATHS MUST BE REMOVED BY JANUARY 9TH (ANY REMAINING WILL BE DESTROYED BY THE MANAGEMENT)

Hilary had had the bizarre desire to add her own notice:

IF WE HAVE TO REMOVE OUR WREATHS,
WHY HASN'T <u>MANAGEMENT</u> REMOVED ITS NOTICE?

She was pleased that she had made one decision – to have her mother's ashes scattered in the quiet area around the other side of the building, where there was a small walled garden, with grass that you could walk on and two cherry trees that would provide a little shade in the summer. She thought her mother would have appreciated the peace and calm. She didn't need or want a rose or plaque to remember her.

Now that the washing up was done, Hilary felt lost and alone. She wiped all the surfaces, polished them with the tea towel, and rearranged the furniture in the living room, putting everything back to the exact spot from where it had been moved in the course of the afternoon, lining up chair legs and table legs with dents in the carpet. She wandered into her bedroom and walked out again. She closed all the curtains. She opened her mother's bedroom door and shut it again without going in.

Going back into the kitchen, she took her mother's apron off the back of the door and put it in the washing machine, adding the tea towels and dishcloths she had used. Selecting the programme, she switched the machine on, glad of the noise that took some of the silence away. Why hadn't she let anyone stay? She sat down at the kitchen table and put her head in her arms and wept. Tears of sadness and self-pity, anger and distress, grief and loss poured from her. She cried all the tears she hadn't been able to cry at the funeral. She cried for herself, for her mum, for her dad, for the past, for the future. What on earth was she going to do? She had never been on her own. Before the funeral, she could pretend none of it was real; she could pretend that her mother would be home soon. But although she hadn't seen the flames or smelt the smoke, she knew now that her mother had gone and would never return.

The phone rang and rang.

Lifting her head, she looked towards it but didn't seem to have the power to get to it. Then her mobile rang. She could hear it but didn't know where it was. Distracted from her tears, she got up and started to look for it. She found it in her coat pocket, just as the ringing stopped.

It was Suzanne. Hilary phoned back, but the phone was engaged. Then it rang again, a message.

"Hello Hilary. It's me, Suzanne, just phoning to see how you are. Phone me if you want to talk."

She couldn't talk, so she just texted back "I'm OK x".

She couldn't talk; she didn't know what to say. She felt such a fool. Everyone was so kind. She didn't deserve it. Suzanne was just doing what she'd do for any patient.

She started crying again. She curled herself up on the settee, hugging a cushion. She must have cried herself to sleep, because the next thing she knew, it was nine o'clock.

She turned on the television and turned it off again. She poured herself a glass of sherry and went to bed, hoping for more sleep. Hoping for oblivion.

She was woken from a very deep sleep by the sound of the phone. It was still nine o'clock, but when she came to, she realised it was morning. After days without sleep, she now seemed unable to wake up. She liked sleeping. She pulled the duvet around her head and let her body drift back into it.

Her bladder woke her at eleven and then the phone rang again. Taking a cup of coffee back to bed, she saw several missed calls and texts on her mobile.

She replied briefly to the texts; she didn't want anyone coming round to check on her; she didn't want anyone worrying. No-one would want to be with her while she was like this. They would all talk to each other, reassure each other that she was OK. She just wanted to be on her own. Well, she didn't really; she wanted her mum with her. A tear fell on her cheek.

And then she was crying again, sobbing into the sheets, wailing like a banshee, banging her fists into the pillow like a toddler mid-tantrum. She smashed her elbow onto the corner of the bedside table, sending a shaft of pain all the way into her little finger. Like a hysteric being slapped, the sudden pain brought her to her senses. Her tears stopped almost as quickly as they had started.

"What would Mum think?" she reprimanded herself. "Keep busy," that's what she always said. "Take your mind off things – no good wallowing."

With her mother's words in her head, she got up and, while her bath was running, she stripped her bed, collected all the other laundry that had mounted up over the last few days and took it to the washing machine. She almost started crying again when she took her mother's apron out of the machine and hung it over the airer to dry, but she held it together and took herself off to have a bath and to try to repair some of the damage the tears had wreaked on her face.

She washed herself, washed all her bedding, then stripped her mother's bed, carefully remaking the bed, ready for her mother's return, pulling the candlewick bedspread over the sheets and blankets and placing a clean nightie under the pillow. She vacuumed everywhere, and dusted, moving the many ornaments. By two o'clock she was exhausted and, getting the last load out of the washing machine, sat down at the kitchen table. She wanted something to eat. She took a slightly stale tea cake out of the bread bin, spread it thickly with butter and put a chunk of cheese next to it. She made a milky coffee and took the whole meal into the bedroom. The curtains throughout the house remained drawn; she wasn't ready for the outside world yet. She got into bed fully clothed and turned on the television, choosing a 1980s police drama for distraction. The tea cake tasted good, the cheese slightly sharp in her mouth, the coffee oddly comforting. She snuggled under the duvet and lost herself in the New York streets. She was soon asleep again.

The next few days followed a similar pattern. She felt safe and she had friends on the television. She didn't need anything else.

Then Suzanne called round. Fortunately, she came late one morning to see if Hilary wanted to go shopping or if she needed anything. Hilary was in busy mode, so Suzanne was reassured that she was coping. She went around opening curtains and Hilary didn't stop her. Hilary asked her to buy some more teacakes and cheese. She wasn't yet ready to go out.

Suzanne came back with some fruit as well as what Hilary had asked for; she had seen the state of the fruit in the bowl on the dining table. When Suzanne met the others, she told them that she thought Hilary was doing all right under the circumstances. She was keeping busy but, after all those words she had spoken in the hours and days after her mother's death, she now didn't seem to want to talk at all.

Hilary was pleased that she had coped so well with Suzanne's visit. She didn't think she'd cried and she'd resisted the temptation to run around after Suzanne had left, closing the curtains again.

A week after the funeral she had to go to the doctor. She'd tried to phone for a sick note, but the doctor wanted to see her. Jag would have just left one out for me, she thought. She was too frightened to go out. She wasn't even sure she remembered how to drive. She still felt very tired. What if she fell asleep at the wheel? She put on her anorak with the big hood. She kept her hood up and her head down until the doctor called her in. She didn't want to see anyone. If anyone was nice to her, she'd cry. The doctor seemed busy, not really interested, and for all she asked her, she might as well have just done the note over the phone. Hilary shoved the sick note into her handbag and scurried out before anyone could recognise her. She almost cried with relief when she got back to the safety of her bungalow again.

She was soon back under the covers with her teacakes, waiting for the TV cop show to start, knowing that the music immediately calmed her, relaxed her, allowed her to escape and, most afternoons, to sleep. It seemed the best way to get through the day. If she was asleep, she wasn't thinking.

Janet called around, nervous and diffident, wanting to know if she could do anything. She made them both coffee and tried to get Hilary to talk, but Hilary seemed to have forgotten how to have a conversation. She was polite and answered all the questions Janet asked her, but couldn't wait to be rid of her so that she could get back to bed.

Carol phoned to ask if she felt up to the anniversary party. She knew it was very soon, but it would be only family and friends, everyone would understand if she wanted to leave early. Carol was unaware that Hilary had only managed to leave the house once since the funeral, to go to the doctor for a sick note. She wasn't aware that Hilary had forgotten how to have a conversation, that she was afraid to leave the house. But, then, how could Carol know? Hilary certainly couldn't tell her; she was too ashamed. So she told Carol that she was sorry but she couldn't make the party. She didn't want to make everyone miserable; she hoped it went well; she hoped they would all have a nice time; sorry, sorry.

Liz called around and took her out. She wouldn't take no for an answer. She waited while Hilary got dressed and they drove into the country, to a pub Liz knew, and they each had a large glass of wine. Liz kept up a running commentary, about what she'd done, what she was going to do, what Siobhan had done, what John hadn't done. She didn't seem to notice that Hilary didn't say anything. Hilary felt almost as relaxed as when she was in bed with her television for company. Liz's calm voice and the wine eased the tension, and the pleasant, quiet surroundings made no demands on her. Liz took her home, gave her a hug and Hilary found herself sad to see Liz go.

Hilary allowed the world to go on around her. Suzanne had a key and kept the fridge stocked with milk and the cupboard with sherry. She was sensitive enough not to disturb Hilary if she was sleeping, not to force her to be normal. Hilary was aware that she must be worrying them all. She was certainly worrying herself, but what was the point? She didn't need to go back to work; she had enough money to live on; she could just stay in.

Too many things made her cry. Making Phyllis a cup of coffee, starting to say something to her as she walked into a room, the jolt every time she realised her mum wasn't there. She also found herself thinking about her dad too, grieving for him anew, grieving for all those she had lost.

She was alternately cross with herself for her loss of self-control and passive and inactive under the weight of it all. There seemed no point in going on. No-one would care if she went. She didn't contribute anything useful to the world. She wasn't a nurse or a doctor or a charity worker. She didn't have children or grandchildren to worry over or to worry over her. Her bungalow would be more useful to someone else. It was too big for her, too grand, too much trouble. What would she do if something went wrong? Phyllis had dealt with the running of the house, knew the plumber's phone number, where the insurance documents were filed, when the boiler needed servicing.

"Oh, Mum, why did you have to leave me like this?" Another bout of crying. Where did all the tears come from? She must be dried out by now.

Her crying was interrupted by the doorbell. Whoever was there was quite insistent. But when Hilary dragged herself from her bed and wiped her face, there was no-one at the door.

Her mother would soon have told her to pull herself together, but she didn't seem to have the strength to do it on her own. "Keep busy," she heard her mother's voice telling her, but she had cleaned the bungalow throughout and swept the garden path at the back. The front of the house needed some work, but she didn't want to go out and risk having to talk to someone. She knew she had to deal with some paperwork, make an appointment with the solicitor and the bank, but she couldn't concentrate. The neatly filed papers were all in box files next to the bureau, marked in her mother's hand; the more recent ones were labelled by Hilary as Phyllis's handwriting no longer met her own high standards. She had continued to write the shopping lists and notes for the milkman or notes for Hilary in her spidery, wobbly hand, but she didn't want that writing on the spine of a file for all to see. Hilary had told her that it didn't matter. No-one went into their tiny study apart from the two of them. But her mother didn't want to take any chances; appearances were all important. All the correspondence with her various committees had been on the computer, her physical weakness hidden behind her strong words and opinions.

She went to the files lined up on the shelf. They had talked about getting the house insurance changed into Hilary's name. Now she would have to do it on her own. All the relevant authorities had been informed. After Phyllis's death, Hilary had been swept along in the welter of arrangements and remembered the kind lady who had taken her in hand and registered the death. She had a vague impression that Janet had been with her; she certainly must have made the appointment. The office had been in another town, a new building on an industrial estate surrounded by plumbers' merchants and car body workshops, light and bright and efficient. Hilary remembered feeling a bit cheated that it hadn't been an office in the splendour of the old town hall. She had been given a number to phone for 'Tell Us Once', which sounded like a friendly group of people being helpful, rather than a link to government computers keeping tax and pension records up to date.

She must have written to people in her mother's address book because cards had come, people had attended the funeral. Opening the bureau, the Basildon Bond note paper and envelopes lay where she had left them. She tidied them into their cubby hole and touched the dish with the dry, shrivelled sponge that her mother kept long after stamps no longer needed licking.

"Right."

"I'll make a start."

She picked up the insurance file, pulled the phone towards her, took a deep breath and started.

It was soothing, in an impersonal way, after the knee-jerk "I am sorry" from the person on the other end. She was asked a list of questions and arrangements were made for her to send the relevant documents for the insurance to be changed into her name.

Encouraged by such a promising start, she pulled out the banking file. "Sorry, we are unable to do that over the phone. You'll need to book an appointment. What day would be convenient? Which branch?" She felt battered and bullied but pleased that she had got through it without crying.

That was enough for one day.

Days passed. The texts and emails kept coming; the day of the party was getting closer. No, she definitely couldn't go.

She had heard from people from work and even a couple of old school friends had tried to get in touch. She hadn't replied. She knew she should, but she didn't want anyone to see her like this; she didn't want to talk or communicate in any way, so what was the point?

Lying in bed on the morning of her appointments with the doctor and the bank, she wondered if she could phone and cancel. She felt awful, looked worse. It wouldn't matter if she lost her job; she had loads of money. As her mother would have said, "You'll be comfortably off."

Perhaps she could rearrange.

A small part of the old Hilary emerged and pushed her out of bed and into the shower. "You mustn't let people down."

As she sat at the kitchen table eating a toasted tea cake, a thought came to her that, apart from the currants and sultanas in her comforting teacakes, she had not had any fruit or vegetables for three weeks. Suzanne had diligently stocked up the fruit bowl each week, replacing the shrivelled grapes, soft apples and brown pears, in the hope that one day Hilary would feel like eating what was in the bowl. Perhaps she'd feel better if she ate a bit better and drank a bit less. She cut up an apple and put it on the plate in the melted butter that had dripped off the tea cake. She took a quarter and bit into the crunchy flesh. The freshness and coldness of it woke her mouth up, woke her up. She felt virtuous and strong. She ate the rest.

"Right, let's get through today."

She put on her work clothes, a navy skirt and white cotton blouse, and felt neat and clean, ready for the world. She felt that she had turned a corner, not quite ready to come out from hiding yet, but less frightened, less negative.

The appointment at the bank went by in a blur. The young assistant manager was more nervous than Hilary and over obsequious. He seemed uncomfortable in his ill-fitting suit, his brightly chequered tie making him look like a caricature of a TV presenter. It felt as though she was reassuring him, helping him through a difficult time. He admitted at the end of the stumbling interview that it was the first time he'd done it on his own; he hoped he hadn't made any mistakes; he hoped he hadn't caused any upset. He was nervous around death even at this distance. His anxiety made Hilary feel stronger.

At the GP's surgery, Hilary smiled at the receptionist and accepted condolences offered by people she hadn't seen. She didn't cry. She told the doctor that she was feeling a bit better but not yet ready for work. The doctor was pleased. She said the whole room felt lighter this week; Hilary didn't seem so bowed down, so low. Perhaps she had turned a bit of a corner. But there was no rush. She should take things at her own pace, get through it in her own way. She seemed full of phrases designed to reassure. Hilary felt less of a burden.

It was turning into a good day, and all because of an apple.

She waved to David as she pulled into the drive and went into her bungalow feeling lighter than she had since her mother had died.

There were a few letters on the mat. Picking them up, she took off her coat, hung it up and went through to the kitchen to put the kettle on. She dissolved when she saw her mother's name on the first envelope. It was a catalogue from Cosyfeet, the shoes Phyllis hated but had to wear as her feet became more swollen and misshapen.

"Oh fiddlesticks, I'm hopeless. It's no good. I'm not going to get any better. There's no point."

She allowed herself a few minutes of misery, then pulled herself together. This wasn't what her mother would have wanted; she had brought her up better than this. When she had been feeling a bit better on the way back from the doctor, she had called in at a local shop and bought some vegetables and fruit, determined to eat properly.

"Right. I'll have a tea cake for lunch, then I'll get something out of the freezer to cook for dinner with proper vegetables, a proper dinner."

After lunch, feeling tired from all her exertions, she treated herself to a couple of hours under the duvet, the New York voices on the television lulling her to sleep. Bliss... She had a proper dinner that evening and watched television in the living room instead of retreating to her bedroom out of sight of her mother's chair, which sat accusingly in the corner, overpowering the room, unplugged and unused, waiting to learn its fate.

The following few days seemed a little easier. She found a routine. She felt more useful. She cried less, and when she did cry it was less unexpected, more controlled. She could think about her mother now without guilt or tears in her eyes.

Suzanne and Janet had both told her how the preparations for the party were going – what they were going to wear and when their hair appointments were. They were keen to keep her involved even though they knew she wouldn't go. They both asked if she wanted to go out for coffee. She wasn't sure. She was out of practice at talking. She'd been into town to buy some bits of nonsense, just testing herself to see if she could do it. But she wasn't up to socialising yet.

She'd unexpectedly caught a few minutes of *The Jeremy Kyle Show* on television, a mother and daughter at loggerheads, screeching at each other, looking as if they wanted to scratch each other's eyes out, hating each other. Hilary had watched with fascination for a few minutes, unable to tear her eyes away. Then, when fresh tears arrived, she turned the television off, pulling the plug out at the wall to make sure the images had gone. She calmly thought about her mother, remembered ordinary times – bickering over what to watch on television, racing each other to solve the crossword clues, swapping books. When Hilary wasn't working, they had breakfast together, discussed what the papers had to offer. Hilary could picture her mother opposite her, resplendent in her maroon dressing gown, voicing her opinions, criticising in no uncertain terms those who didn't fit with her views. Hilary hadn't always agreed but she had learned to keep quiet. She remembered her school report one year: "Hilary is too suggestible. She must learn to form her own opinions, not be constantly swayed by others." She had been hurt. It was just the way she saw things; she could see things from all sides and she hated to hurt people, so she stayed on the fence. Her mother had told her off for not standing up for herself. She didn't argue.

Hilary and Phyllis had always agreed about clothes. She thought of the girls at school who had argued with their parents about clothes, wanting to wear short skirts and revealing tops, rebelling against the outdated school uniform. Hilary had learned to keep quiet there too, secretly thinking the outfits tarty, and not quite nice.

She hugged herself. She supposed she had loved her mother. Neither woman was demonstrative, neither ever said anything about loving the other. Hilary always cringed when she heard people at work talking to their children, signing off with "Love you" and "Love you lots". She hadn't needed her mother to say anything like that. She would have curled up in a ball if her mother had been like some of the mothers at school sending elaborate cards and gifts to their "darlings". Her mother had been in charge, bossy, noisy, but always there for her. Always. The bungalow was so quiet now. So quiet.

The doorbell rang, interrupting Hilary's thoughts, making her jump. She went reluctantly to see who was there.

Chapter Six

Celebrations

Carol waved as she drove past Hilary's bungalow. She wasn't sure if Hilary had seen her but at least she was up and dressed and it looked as if she was sending some poor door-to-door salesman away with a flea in his ear.

The day of the party had come all too soon. Sixty people were expected; the food was ordered, the disco booked. She really wanted to enjoy this. She was on her way to decorate the function room at the golf club and to check on the details of the buffet. At this rate she'd be exhausted before the party started.

Two hours later, as she was driving home again, she wondered whether she should pop in on Hilary. But seeing that the curtains were drawn, she continued on past. She was disappointed that neither her own mother nor Jonathan's father would be at the party. It was too far for them to travel. Even if she could have organised it, her mother wouldn't have liked the food, it would have been too late to get her back to the nursing home with its rigid timetable, and the toilets would have been a nightmare. She could almost hear her mother moaning. It would have been too noisy for Jonathan's father with his hearing aids and, anyway, he wouldn't have known where he was or, for that matter, why.

Stopping at traffic lights, Carol remembered the agony of settling her mother in the home. She'd complained about the food, the other residents, not enough visitors, too many visitors. She had even complained that Carol had conned her into distributing her belongings to the grandchildren to prevent her from going home. It had been a nightmare.

The lights changed and she pulled forward into the traffic, wondering if she'd get back in time to have a nice bath.

Her mother had settled, eventually. Carol became anxious thinking of those agonising months. She'd tried not visiting, but then she had nightmares wondering what was happening to her mother. She'd tried taking her out more, but her mother just moaned the whole time. She'd tried taking the grandchildren, but then she couldn't bear it when her mother cried in front of them. She'd tried ignoring her, shouting at her, cajoling her, crying. She contacted her brother but he was working abroad and said he'd leave all the decisions to her. She'd even considered taking her home. Then the resident in the adjacent room changed and her mum had an ally. Someone to moan with about the staff, the food, the other residents, neglectful daughters. Gradually, the visits became less of a trial. Her mum had stopped asking to be taken home. Instead it became difficult to take her out at all as she was too busy. Her mum started knitting again, taught others how to knit. Carol found herself admiring their misshapen efforts with the same patience and tact that she afforded the grandchildren.

She remembered how she'd told everyone at New Year how lucky they were to have their parents cared for and settled. The difficult times with her mother had been obscured by a haze of alcohol. It's just as well the mind allows us to push painful memories down; we'd never do anything else if all that pain stayed at the front of our consciousness, she thought to herself, as she pulled up in front of the house. She shook herself as she got out of the car, shaking off the memories.

She went inside to find children and grandchildren in her tiny living room, watching a cartoon. Jonathan made her a cup of coffee, sat her in his chair, and two of the grandchildren climbed onto her lap. She almost fell asleep. Then, with only two hours before the first guests were to arrive, she shooed the whole family out, back home and to their hotel, and went upstairs to change.

Her new dress was hanging on the wardrobe door, a beautiful, soft, silky material in yellows, golds and browns, a lovely dress – but it looked enormous. How had this happened to her? The bath was running. The bath, her only indulgence, the only guilt-free me time she allowed herself. As she lay back in the hot water, she wondered how she had become this person who put everyone else first, who looked after everyone else, who ignored her own needs. When had she become so passive? Had it started when the children were born? Everyone said how lucky she was to have such a helpful husband, and he *was* a helpful husband and she knew she was lucky. She worked part time for a charity, helping to organise the shop, doing the accounts, helping at fund-raising events. She loved her work, but even there she felt as though she was a bit of a dogsbody and was always the one to fill in if someone else was off. When the children had left home, she thought she might do more, but then along came grandchildren and her parents became progressively more needy. She just ended up with a different set of people clamouring for her attention.

I've got to fifty-five and I've lost who I am, she thought, ducking her head under the water to wash her hair. I don't know where all these negative thoughts came from; this isn't me. I'm going to plan something. I'm going to take a whole day for myself and just see if the world falls apart. I wonder if any of the others would fancy a day at that new spa I saw advertised.

Her thoughts were interrupted by Jonathan putting his head round the bathroom door (one day she would dare to lock it). "Have you drowned? It's quarter to, we need to leave in half an hour." "I'll be ready," she replied. "You go and sort yourself out." The moment had gone. Carol heaved herself out of the bath, feeling grateful that they'd chosen the one fitted with handles.

Half an hour later they were both downstairs in their glad rags, gathering handbag, coats, keys, switching lights off, moving towards the door in a way they had hundreds of times before. Outside, Jonathan gave the door a push to check that it was locked. The same routine as always. Their life was made up of lots of comfortable routines. Was it going to be possible to break away even for a day?

They arrived at the golf club just before the cars bringing family and friends. A flurry of hellos, hugs and kisses. Everyone congratulated Carol on the way she had decorated the room. The white streamers and pearl drop balloons brightened the rather dull, square meeting room that they had hired for the evening.

Looking around, Carol smiled at the people who'd come to celebrate with them. As well as their children and grandchildren, there were friends and neighbours and a few old friends that she had hardly seen since her wedding day thirty years ago. She was glad she'd managed a quick call to her mum in the taxi on the way; she'd sounded happy and, uncharacteristically, had wished them a nice time. Old and young mixed together. No-one seemed to be on their own, but she'd have to keep an eye on the younger grandchildren; they could get a bit boisterous and over-excited.

Greetings over, groups formed and reformed. The men clustered round the bar, shouting and laughing loudly, and the children were, for the moment, behaving. The disco started and in the small dance space a few people danced. The youngsters looked on in a mixture of horror and amazement as their parents threw themselves about to music from the seventies and eighties, singing along, hands in the air, some looking more comfortable than others, looking just as they had when they danced around their handbags at the university union discos. The dance floor population ebbed and flowed as the DJ tried to gauge his audience, never getting it quite right but gamely carrying on. Even when no-one else was dancing, Carol and Jonathan's grandchildren ran across the floor, dragging balloons and streamers behind them, so the DJ was never quite on his own.

Suzanne, Liz and Janet sat down, Liz looking very red-faced and hot after dancing particularly energetically to 'Jump' by the Pointer Sisters. They had retrieved their drinks and found a quiet corner in which to catch up. Suzanne and Liz both thought Janet was looking tired, but neither of them said so. Their talk turned to Hilary and what a shame it was that she and her mum had missed this do. Phyllis had bought a new dress for the occasion just after Hilary's birthday lunch, but had never had the chance to wear it. None of them could believe how hard Hilary had taken her mother's death. She was always so sensible, considered and calm.

"Actually, I don't feel that I'm coping very well with my parents at the moment," said Janet. "Hilary was such a good sounding board but I daren't say anything to her now. I just go and listen and make coffee. I'm exhausted from travelling up and down the motorway every week. I don't even like driving and I feel so threatened by the massive lorries, thundering past. They seem to go faster the wetter it is, producing spray that blinds and disorientates. You'll think I'm daft though, because I've realised that I feel less threatened by lorries with pictures of babies or soft white bread on the side, however big and badly driven they are."

The others nodded in agreement. "I'd never thought about it, but you are right. You imagine the driver of a lorry with a cute picture to be better and somehow nicer. Our minds are strange the way they work, aren't they? No wonder advertisers have a field day with us," commented Liz. "I really don't know how you cope with all that travelling. At least the weather is OK at the moment."

"You know, perhaps we ought to try and do something to make us all feel better, Hilary included. We all seem to try to pack too much into our lives trying to please others," mused Liz, tapping her foot to the opening bars of 'Come on Eileen', obviously itching to be back on the dance floor.

"Come on, let's dance. That's guaranteed to make us feel better." Suzanne dragged them back to the dance floor, squeezing between all the others who'd been tempted back.

Throwing themselves around to the frenzied rhythm, surrounded by smiling faces, they couldn't help but momentarily forget all their troubles. An unknown 'modern' track with a beat they couldn't get their feet in time to sent them laughing back to their seats, followed closely by Carol who had danced almost every dance.

"Phew, I'm getting too old for this. My knees will hurt tomorrow," she said, as she flopped down next to Liz.

"We were talking about getting ourselves out for the day to make ourselves feel better."

"Really, that's just what I was planning in the bath tonight," countered Carol. "What about that new spa that's just opened? They've got some really good deals on, as they are trying to drum up custom."

"It's lovely. We got shown round when we went for coffee in the hotel the other Saturday," said Suzanne. "They were trying to get David to treat me to a treatment but he didn't take the hint. Sometimes he is just so dense."

"Well, why don't I get some details and email everyone with some options. I'll include Hilary. I think we need to try to persuade her to come, even though she will probably say no."

"Definitely. I've been a bit worried about her. She's a funny old thing. I didn't want her to feel pressured, so I've just been popping in from time to time, but half the time she's been in bed. I think she's been living on teacakes and sherry, although last week some of the fruit had gone and there was a bit more in the fridge. I think she'd been shopping. It's so hard to know what to do. If she doesn't want to talk, you can't make her. She's still off sick."

"I know, Suzanne, it's really difficult, isn't it? I invited her out for coffee but she didn't want to come. What surprised me more, actually, is that she hasn't asked about my mum at all. It's just not like her. I miss her." Janet twisted the gold bangle on her wrist.

"We'll start working on her straight away." Carol was feeling extra confident as a result of deciding that she needed to do something to change her life, and having drunk several glasses of bubbly. "I'll look into it," she said over her shoulder as Jonathan took her onto the dance floor for a slow dance to Joe Cocker's 'You are so Beautiful', the first song they danced to as man and wife, thirty years earlier.

They all got a little tearful then – perhaps it was the alcohol. But the DJ followed that with the Traveling Wilburys, which put a stop to any soppiness and everyone was soon laughing and moving on the dance floor with varying degrees of skill and rhythm.

The bar closed at midnight and it was time to start thinking about going home. Drinks were finished, handbags retrieved from under tables, phone numbers and email addresses exchanged with a "We must keep in touch". Jackets and wraps were donned and a slow-moving snake of people moved towards Carol and Jonathan to say thank you and goodbye. Soon there was only family left. Carol and Jonathan were persuaded to call at the Travel Inn for a last drink with the family before going home and, not wanting the evening to end and reality to intrude, they agreed. Tired but happy, they piled into taxis for the short journey. As soon as they got to the hotel, the grandchildren fell asleep on the red plush banquette seating and Carol, Jonathan and their three children were able to talk for a few minutes – how well the party had gone, how well Uncle Alf looked, how drunk Auntie Joyce got, but how quietly she slept in the corner, how much Champagne had been drunk by everyone, how nice it was for the whole family to get together and why did it only happen for weddings and funerals? The comments went back and forth until Carol could no longer keep her eyes open and persuaded Jonathan to order a taxi to take them home. He must have been feeling mellow or tired, because he agreed straight away, even though it was only a fifteen-minute walk from the hotel to their house.

With further goodbyes, the children were woken or picked up, and arrangements were made to meet at lunchtime the next day. The children saw Carol and Jonathan into the taxi. It reminded Carol of their wedding day, only this time it was their children and grandchildren and not their parents and siblings who waved them off. "A jolly good do," they both agreed as they made their way home.

Hilary thought of them all that night, enjoying themselves. She stayed up late watching the television, not really concentrating, thinking of what they would be up to. She knew that there would be lots of drinking and dancing. She wasn't much of a dancer, too self-conscious, and one drink and she worried she'd say something stupid or make a fool of herself by falling over. Phyllis had been looking forward to the party far more than Hilary. Her mother had oozed confidence; she'd had enough for both of them. Hilary could never think of anything to say and when they all got on to children and grandchildren, she had nothing to add. She needed something to do, like at Suzanne's New Year's party, or a role to play like at her birthday lunch. She liked to know where she stood.

Bored with the television, she dared to go into her mother's room and look at the dress her mother had bought for the party. She held the royal blue dress to her face, rubbing it against her cheek, remembering going into town to choose it, her mother struggling to try things on in the shops but determined to find something, getting a bit cross with the assistants who tried to rush her and with Hilary for not being helpful enough. Hilary hadn't really liked the dress, but she hadn't told her mother. The material seemed a bit flimsy and cheap, although the dress wasn't. Her mother loved the colour. There had been no discussion. Hilary gave in as always and justified it to herself – it didn't matter if the dress wouldn't last, as long as her mother had the pleasure of wearing it. But in the end, she hadn't worn it. Hilary hung it back in the tightly packed wardrobe, and shut and locked the door to stop it from springing open.

"Perhaps next time someone asks, I will go out," she said to herself. As she locked the front door, she saw the lights of David's car turning into the drive opposite.

"Gosh, it's nearly one o'clock. Better go to bed."

She turned out the lights and checked that the back door was locked before finding her way to the safety of her duvet.

Chapter Seven

In the Local

"Anyone ready for another drink?" asked Richard, as he headed past the table where John and Jonathan were already sitting. "Excellent party at the weekend – thanks."

"Glad you enjoyed it," replied Jonathan. "It was all down to Carol's hard work as ever. I'll have another pint of bitter, please. This week's guest beer, can't remember the name," he said, twisting round in his chair to try to see the pump.

"Is it all right then? I think I'll try it. The IPA is terrible tonight."

"Cheers!" said Richard, putting the beer down and squeezing past Jonathan to sit down. "I can't believe you two have been together thirty years. Janet and I'll be seventy-five before we celebrate our thirtieth anniversary – and looking at poor Janet running herself ragged looking after her mum and dad, I'm not so sure getting old is all it's cracked up to be."

"I noticed she looked a bit tired at our do, but she seemed to enjoy herself."

"Oh, she had a great time, but eight o'clock on Sunday morning she got a call from her dad. The carer hadn't turned up and he was trying to help her mum wash and dress. They all sounded in a right state. I couldn't let her drive all that way again so we both drove up. Her parents are OK, but I find her mum very difficult to cope with. You know what I mean. Constantly repeating everything and crying for absolutely no reason. I don't know how her dad puts up with it. I'd have to put her in a home."

"Getting Dad and Carol's mum into homes wasn't easy, but it certainly takes some of the worry away, once they are settled, although Carol still goes to see her mum at least once a week and the rest of the time we seem to have Lucy's two to look after. I love it," said Jonathan, "Playing with all their toys, watching CBeebies. Carol is too grown up to enjoy small children."

John took a long drink from his pint, wiped his lips and sat back, listening to the other two. He'd had a long day at work and had come to the pub on his way home. Liz never expected him home before seven thirty. In fact, he felt positively in the way sometimes. She occasionally joined him in the pub, but more often left him to it and had a glass of wine as she made the dinner. They had, over the years, worked out what the other needed and they muddled along amiably. Neither had much ambition or passion and they had a comfortable life, without the trials and tribulations that the others seemed to go through (and seemed to spend a lot of time moaning about). His parents were both dead. They had died as they'd lived, tidily and without drama, heart attack and stroke within a year of each other, no lingering, no suffering, active and independent until the last. A shock for him and his sister, of course, but they had been a good age and they'd had a good life. He counted himself lucky. Liz looked after their only grandchild, Siobhan, while their daughter, Lisa, worked, but Siobhan was long gone before he got in from work in the evening. He occasionally saw Siobhan when Lisa had a weekend shift, but most of the time he wouldn't have known she had been at their house – all traces removed before he got home. Their son, Edward, was doing very well for himself, working in insurance in New York – John was very proud of him. That was something he was happy to tell the others about. Edward had succeeded beyond everyone's expectations. Perhaps the ambition that should have pushed his own career forward had all gone into Edward.

"Come on, drink up, John. It's your round." Richard was holding his empty glass up for him. "You're very quiet."

"Long day, mate. Is everyone having the same again?" John asked, as he got up, collected the glasses and went to the bar.

"Oh good, I timed that right," shouted David from the door. "Pint of lager, please," he said, as he made his way towards the others at the table, playfully punching John's arm as he walked past him.

"Great party, Jonathan. Have you recovered? Have all the family gone back now?" asked David, sitting down in the chair John had vacated.

"They all went back Sunday. I was so pleased it went well, made up for all the other celebrations we've had to miss for one reason or another. Know what I mean?"

"Jump in my grave as quick, would you?" asked John, as he put down the three drinks he was carrying and went back for his own. David shuffled across to the next chair and drank almost half his pint in one gulp.

As ever, he managed to monopolise the conversation, full of jokes and bonhomie, calling out to others across the pub, dragging all the attention to himself, his loud voice and louder laugh commanding attention.

"Car going OK, John?" he boomed. John had bought a second-hand convertible when he turned fifty. It was his pride and joy. He loved to get it out as soon as the weather was warm enough to have the top down and he and Liz could be seen speeding along the roads, heading out of town. David, who had a new car every two years, took the mickey out of him for all the love and attention he bestowed on the ageing relic.

"Had the top down last Sunday – great way of clearing the head after the party. I shall have to take it and get it serviced though, before we take it down through France again."

There followed discussion and banter about the best way to keep the car on the road, until David got up and replenished their glasses.

"Last one," they all agreed.

David came back from the bar looking thoughtful. "Just been talking to George." They looked up and acknowledged a mutual acquaintance at the bar.

"Remember Stephen who worked behind the bar and then left to go and run his own pub? He's just been diagnosed with bowel cancer. He must be our age, if not younger. It doesn't bear thinking about."

"But he always kept himself fit," said John. "I don't think he drank and he certainly didn't smoke. How unfair is that?"

"Carol will be upset," said Jonathan. "I think she had a bit of a thing for him years ago."

They drank in silence for a few moments in the bustle of the pub. The news seemed to leave them all thoughtful, considering their own mortality.

One by one, they finished their drinks and got up to go. It seemed wrong to continue enjoying themselves in the face of this news.

Two weeks later, Jonathan once again pushed his way into the pub. He could hear shouts of laughter, words and phrases flung into the air above the general noise of the bar. He had been coming to this pub for years, but none of the previous landlords had got it quite right until Ben and Sheila had taken over five years earlier. The staff reflected the personalities of the owners and couldn't be more friendly or helpful, without being obsequious or intrusive. The food was good (although Carol thought it a bit pricey). More importantly, the beer was well cared for. On the rare occasion when none of his friends were there, Jonathan felt comfortable, sitting quietly with a beer and the paper. He had struck up a conversation with some interesting people over the years.

Tonight, he expected that John and David would be in, but he wasn't sure about the others. As he got his drink from the bar, he saw David holding court on one of the high round tables, and went over to join the noisy crowd. Jag and a couple of his colleagues from the local hospital had joined John and David and they were all in high spirits. Jonathan was quiet at first. He was halfway down his drink, listening to the talk of cars, golf and football batting back and forth across the table, when David bellowed, "You're quiet," as if he was the other side of the bar, rather than merely a couple of feet away.

"Just taking it all in, winding down, you know?" replied Jonathan. "Have you heard how Stephen is getting on?"

"Surgery yesterday – apparently it all went OK but he's got to have a bag. Ugh, can't imagine having to deal with that." David brought Jag and his colleagues into the conversation, dragging them away from their beloved cars. He asked them about Stephen's chances, about what would happen next, grilling them. They didn't seem to mind, although the three all seemed to have slightly different opinions, and they disappeared into medical speak that started to go over the others' heads until David dragged them back again.

Jonathan, now more relaxed and halfway down his second pint, chipped in. "I couldn't believe Carol's reaction two weeks ago when I told her. You remember I mentioned she'd had a bit of a thing for him before we married. I went home from here, told her while we were having dinner and she just broke down."

"Oh no, you were obviously second choice."

"She got you on the rebound."

"Perhaps she still fancies him."

They ribbed him, the comments becoming lewder, but now he put his hand up to quieten them all. "No, it was worse than that. She'd found a breast lump. She'd already been to the doctor and been referred. She didn't want to tell me, but hearing about Stephen, it all came out."

That shut them up. They all looked suitably chastened, but Jonathan reassured them by saying, "Believe me, everything you've said – and more – about her and Stephen went through my mind before she was calm enough to tell me what she was crying about. Until her news sank in, I thought my world had come to an end. And then when her news did sink in, I realised that my world could come to an end. I was completely shell-shocked."

"Can't imagine."

"What happened?"

"How is she?"

"Do the others know?"

"It's been a hellish fortnight, but after going through all the tests, it was just a cyst and the doctor drained it. She wouldn't let me tell anyone until now. She's kept it all to herself and, to be honest, if the news about Stephen hadn't shocked and upset her, I don't think she'd have told me either. I can't bear the thought of her going through all that on her own. When they put that needle into her breast, it was me that needed the anaesthetic." He shuddered.

"Did you go privately? I'd make sure Suzanne did. The waiting is the worst."

"No. The NHS was brilliant. After all, it's only a fortnight since we were in here talking about Stephen and she's been referred, investigated and treated. I couldn't fault the care, although it's a bit like a conveyer belt. I suppose it has to be with the numbers. And, although the staff were all very good, they treat the whole procedure as routine, which I suppose for them it is, but certainly not for us. Carol was very good and I feel most of the time she was looking after me instead of the other way round. I'm hopeless with illness."

"Women are a lot braver than we are," countered Jag. "I wish there was a way of making all these processes more humane, but when there is a possibility of cancer, speed of diagnosis is of the essence and the niceties get lost. Does she know you are telling us all about this?"

"Of course. It's been agony not being able to talk to anyone about it, you know what I mean. Carol doesn't seem to need to talk. She thinks very deeply and the more difficult a problem or issue, the quieter she is. After all these years, she knows me – she knows I need to talk and she knows it's you lot I'll be talking to. She just didn't want the discussion going on before the outcome – whatever it was – was known."

"The girls are all having a spa weekend soon, aren't they? That couldn't come at a better time, could it? What with all the traumas they've had to deal with, they deserve a break. I thought it was a bit extravagant at first, but now I just don't blame them. Perhaps we should have booked up too. Although, it wouldn't have been a break then would it?" They all laughed.

The others agreed with Richard and the talk turned back to the more comfortable subjects of cars, work, arrangements for golf while the 'girls' had their trip to the spa.

Chapter Eight

A Spa Weekend

The spa was in a hotel just far enough out of town for the trip to feel like a real break. Set in beautiful surroundings, the Georgian house looked as though it was welcoming guests to a weekend house party, rather than paying guests who were there escaping the rat race, treating their mothers or meeting with friends for a day out. Most of those driving up the long drive were women. The car park was discreetly hidden among the trees so as not to spoil the grace and symmetry of the building and its circular driveway. Low, weathered, wooden signs pointed towards the reception. All was calm and luxurious, and felt like a treat even before you entered the building.

The receptionists and staff were perfectly made up and polite. They wore white coats, which gave the place the feel of an eighteenth-century asylum for the mad and demented rich. You had the impression that you would be cared for, looked after, cocooned in comfort and safety, away from the outside world. Hundreds of thousands of pounds had been spent to create this impression, which explained the steep prices.

And, thought Carol, as she trundled in with her weekend case, it will be worth every penny.

Almost as soon as Carol's family had returned to their own homes after the anniversary party, emails between Carol and her friends, and between Carol and Holden Hall spa started to fly about. They managed to persuade themselves and each other that a weekend would be better value than a single day. They settled on a date.

Hilary had agreed to come just for the day. Having made the momentous decision that she'd accept the next invitation, she decided it must be fate that it turned out to be something so exciting. She had been the first to respond to Carol's email, but fearing how she might react had decided a day at the spa would be enough. She had always wanted to go to a spa. She had never had a massage or a facial; that was something other people did. Now the day had arrived and she actually felt excited about it. She felt a little guilty too, not sure that her mother would have approved, but she managed to justify the trip by telling herself that she had promised to accept the next invitation she received. Her mother had always said that you must never break a promise. She had a memory of being seven, and let down by a friend. In floods of tears, she had fled to the swing seat in the garden. Her mother had followed and sat down next to her. She remembered the smell of lily of the valley wafting up from the border as her mother gently explained why it was so important never to break a promise, not to let others or herself down, not to make others suffer for a broken promise. She remembered feeling very grown up, as if she was being trusted with a secret.

Janet was staying for the whole weekend. She hoped that nothing would happen to spoil her stay. Her father was again managing brilliantly and the care agency they had chosen was very efficient. But you never could tell, and no-one could predict illness either in her parents or the carers. Janet would always worry; Carol hoped she would manage to relax. Suzanne had already been to the spa a few weeks earlier and had returned with glowing skin and glowing reports about the venue and the treatments. Liz had made it clear to her daughter that she wasn't available for childcare that weekend. Even Chahna hoped to be home from a business trip to

Paris in time to join them for at least a meal and perhaps a swim. All the men had enough food in the fridge, plans for at least one game of golf and phone numbers in case of emergencies. Although they were only going thirty miles up the road, it felt like preparing for a military exercise.

As Carol was signing in and getting her room key, Liz, Janet and Suzanne arrived in convoy up the drive. They'd decided on separate cars, just in case they were needed elsewhere. That way if one had to leave, it didn't disrupt the weekend for anyone else. They were directed to adjoining rooms in a recently added extension. The rooms were disappointingly not the Georgian splendour they had imagined, but comfortable standard en-suite hotel rooms that could have been anywhere in the world. Still, they agreed, the rooms were clean and to a good standard, with comfortable beds and everything they could want or need. They simply lacked character. Determined to make the best of everything, the women unpacked quickly, deciding the rooms were only for sleeping in anyway, and went off to explore the facilities.

The dining room made up for the business-like style of the bedrooms –fabulously ornate mirrors over the two fireplaces, mahogany sideboards with spindly legs, beautiful highly polished mahogany tables and chairs, all set with what looked like Georgian silver (surely you can't put that in the dishwasher, thought Janet), and a painted floor. They were all impressed by the attention to detail. The sash windows extended down to the floor, opening out onto a beautiful paved patio area with steps leading down to a formal garden. None of them was sure enough of her architectural history to know whether this was correct for the period, but it looked stunning.

Looking at her watch, Carol said, "Right. My first treatment is at eleven o'clock. I'd better find out where I have to go."

"Is it OK if I come too?" asked Janet. "I think we are both having a pedicure to start off with. I think our treatments might be in the wrong order. I shall chip my toe nail polish getting onto the couch for the body wrap. Or will the polish just melt in the heat?" Janet was ever the worrier.

"Don't worry, Janet, just relax and enjoy the day. I've got some time before my treatments start," said Liz, consulting her paperwork. "Shall we meet up for lunch?"

They agreed to meet back at their rooms before going for lunch. Janet and Carol went off to find the treatment rooms, still feeling slightly self-conscious in their white towelling bathrobes. Suzanne and Liz headed back to reception to find out if they could get a cup of coffee. Would that be allowed or would they have to settle for herbal tea? At reception, they found Hilary, looking like a frightened rabbit, holding a bathrobe at arm's length as if ready to hand it back and run out the door.

"Oh, Hilary, how lovely."

"Brilliant timing. We're just going for coffee."

As they hugged each other, Hilary felt her eyes fill with tears. "I'm still not sure I should have come. I'm such a misery. Sorry. Oh dear. Oh dear," she said, roughly brushing the tears away. She had been so determined not to cry. She had put her things out the night before, finding her swimming costume, deciding what to wear. But, on the drive across, she had started to worry that she shouldn't be going out to enjoy herself. What would people think? Her mother hadn't been dead long. She felt her mother's disapproval, as if she was sitting on her shoulder telling her that this wasn't the sort of thing nice girls did. She'd gone all the way around one roundabout and started to go home again, but then she'd stopped the car, and thrown her shoulders back, feeling as though she was throwing her mother off. She'd turned around again and continued on her way to the hotel. Arriving hot and flustered, she'd then worried because she was late – how would she find anyone? But fate intervened and she'd been rescued.

"Nonsense," said the ever-sensible Suzanne. "Come on, it'll do you the world of good. I just wish you were staying."

"Where do I go? What do I do? Where shall I get changed? Oh dear. Oh dear." As she fumbled with the strap of her bag, trying to hitch it onto her shoulder while holding the bulky bathrobe and papers she'd been given, her look of fear intensified.

"Come on. You can use my room, so much nicer than a changing room and a locker." Liz put her arm across Hilary's shoulders, pushed the strap of her bag further onto her shoulder and guided her towards the corridor leading to their rooms.

"Oh dear, this is a bit of a disappointment after that beautiful entrance, no...er... I mean it's lovely, but I thought it would..." Hilary trailed off.

"That's what we thought. Still, it's adequate for what we need. You get changed," replied Liz, as Hilary squeezed past her into the bathroom and shut the door.

"At least everything is lovely and clean," Suzanne chimed in. "David and I went to Paris last month and the place we stayed in was awful. It got a brilliant write-up in *The Telegraph* and, yes, the ambience was lovely, 'French style as we like to imagine it,' but it was *filthy*. You didn't have to run your finger along surfaces to find the dust. It was fighting for space with the cobwebs and grease, ugh."

"You two are never at home," said Liz over her shoulder as she tidied away some of things she had flung on the bed, not wanting Suzanne to criticise her housekeeping skills. "How do you manage to keep your house so beautiful when you are always working or travelling?"

"I'm not sure. I like housework when I get the time, but I think you've just answered your own question, we're never there! David insisted on keeping a weekly cleaner when I moved in and although I thought it very decadent and unnecessary at the time, it's amazing how quickly you get used to it."

"What on earth is Hilary doing? She only had to undress and put a swimming costume on."

Hilary was now struggling into her swim suit; she couldn't remember the last time she'd been swimming. She got into it but then stared in the mirror in despair; how could she face other people looking like this? The bandeau top of her purple-patterned costume was stretched across her chest, flattening where it touched, the top of her breasts spilling over the straining material. The high legs dug into her hips, the cellulite spilling out at the sides. She looked like a picture on the naughty post cards she and her dad had loved to giggle at.

She stood looking in the mirror for a while. She felt like crying. She felt like giving up and going home. Coming here was a mistake. What had she been thinking? Why had she bothered? She was just deciding to go home when Liz knocked on the door and, without waiting, walked in. She burst out laughing.

Suzanne came up behind her and looked over her shoulder and started giggling too and soon, in spite of herself, Hilary, for the first time in weeks, although she could hardly breathe, was laughing uncontrollably.

"You look like a purple larva," spluttered Liz.

"No wonder you took so long," laughed Suzanne. "How will you ever get out of it?"

Hilary couldn't answer for laughing, the giggle bubbling up, as uncontrollable as the tears had been. She couldn't believe how good it felt to be laughing. It seemed to release something inside her and, for the first time since her mum had died, she felt the sadness that had enveloped her lift. She was so glad she had come, and made the instant decision to see if they had a room for the night (if she could ever get out of this darn costume and find another). Why on earth had she thought that her mother wouldn't approve? Phyllis had loved luxury. She would have loved the surroundings, even if she didn't like the treatments. She had loved to have fun. She had loved to laugh. With sudden insight, Hilary realised that it was her anger that was allowing her to remember only the harsh bossy side of her mother. The mum who had loved her, whom she had loved, had been softer and lots of fun.

They all fell on the bed like teenagers, giggling uncontrollably, trying not to wet themselves, pulling at the straps on the purple costume, trying to free Hilary.

"Let go," cried Hilary, tears of laughter streaming down her face. "We'll have to cut it off." Their laughter gradually subsided – until they looked at each other, and, like school children, they started again.

"Right," said Suzanne, taking charge, "I'll go to reception and see what they have for sale. I saw a rail as we came in. Obviously they are prepared for moments such as these." Trying to be serious caused more giggles.

"Ask if there are any rooms available for tonight. I'm probably too late but I think I want to stay…if only to get my own back on you two somehow."

"We're not going to have time to get a coffee now. I'll put the kettle on in here." Liz got up and filled the kettle in the sink, still quietly chuckling to herself.

"Have you got scissors? I'll start trying to get out of this monstrosity before I am completely strangled. Oh dear."

As Suzanne went out of the room and Liz busied herself with the kettle, Hilary said to their backs, "I don't know how you've put up with me all these weeks. I think I'm finally finding my way back to being me. I'm sorry I've been such a misery."

"Don't be such a twit," Suzanne said. "I'm just sorry we couldn't do more."

"Mum would have been so ashamed of me, grizzling all the time like that. She was so strong."

"You daft ha'porth, she would have been worried and upset to see you like that, like we were. We spent ages discussing how best to help you. Anyway, she wouldn't have been ashamed. You dealt with everything about the funeral, told everyone, you coped really well."

"Did I? I had no idea what I was doing. I have very little memory of the last few weeks, must have been on automatic pilot. Oh dear, do people really think I coped OK?"

"Of course. Right, now, come on, let's have coffee and get on with whatever this place has to offer." Liz got out her programme and moved the subject on to their plans for the weekend.

Janet and Carol were admiring their newly painted toenails and comparing notes on the skill or otherwise of the practitioners, when they saw Suzanne coming from reception.

"Great news – Hilary has decided to stay and I've just confirmed they've got a room."

"Oh lovely, how come?"

"That's wonderful – how on earth did you persuade her?"

"Well…she'll have to tell you herself," answered Suzanne, as a giggle bubbled to the surface. "She certainly does seem better though, coming round a bit. I think she might finally be coming to terms with it."

She walked off, carrying a small carrier bag, back towards the bedrooms. "See you at lunch," she called over her shoulder.

"How does she manage to look elegant in a dressing gown?" mused Carol, pulling the tie on her own gown tighter around her ample middle. "You always look lovely too, whatever you wear," she said to Janet. "And I wish I knew how you manage to have hair that always looks perfect. Mine never seems to go right, whatever I do."

"Carol, why do you always put yourself down? You're lovely and everyone loves you."

Carol noticed that Janet had not said anything about her appearance. She didn't want to just be loved because she looked after everyone; she wanted to be gorgeous and glamorous, not plump and homely.

They consulted their timetables and realised they had time for a swim before lunch.

The pool was at one side of the building in a long orangery full of natural light from the wall of glass down one side and the three domed roof lights above. Loungers and chairs were dotted around; plants and trees gave the impression of an island paradise. Hilary was lounging on one of the loungers reading, looking lovely in a red polka-dot halter-neck swimming costume.

"You're staying after all?"

"Yes," said Hilary, smiling. "Suzanne organised the room and this costume. You've all been so kind. I'm sure I don't deserve it – I must have been a real pain. I'm really sorry."

"Come on, let's have a swim," said Janet.

The three of them swam a few lengths of the pool, setting a leisurely pace suited to the surroundings, and then sat in the sauna to dry off.

"It's good to see you smiling again, Hilary," said Janet, settling herself on the top bench.

"I really miss Mum, but it sort of feels as though she is still there. I think that's one of the reasons why I've hardly been out. It would feel like betrayal to go out, even to do the shopping. I have to go to Sainsbury's these days. I don't think I'll ever be able to go into that Tesco again – although at least I can now mention the name without crying.

What a fool I've been. If it hadn't been for your kindness – or bloody-mindedness – you'd have given up on me. Liz and Suzanne laughing at me – I'm sure they'll tell you later – did me more good than you can imagine. I think it was the first normal reaction towards me for weeks. Everyone has been so kind, so sympathetic, so careful, that I have been allowed to wallow in self-pity. I can't remember the last time I asked you, Janet, how your parents were getting on, and I've heard on the grapevine, Carol, that you've just had a bit of a scare."

Janet turned to Carol. "What scare?"

"Really, you haven't heard? I'm surprised Richard hasn't said anything. I know Jonathan told the whole pub the other night."

"Actually, I've been so preoccupied with getting Mum and Dad sorted for me to have this weekend away, he probably forgot or thought it was wise not to burden me further, but I wish he had. What happened?"

"I found a lump in my breast." Janet and Hilary remained quiet, waiting for Carol to continue. "Fortunately, it was just a cyst."

"But that must have been awful. Why on earth didn't you say anything?"

"I didn't want to burden anyone really, and there's a bit of me that says if I don't say it out loud, it won't be true. I didn't tell Jonathan until I'd been to the doctor and got a hospital appointment. The doctor was brilliant, organised it all very quickly, not giving false reassurance or causing alarm. It was that locum who came to see you after your mum died, but you probably don't remember her."

"Yes, I've seen her since for sick notes. I'm still not back at work – I'm so ashamed, but I haven't been able to face it. She's very efficient, but Jag will always be my favourite. He always says the right thing."

"But how did you keep it to yourself?" asked Janet, taking the conversation back to Carol. "Didn't you feel the need to talk it through? I'd have talked to anyone who'd listen. I'd have had to look on the internet to find out what would happen. I'd have written myself off before I got to the outpatients. Eulogy written, the lot."

"I was really frightened and things do go through your mind, even when they found that it was just a cyst. I was thinking of all the times diagnoses are wrong. But talking doesn't help me. I think a lot and I wrote a lot about my fears in my diary over the two weeks between finding the lump and being reassured, but after the appointment when the cyst was drained, I got rid of all those pages in the diary, end of episode. I wouldn't want to read them again. It would take me through it all over again. Jonathan was lovely, but he's a bit of a coward about medical procedures. I thought he was going to faint when they drained the cyst and he wouldn't touch that breast until the bruising had cleared completely. Not sure what he thought would happen!"

Hilary and Janet laughed.

"Well, I think I'm dry and I think it's about time we made our way to meet the others for lunch. I wonder how their massages went. I'm not sure I fancy eating lunch in my dressing gown. Oh well, when in Rome..."

It was a bit surreal, the sight of thirty or so women (and a couple of men) sitting in towelling dressing gowns in the beautifully appointed dining room being served by smart waiters and waitresses. Thoughts of the eighteenth-century genteel asylum once again went through Suzanne's mind, but everyone looked pretty sane and the conversation at their table was certainly close to normal.

Chahna had joined them for lunch and had taken a cancellation for a facial after her swim. She somehow managed to look the most relaxed, even though she had come from work. She had a serenity about her that English women never seemed to achieve.

Liz was telling them about Hilary's swimming costume and the story was taking longer than it should because she kept dissolving into giggles. The others were laughing more at her inability to control her giggling than at the story itself.

Janet chipped in, "Actually, I had to go out and buy a new swimming costume before coming here. I can't remember the last time I wore one and while I'm willing to wear a bikini on foreign beaches, I couldn't show off that much old flesh so near to home. I spent ages preparing. I nearly went as far as booking myself in for a leg and bikini wax but settled for a Bik razor in the bath."

There were murmurs of assent. They were all conscious that their bodies needed more attention before being shown off, even among friends.

The food was excellent; they had all been concerned that it might prove too healthy or that there wouldn't be enough, but it was well cooked and plentiful. There was even wine, but they decided to wait until dinner. The only dissenter was Liz, but the others soon talked her around.

The mood was gentle and relaxed. There was laughter from some of the other tables and the place seemed to be living up to its reviews. Carol was relieved, as the idea had been hers and she wasn't sure she'd have been confident enough to laugh it off if it had been terrible. She would have been afraid to ever suggest anything again. As it was, ideas for future trips were already going through her mind.

Carol and Liz left the table before the others, as they both had treatments booked; the others were interested to see what they would think of their seaweed wraps. Plans were discussed, arrangements made for the afternoon and evening, and they gradually dispersed.

Carol was a bit apprehensive about the detox wrap treatment she had booked. It had sounded so exotic when she read about it, but now she wasn't so sure. Liz looked as though she was going to a dentist's appointment as she was led away by a tiny immaculately turned-out therapist. The two friends exchanged glances as they were led to their fate.

The room was warm with dim lighting and relaxing music in the background. Carol was relieved it wasn't whale song, as had been in vogue the last time she treated herself to a facial. The room contained two couches and a shower in the corner. Help, she thought, as she was left to take off her swimming costume and put on a bizarre pair of paper knickers, which looked for all the world like a male posing pouch. I hope there isn't someone else having a treatment in the same room.

As instructed, she lay down on the warm couch under the towel, waiting for her therapist, Jane, to creep back in. Carol felt very self-conscious wearing nothing but the paper knickers, but Jane put her at her ease, describing clearly what was going to happen, making small talk about lunch, and asking where Carol had travelled from. The tinkling piano music and occasional birdsong carried on in the background as Jane covered Carol's arms, legs and back with unpleasant-smelling red scratchy stuff that made her skin tingle. No sooner was she covered than Jane instructed her to shower. Getting up from the couch was a challenge because she had been lying on polythene, which now stuck uncomfortably to her coated skin.

Jane showed her the controls of the shower and left her alone. It took some time to remove all the red stuff and she had to shuffle her feet around to get it all down the drain. She hoped the therapist wouldn't come back too soon and see her doing this bizarre dance in the shower. She finally felt that she and the shower were sufficiently clean and stepped out of the cubicle after turning off the water. Her skin felt beautiful, soft and silky. Jane came back into the room just as Carol stepped out of the shower, as if she had been listening for the shower to stop running.

The reason for the second couch soon became clear. Because the first couch was such a mess from the first phase of the treatment, Jane instructed her to lie on the polythene-covered second couch, where she smothered her in green slime from the bottom of the sea. It certainly smelt fishy!

Wrapped in polythene, Carol relaxed as Jane massaged her head while the algae went to work on her toxins.

But she wasn't done yet. After twenty minutes, she had to untangle herself from the polythene and walk, like a monster in Dr Who, back into the shower to wash off the green gunk.

There was no denying that her skin felt better – but this wasn't the relaxing experience she had anticipated, and she wondered how Liz was getting on.

After another long shower, during which worrying thoughts about blocked drains filled her mind as the green sludge slowly drained away, Jane instructed her to lie on her front on warm towels covering the now cleaned first couch. Carol covered herself with a thick soft towel, feeling clean and smooth, ready for the next stage.

"I'll be applying some firming cream to your skin now," Jane said, and, starting on her back, she expertly massaged away all the tension as the cream was gradually absorbed. Each leg was uncovered and massaged in turn. "I'm massaging all the toxins to the lymph nodes to help clear your system," Jane informed her. Carol didn't really care about the toxins; it just felt wonderful and she hoped all the others experienced something as good as this while they were here.

All too soon the ninety minutes had elapsed and Carol was getting back into her swimming costume and dressing gown. When she emerged from the treatment room, she saw that Liz was waiting for her.

"What did you think of that then? I wasn't at all sure when it first started and then when I was wrapped in all that polythene," Liz said. "You know, I was dreading having a hot flush – that would have been a nightmare scenario, but fortunately I was spared. I'm not sure I'm detoxed but my skin certainly feels wonderful."

"The massage at the end was really wonderful, wasn't it? The best I've ever experienced, although I suppose I don't have extensive experience really. I feel fabulous – but I did feel a bit silly with all the red and green stuff all over me," Carol confided.

They headed off, feeling calm and relaxed, in search of herbal tea, as coffee seemed sacrilegious after all that detoxing.

"What a brilliant day," said Liz, as she and Janet sat on the terrace and sipped long gin and tonics, relaxing in the evening sun. Chahna had had a swim and a facial after lunch and then shot off home in her Porsche. Suzanne, who had packed as many treatments into the day as she could, was now waiting for her nails to dry before getting changed. Carol was changing and phoning home to check that no disasters had befallen anyone in her absence. She filled Jonathan in on the treatments she had tried. He was rather bemused by her descriptions, but happy that she sounded so relaxed. Hilary had rushed home to get her overnight things and some other clothes and had promised she would be back in time for a drink before dinner.

Liz was in a long floaty dress, her long hair loosely held in a ribbon, bangles and beads giving her a slightly Bohemian look. Janet, tidy as ever, had put on a shirt-waister, the belt emphasising her still slim waist.

"How are your parents now?" Liz asked. "Are you still going up to see them as often? Every time I'm driving, I think of you, you know, and your soft lorries. You are right – they are somehow less threatening."

Janet laughed. "You must think I'm potty. Yes, I still go every week. Actually, Dad is coping really well and the carers are great, but I feel that I still need to go, even though sometimes I drive all that way and they don't need anything. I think it's me that needs to feel that I'm doing all I can. Does that sound silly?"

"No, of course not. We all need to feel needed, you know, and you must have felt awful when you realised what your dad had been coping with without telling you. Guilt is horrible."

"Actually, I did feel guilty at first, but I don't think I do any more. Dad could have asked us for help. I think that not only was he trying to protect Julia and me, but I think he felt a bit ashamed of how Mum was and wanted to shield her from our sympathy. I think he was also a bit afraid that if we knew how bad she was, we'd insist that she go into a home and he couldn't bear that. Does that make sense?"

"You always make sense," said Liz. "You spend a lot of time analysing things, don't you? You know, I've no idea how I'd be in your situation. At least Mum is still fit and healthy. When Dad died, she was low for a bit, but she's a very strong person and she just picked herself up and got on with life. I do admire her. I love looking after Siobhan. She's nearly four now and an absolute delight. Tiring, definitely, but at least children grow and develop. There is only one outcome with old people."

Carol joined them. "I know. I have our grandchildren, although Jonathan does more of the looking after than I do. He just loves playing. He is such a child. But that is much less tiring than seeing Mum or Jonathan's dad in their respective nursing homes. I go to Mum every week – I'm not sure why. The days all blur into one for her. I think it's more for me than her."

"That's what I was saying", interjected Janet. "It must be a woman thing. Richard phones his mum every week but we only see her on high days and holidays and when we do go, he's treated like the prodigal son."

"Yes," replied Carol. "Jonathan has to be persuaded to go and see his dad. I go more than him. He hates illness. He got really upset when he went to see his dad a few weeks ago. His dad was confused because of a urine infection, in a bed with cot sides, shouting out, trying to climb out of the bed...no-one should have to see a parent like that. The reality of getting old is hateful."

"This sounds really jolly," said Suzanne, joining them and looking elegant in her Ralph Lauren shift dress. "Hilary's just come back with her overnight stuff. Let's change the subject. Time for another drink I think."

After a meal better than any of them could have imagined, they went outside to enjoy the last of the warm summer evening.

"I shall have to go and phone Julia." Janet was the first to break the moment with talk of their responsibilities.

"Surely she would have phoned if there'd been any problems," said Liz, not wanting to think about anything but the beauty of their surroundings and the evening.

"I hope she would, but actually, I just want to reassure myself that all is well and then, for the first time in months, I think I'll sleep well tonight. I can't remember the last time I felt this good." Janet finished the last of her drink and got up, saying goodnight to them all, and made her way back to her room.

Janet phoned Julia, her dad and Richard and was reassured that everything was fine. Julia was a bit short with her, failing to understand why she needed to check up all the time; her dad sounded tired but in control; Richard was just happy to hear her sounding so relaxed. She could hear the sounds of the pub in the background. She wanted them to rely on her, but they had to be reminded sometimes that she had her limits.

Luxuriating in the peace and quiet of her room, the darkness of the countryside and the inner calm that she felt, Janet fell asleep quickly and didn't hear the others pass by her room when they turned in much later.

Liz, Carol and Suzanne persuaded Hilary to stay up with them and share another bottle of wine. Hilary's sleep pattern had gone completely to pot over the last few weeks. Before her mother died, she was in the habit of going to bed early, matching her hours to her mother's, telling herself that she needed the early nights because of work in the morning, rarely accepting invitations in the evening. Phyllis's death had left her with no pattern. Days of hardly getting up alternated with hours of wakefulness. She felt tired now, but didn't want to end the moment.

"If I fall asleep, you'll have to carry me to my room. Sorry it's not anywhere near yours…you ought to see it. Because I got a cancellation, I'm in one of the rooms in the main house. It's beautiful. It's right at the front with a view down the drive, on two levels with two big sash windows, and the bathroom is completely over the top! Here's the key. Room 3. Go and have a look. I'll sign for the wine when it arrives."

The others didn't need second bidding and shot off like eager teenagers. They discovered the room at the top of the grand staircase leading up from reception. The wide door opened into a light airy room with blue-grey striped wallpaper. Pale blue curtains framed the view of the drive through the windows. A fireplace with pale flowers in the grate, a simple four-poster bed and antique mahogany bedroom furniture completed the room.

"Wow, look at this."

The bathroom faced the side of the house. A massive claw-footed bath dominated the room, a huge basin set in a chrome frame sat to one side and the toilet had a cast-iron cistern set impossibly high on the wall. Black and white tiles made up the floor. Old bottles filled with coloured concoctions were ranged along the mantlepiece above the fireplace and a gilt mirror stretching from mantlepiece to ceiling reflected them back onto the white tiles.

"It's brilliant that Hilary's staying in this room. Just perfect for her. She really does deserve to be spoilt," said Carol generously.

"Yes," agreed Suzanne. "But next time I come, I'm going to make sure I get a room in the main house!"

Hilary was smiling when they re-joined her at the table. "Oh dear, I wasn't sure whether to say anything. It seemed a bit unfair that I'd got the best room when I turned down the trip in the first place."

"Don't be so silly. I think it's great. I just said to the others that you deserve to be spoilt." Carol gave her a hug, then held out her glass for more wine before leaning back in her seat. "I can't believe how lucky we've been with the weather. Who would have thought we'd be sitting outside at ten o'clock at night, especially after all that rain last week?"

They chatted for another hour and then one by one started yawning.

"It's catching. I think we'd better turn in," Liz said. "What time do we need to be up? I want to have a swim before breakfast."

"I'll join you, Liz. I've got to get my money's worth from my new costume." Hilary went up to her room, hearing the others giggling behind her. She shut the door, taking one last look at the view before drawing the curtains, undressed for bed, said night-night to her mum and fell immediately into a dreamless sleep.

Liz, Suzanne and Carol found their way back to their rooms. Carol sent a 'Goodnight, sleep tight' text to Jonathan. Liz chatted to John on the phone about her day, while sipping a whiskey from the minibar. Suzanne knew David would still be in the pub, as she'd spoken to him before dinner, so she got into bed with her book, enjoying the luxury of being able to read without the constant pestering of "When are you going to put the light out?" from the other side of the bed.

"Well done, Carol," said Suzanne as she joined the others at the table for lunch. "What a wonderful couple of days."

"Actually, we could all have come in one car. All our 'dependents' and hangers-on have managed without us, no disasters, not even a worrying phone call." Janet breathed a big sigh and sat back in her chair. "You know, sometimes I think I have to stand back and not constantly wait for things to go wrong. I'm wearing myself out to no purpose." She laughed ruefully.

Hilary turned to her. "I've been thinking over the weekend. You can't believe how much good it's done me. I have to admit, I'd got myself into a spiral of self-pity and wouldn't let anyone help. Of course, I have to mourn for Mum, but she would have been the first one to tell me to pull myself together and get on with things. I have allowed myself to sink so low thinking I had let her down – guilt was the biggest problem that I couldn't get around. But this weekend… I don't know what made me think of it, but I remembered what Jag said, soon after mum died. He said that life isn't about the last few minutes, it's about all the days, weeks and years that go before. That wasn't a comfort at the time. I couldn't see beyond the stupid minor things. But now I seem to have got it into perspective and last night I was thinking for the first time about some of the lovely times Mum had. Sorry, I'm wittering on."

"No, no," the others murmured.

"Yes, I am, but to get to the point of all this rambling, I wanted to ask you, Janet, if you'd let me come with you one time when you go and see your parents. They met Mum last summer when they came down to stay at yours and you had that lovely garden party and I know your mum and mine had a lovely time talking about the good old days. I could take some photos that I haven't dared go through. It may bring back some old memories for your mum – I know she won't know any of the people but the fashions and the scenes could stir memories. Please say if you don't think it's a good idea. I don't want to make things any more difficult for you."

"What a brilliant idea," Suzanne chipped in, as she saw that Janet was a bit overcome with tears in her eyes.

"I'd love you to come," said Janet, her voice slightly thick with tears. "I've so missed our chats but I haven't wanted to put on you. Actually, it would be great to have some company on that awful journey too. Mum loves company, although half the time she hasn't a clue who I am. And, if we plan it right, perhaps Dad could go and have a couple of hours out with a friend. I think when I go, he feels he has to be there. Oooh, I can't wait to get it organised and that's the first time in a long time I've thought about going up there in a positive way."

They immediately got out their phones and sorted a day. There was a feeling of relief around the table, as if a weight had been lifted. Hilary had been so much like her old self in the last twenty-four hours. Later, on the phone, Carol confided to Liz that she hadn't realised what an impact Hilary's depression was having on them all until it lifted.

They ordered coffee, more to prolong the lunch and delay packing and departure than because they really wanted it. They chatted about the week ahead and the possibility of returning to a tidy house. There was a brief silence when they all realised that of course Hilary would go back to a tidy, empty house. A shadow passed across her eyes but she soon smiled and recalled how her mother had been so tidy and insisted on everything being put away before going to bed every night. When they'd gone on holiday when Hilary was young, Phyllis almost spring cleaned before going, so the house would be ready for their return. It used to drive her dad mad.

Bags packed, bills paid, they set off down the drive and back to real life.

Chapter Nine

The Visit

"You know, I actually felt jealous of you."

Janet and Hilary were in Janet's car, driving up the motorway to see Janet's parents. The day was dull, not at all like June. There was an annoying drizzle that reduced visibility but wasn't quite enough for the windscreen wipers, so that Janet had to keep switching them on and off to stop them from scraping noisily across the windscreen.

The trip had been arranged soon after they returned from the spa, as neither wanted to lose the impetus. Janet was afraid that Hilary would go back into her shell as soon as she got home and Hilary was afraid that Janet would think it wasn't such a good idea after all.

The road was as busy as ever. Janet could never understand how so many people, at any one time, had to be somewhere else.

"Oh dear. How on earth could you be jealous of me?" said Hilary, turning slightly to face Janet as she drove.

"Please don't be upset if I tell you. It's a bit of a guilty secret that I couldn't tell anyone else, and you'll think me awful when I tell you."

"Tell me what?"

"When your mum died, I was jealous because I couldn't understand why your mum, who was full of life and had every reason to go on, died, and my mum, who has no quality of life, had to carry on. The worst of it was actually I was feeling sorry for me, not Mum. Mum doesn't know if she's on this earth or Fullers. But how could I feel jealous of you when you were feeling so bad? Oh, I did get in a muddle. I tried to be there for you as you would have been for me, but I don't think I was much help." Janet's eyes filled with tears. Her vision blurred and she was relieved to see the sign for services in half a mile. "I shall have to stop."

Hilary felt the familiar lump in her throat and the tears build, but she said nothing as Janet pulled into the inside lane and followed the slip road. With luck and no help from the multitude of signs, they found their way to the car park and, parking next to a scruffy Vauxhall, headed for the café. They had to squeeze between two cars and managed to wake a terrier who, throwing himself against the window, barked frantically at them. They didn't know whether to laugh or cry and hurried towards the concourse before the owner returned and told them off for upsetting the dog. They joined the queue in the café and, after a long wait, sat down with their coffees. "I feel so guilty for not noticing, not doing anything and now for wanting her dead." Janet emphasised the last word, causing the woman on the next table to look up from her crossword in surprise. Hilary smiled at her, challenging her to comment. Her eyes dropped back to the paper.

Janet was staring at her coffee, stirring it around and around with the wooden stick that made no impression on the froth. Hilary gently took it from her and said, "You don't want her dead. You want her back. My mum's greatest fear was losing her mind. She always said, 'If I ever get like that, shoot me,' and I think she meant it. I *do* understand your feelings. I think I'd have felt the same. I can't understand why some people have to carry on living when all the joy has gone. It's not as if you can blame medical science for keeping her alive. She just is alive. You must feel worn down by it all and, not wanting to be a prophet of doom but, physically, she is very fit and could go on for years."

Janet smiled through her tears. "Huh, I knew you'd know exactly what to say to cheer me up," she said ruefully. "Let's change the subject."

They both sipped their coffees thoughtfully for a moment. As she picked up the heavy mug, Hilary wondered aloud, "Whose idea was it to serve buckets of coffee? They certainly weren't thinking of travellers with bladder weakness."

"Or men with prostate problems."

"The only way to get a small cup of coffee is to have an espresso and that's so strong that if you're not careful it gives you palpitations."

"The joys of getting old. I'm not going to drink all of this or we'll have to have another stop before we get there!"

Hilary and Janet drank what they could of the coffee and then after a trip to the Ladies went out into the depressing drizzle for the final ten miles of the journey.

George was at the door as they pulled onto the drive. He'd obviously been waiting for them.

"I thought you weren't coming."

"Actually, I said between eleven and half past. You know you can't always judge the traffic," said Janet, already feeling guilty for having that coffee, knowing what a stickler for time her dad was.

He was smartly dressed in his suit trousers (now a little too big for him, Janet noticed, and a bit shiny down the front), white shirt and tie. His sports jacket was hanging on the hall stand. He had arranged to go out to meet a friend for lunch. He'd needed no encouragement when Janet had phoned him and told him she was bringing a friend to chat to Mum and between them they'd look after Mum if he wanted to go out. He was obviously excited about going out.

"This is Hilary. Do you remember you met her last year?"

He shook her hand formally.

"Hello Hilary, I'm sorry for your loss."

"Thank you, I do miss Mum but I'm gradually getting sorted out."

Niceties over, George was keen to go through the routine for caring for Beryl while he was out. He went through it carefully, Janet resisting the temptation to tell him that the routine he was describing to her was the one

100

she had set up while he was in hospital. When he was finally happy that she understood and would remember all that needed to be done and what to do in all conceivable eventualities, he put on his sports jacket and put his head round the door to check on Beryl, who was sleeping in the chair. Then he went into the front room and sat down by the window to wait for the taxi he had booked, because he couldn't drive any more. Janet had offered to take him the short distance to the pub but this was his last bit of independence and he didn't want to give it up. Besides, he didn't know Hilary well enough to be happy for her to stay alone and look after Beryl.

Soon after George was whisked off in the taxi, the carer, Gail, arrived to help with lunch. Janet kicked herself for not thinking to cancel her.

While Gail went in to see Beryl and helped her to the toilet, Janet and Hilary went into the kitchen to start on lunch. A few minutes later, Gail came in with a pile of washing.

"Your mum's had an accident. That's really unusual for her, so I'll take a sample into the surgery in case she has an infection."

"Thanks, Gail, that's a good idea but, actually, I think that it might be that Dad didn't take her to the toilet at ten this morning. He's been preoccupied and excited about his trip to the pub for lunch. You know what he's like for his routines – the slightest thing throws him off track."

Janet turned to Hilary. "Dad has strict routines for everything. As mum can't always say when she wants the toilet, he takes her every two hours and sits her on the toilet and, so far, that has avoided accidents or embarrassment. When we were young, everything was done to a time, woe betide if Mum didn't have his dinner on the table at six o'clock. Julia used to drive him mad because she was completely chaotic. I think Mum was a bit like Julia before she married Dad but she soon found it was best to fit in with his routines. They've been married sixty years, so it can't all have been bad. Dad always says that it's his military training, though he only did National Service for two years. But, I suppose, during the war it would have had quite an impact on a young mind, and if routine got you through that nightmare it could get you through anything."

Gail wrote up her notes, put the washing in the machine and left them to it.

Janet and Hilary took lunch through to Beryl, who was sitting looking at the television. Janet placed the tray on her mother's lap and put a spotless ironed linen napkin around her neck. She wondered who was doing all the ironing and made a mental note to ask her dad. Beryl's clothes had been changed; they looked clean but worn. She was wearing a bright red hand-knitted cardigan over a floral print dress, pink skin showing between the hem of her dress and her American tan pop socks. Tartan slippers completed her outfit.

"Hello, Mum, it's Janet and I've brought Hilary to see you. You met her and her mum at my house last summer, do you remember?"

Beryl smiled and looked at them both with little recognition. "Where's my lunch?"

"It's here on your lap," replied Janet, going to sit nearer to her. "Oatcakes and cheese, just how you like it." She put a piece of oatcake in her hand and Beryl slowly took it to her mouth.

They ate lunch in relative silence, the television on in the background.

When Janet took the tray and plates out to the kitchen, Hilary untied the napkin from around Beryl's neck and folded it neatly.

"I love your cardigan. Did you knit it?"

Beryl looked down at her cardigan as if she'd never seen it before.

Realising that conversation was impossible, Hilary retrieved the photograph album from her bag at the side of the chair.

She opened it on Beryl's lap. "I found this picture of you and Mum from the party last year. It's a really nice one. I haven't got many pictures of Mum as she hated having her picture taken, so I treasure the ones I have got. She died suddenly earlier this year."

"That's nice, dear," said Beryl.

"Oh no, sorry, Hilary," garbled Janet as she came back in with coffee, hearing the last couple of sentences.

But Hilary was smiling. "It's OK. She doesn't know what she's saying and the picture *is* nice."

Beryl was turning the pages, looking at the photos without any recognition but seeming to enjoy the pictures. Janet went upstairs and returned with an armful of photo albums. They had a lovely time looking through them. Beryl put names to some faces, but Janet didn't know if she was right or not. They were having such a lovely time that Janet almost forgot her mother's medication, but a look of discomfort on Beryl's face as she moved her arm to turn the pages of the album reminded her just in time before George came home.

Hilary and Janet were helping Beryl back from her two o'clock toilet trip when George arrived home, slightly flushed from his beer but looking relaxed and happy.

Seeing the photo albums all over the floor, he raised his eyebrows but soon joined in the talk of holidays and trips from years gone by.

Even though it wasn't long since lunch and an even shorter time until the carer came to make the evening meal, tea and cakes at three was the rule.

After tea, Hilary and Janet collected up the albums and put them away in chronological order.

Before they left, Janet remembered to ask about the laundry and it turned out that George was paying a young neighbour to do the ironing. The neighbour couldn't go out to work because of a disabled child but was glad of the extra money. Janet needn't have worried; Dad was still in charge.

Hilary said goodbye to Beryl and promised to visit again soon. They were soon back onto the motorway. They'd missed the school traffic in town but the motorway was as busy as ever. While they had been inside, the weather had brightened up and now they were driving under a clear blue sky.

"You're quiet," said Janet, pulling out to overtake one of the many lorries on the road. "Are you all right?"

"Sorry. Full of cake," laughed Hilary. "But apart from that, yes, I'm fine. Bizarrely, I'm thinking how lucky Mum was. Oh dear. Your mum is lovely, but such hard work. Your dad must be a saint to put up with her."

"Yes. He can be incredibly annoying with his routines and his timetables, but actually he does what most of us couldn't. Richard would never cope and I don't think that I'd want him to. I certainly haven't got the patience. Thank you for understanding and thank you for coming.

I really enjoyed today. I haven't a clue if it did either of them any good, but it did me the world of good!"

She pulled out into the outside lane, for once enjoying the speed, smiling at the sunshine, smiling just because she felt all right.

"Do you know what I'm going to do?" Hilary asked. "I'm going to get a dog."

Janet turned to her in amazement and then flicked her eyes back to the road. "You don't like dogs."

"Who said I don't like dogs? I've always wanted one."

"But you were always moaning about that one that barked all the time and you were the first to complain about dog mess."

"That doesn't mean I don't like them. I just don't like badly behaved dogs or owners."

"How will you manage with work? And anyway, if you've always wanted one, why haven't you had one?"

"I'm not sure about work – I'm thinking of reducing my hours. Anyway, the reason I never had one was Mum. When I was little, both Dad and I wanted one. He even brought a puppy home once but Mum made him take it back to the animal shelter after a few days because she said she'd end up having to look after it."

"When Brian was killed, the school psychologist suggested a pet, as if that could replace a best friend, so we got a cat. He was a nasty spiteful thing. That put Mum off the idea of any other animal."

"Brian?" asked Janet quietly.

"A boy at school. We were fourteen. I thought he was *the* one, then he got killed, knocked off his bike. I didn't deal with it very well and his death took on a much greater significance than it should have. I had a few boyfriends after Brian but, somehow, never trusted them enough not to leave me. Sorry, I'm a bit of a psychological mess. Still, it meant I was there for Mum when she needed me as she became more disabled. We had a great relationship but I was aware that it was her house and, being the good girl that I am, I abided by her rules. Hence, no dog. I could have moved out, but I would never have found anywhere to match the space and facilities that I enjoyed so near to town. Anyway, now the bungalow is mine, I'm getting a dog. It'll be company, security, something to look after – and you never know – it might be like *101 Dalmatians* and I might meet the love of my life."

Janet laughed. "Right then, if that's the plan, what breed are you going for?"

They spent the rest of the journey talking about puppies, training, costs, dogs they had known.

"Could I go with you when you go to choose it?" asked Janet finally, realising that they were nearly home and she hadn't had time to be frightened or frustrated by the other drivers on the road. "And if you feel you could, I'd love you to come to Mum and Dad's again. I've actually really enjoyed today."

"Of course, I'd love to. I'll keep you informed on the dog front. It's not going to be straight away. These things take time to arrange."

As Janet pulled up onto her drive, Hilary said, "Would you like a coffee?"

"No thanks, I'd better get back to get the dinner on. I think Claire might be calling in this evening. See you soon." She pulled back onto the road, waving to Suzanne, who was just driving into her own driveway.

Chapter Ten

In the Pub

"The girls had a good time at the spa, didn't they?"

Richard inwardly cringed at John's derogatory use of the word 'girls'. He knew there was no malice or insult intended, but one of these days John would say such things in the wrong company and get himself into trouble.

"It did Janet the world of good, but Janet said the biggest change was in Hilary – she apparently just suddenly snapped out of her depression and back to her normal self."

"Yes, but even Hilary's normal self isn't very exciting or dynamic is it? I've always found her a bit too quiet, and disapproving. You know what I mean? She hardly ever comes into the pub or goes out when the rest of us get together."

"Are you talking about the Hilary who lives opposite the golf course?" interrupted Sheila, who was collecting glasses.

Richard and John nodded as they passed her the empties and moved newspapers and crisp packets to allow her to wipe the table.

"She and her mum came almost every week for lunch. They always sat in that corner and always had half a lager, soup and a sandwich. I was really sad to hear her mum had died. She was great fun, really wicked sense of humour. She did seem to keep Hilary in check, though, and was a bit bossy with her. I didn't hear about her death straight away, so I didn't get to the funeral. I wanted to go round and see Hilary but I thought it would look a bit odd, landlady going round to try and drum up custom." She laughed at herself, a loud, deep, throaty smoker's laugh, ending in a horrible cough that made other customers' heads turn.

"I would never have guessed," said John, with some admiration in his voice. "I've never seen them in here but I suppose I tend to come in more in the evening. Well, she's a dark horse."

Having recovered from her coughing fit, Sheila picked up her cloth and leaned on the back of the chair next to Richard. "Hilary came in last week. She sort of crept in, got her drink, ordered her soup and sat in the same corner. I was really pleased to see her. She'd got her book and I thought it best to leave her to her own devices, but my regulars had other ideas. Mad Bill broke the ice by going and giving her a hug. Ugh, he's a bit smelly but she didn't seem to mind and, then, after that, as she sat and had her soup, there was a steady stream of people talking to her and, judging by the laughter coming from the corner, it wasn't all talk of death and loss. She said she misses her mum dreadfully but she's coming to terms with it now and getting her life back together, so she thought she'd test herself by coming to the pub. I really admire her – she's so strong. Hopefully, she'll be a regular again."

"She and Janet went up to Janet's parents a couple of weeks ago. Janet struggled when Hilary was so depressed – she relies on her a lot. Anyway, you'll never guess what Jan told me when they got back." Richard paused for effect, but neither Sheila nor John offered any suggestions. "Hilary says she's getting a dog."

John didn't show a lot of interest in this revelation but Sheila looked thoughtful and said, "Oh that'll be brilliant for her. She's the sort of person who needs to be caring for something – or someone – and it'll be company for her."

"I'm coming," she called to her husband, who was looking slightly disgruntled behind the bar as the evening was getting busier and a crowd of youngsters came in, as ever, all wanting to buy their drinks individually. She gathered up the glasses and crisp packets and, with a final flick of the cloth, joined Ben behind the bar, where she efficiently helped him clear the queue.

"I worry about Liz you know," admitted John. Richard hid his surprise. He liked John but he always thought him a bit selfish and he certainly seemed to leave Liz to do everything at home.

"Yes, I do," he continued, as if Richard had disagreed. "She takes on too much. Lisa is a constant worry to her, although I'm more inclined to let her get on with it. She dotes on Siobhan, spends more time with her than Lisa does. Lisa's got the life of Riley. I know she works hard, but if she didn't have Liz doing all the child care she'd struggle and she certainly wouldn't be able to go out as much. That's partly why I'm in the pub more now, because Liz knows I don't agree with her doing so much, so we seem to be playing this game where we pretend it's not happening. When I get home from work or the pub, all signs of Siobhan are hidden. I keep a check on the calendar so I know when to keep out of the way. It's ridiculous, but if we try to talk about it, we just argue. My feeling is that if we can ride this out, time will sort it out. Siobhan will get older and Lisa might find someone else – or even move away. I know, I know," he flapped his hands, as if Richard was disagreeing with him. "I'm being a bit of an ostrich. But what else can I do?"

As if he had said too much, he picked up the glasses and went to the bar to get more drinks, leaving Richard in a thoughtful mood. We really have no idea what goes on behind closed doors, he thought to himself. I thought I knew John and Liz quite well. We see them often enough. But what we see is what people show us. He was still musing when John returned from the bar.

"I know everyone thinks I'm a bit of a male chauvinist but Liz knows me well and I do care about her an awful lot. This is the only way I can see that we can get through it. At least her mum is well. I don't know how you and Janet cope with looking after her parents. At least with children there are some positives." He smiled ruefully.

"I haven't seen Liz's mum for a bit. I used to see her cycling up to the allotments."

"Oh, Pearl is still about. She's great – she'd give all of us a run for our money. She doesn't sit about in pubs moaning. She's on all the local committees. She used to be a local councillor, you know."

"Who was a local councillor?" asked Jonathan, sitting down with his pint.

"Pearl, Liz's mum," answered John, moving his chair slightly to give Jonathan more room.

"I think you have to be a certain sort of person to want to go into local politics," said Jonathan. "It's certainly not my cup of tea."

The others agreed. There was more shuffling of chairs to make space for David, who had now turned up.

"The local council could do something about parking in the centre of town. It's getting beyond a joke." David plonked himself down and launched into a long and involved story about parking tickets and fines. From there, the talk turned to cars and they settled down to another pint before making their respective ways home.

Chapter Eleven

Charity Coffee Morning

CAKE SALE, TOMBOLA

5TH SEPTEMBER

11.00AM TO 1.00PM

PLEASE COME, BRING YOUR FRIENDS, ALL WELCOME

ALL PROCEEDS TO ST MARK'S HOSPICE

Hilary's address and phone number were on the back of the yellow cards that she delivered through her neighbours' and friends' letter boxes, together with a request (plea) for cakes to sell and tombola prizes.

Phone calls and emails flew back and forth in the week before the coffee morning. Cakes and biscuits were baked, prizes were delivered to Hilary's house or left on her doorstep – unpronounceable liqueurs, slightly dodgy-looking chocolates, bath goodies, cheap wine, hideous ornaments, beautifully knitted toys, tins of food, including marrowfat peas (who ate marrowfat peas these days?), a tiny set of screw drivers that must have come from a Christmas cracker, coasters, a cruet set in the shape of S and P, a boxed set of Inspector Morse DVDs, and, of course, a large and slightly deranged-looking teddy bear. Hilary hoped that, as usual, lots of people would come to her coffee morning and leave having won these tombola prizes. She missed her mum; they had run this event together for years. In more recent years, Phyllis had had more of a supervisory role, but at least she was there. Hilary had been baking for weeks. She loved baking and loved having an excuse to make huge quantities of cakes and biscuits. Her pantry was full.

That morning, she was up early. She went downstairs in her dressing gown and said hello to Hector who lay in his basket in the kitchen. She still couldn't believe that only a couple of weeks after telling Janet that she was thinking of getting a dog, she was now the proud owner of Hector.

Sheila had turned up on her doorstep a few days after Hilary had braved lunch in the pub on her own. Seeing her there, she thought she must have left a scarf or something behind, but Sheila stood on the doorstep and said that she had a proposition.

Hilary invited her in and put the kettle on. They sat at the kitchen table, and Sheila told her about her conversation with Richard and John in the pub, and how Richard had said that Hilary was looking for a dog.

"That set me thinking," continued Sheila. "I have some customers who come in regularly who are in a bit of a quandary. A lovely young couple who live on the estate up near Tesco." Hilary shuddered. "They've had this dog about three years, but Sarah's just had a baby and the dog is simply not coping. He's been the centre of attention for too long. They did tend to spoil him a bit, always sat on the bench between them when they came in the pub. Anyway, to cut a long story short, he keeps snapping at the baby and they are getting really worried. They are talking about taking him to the animal shelter, but I can tell they are putting it off, hoping for a miracle. Well, when I heard Richard talking, I wondered if you might be that miracle."

She stopped. Hilary was silent.

"I haven't said anything to them, of course," she said hurriedly.

"What's he called?"

"Hector," replied Sheila, not thinking that it was at all odd that Hilary hadn't asked about the dog's breed, age or temperament.

"I'd like to meet them, and him. It does sound as if fate could be intervening to help us both. Since I spoke to Janet, I've been wondering how on earth I'd go about choosing a dog and I certainly don't think I could have a puppy at the moment. What's he like?"

"He's a delight, a Hungarian Vizsla, russet brown, very aristocratic looking – but loopy and loving. I think they were originally bred by the Hungarian aristocracy for hunting but now they're reduced to hunting tennis balls and toys. A little bit like a posh lurcher. He seems well trained though, doesn't leave their side when they come in and he walks nicely to heel when he's with Tom – but he hates the pushchair. I've seen him really pulling when Sarah has him and the baby."

"Do you think I'd be able to cope with him? He sounds a bit of a handful. My only experience of dogs is the one on wheels that I used to push around when I was a toddler."

"Well, you won't know until you meet him. Do you want me to speak to them? Tom gave me their number in case I heard of anyone. They are really upset about it. They particularly went for that breed because they are good with children. But they didn't bargain for this level of jealousy. I could phone them now."

"Yes, please. You know, I thought I was being selfish, as if I was going against Mum. This way I'll be helping someone else, salve my conscience a bit. Sorry. Mum is still making her presence felt," she laughed ruefully.

Sheila needed no second bidding and was already rummaging in her bag for her phone.

"Hello, Tom, it's Sheila from the pub... Yes, fine, thanks... Yes, he's all right... Anyway, I think I've found someone for Hector."

She could hear yapping and a baby crying in the background and hoped nothing serious had caused the racket. As she explained to Tom about Hilary and asked when she and Hector could meet, Hilary cleared away the coffee cups and went to the toilet to give Sheila a chance to talk without feeling that she had to be careful about what she said. She picked up her handbag and jacket from her bedroom before returning to the living room, just in case they could go around straight away. She felt excited, anxious and childlike all at the same time. A dog of her own. She'd always wanted one.

She went back into the kitchen and Sheila mouthed, "Do you want to go now?" as she listened to Tom.

Hilary nodded furiously.

Sheila mimed writing in the air with her free hand and Hilary put a notepad and pencil in front of her so that she could write down the address. She told Tom they'd be there in fifteen minutes. Hilary was already at the door, keys in her hand.

"We'd better take both cars because I need to get back to open up. You follow me there. I'll introduce you and then I'd better get off."

After a short drive, they parked outside a neat modern semi, with a clean hatchback on the drive, and tubs of purple pansies on either side of the front door. Sheila rang the bell and Tom answered. They saw him through the glass, carefully shutting the living room door before opening the front door.

He was tall and thin, and wore jeans and a t-shirt. His blond hair stuck out in all directions and looked as though he had run his hands through it a hundred times. He gave Sheila a brief hug and shook Hilary's hand as Sheila introduced them. Hilary liked him straight away.

He led them into a tidy and warm living room. Sarah was sitting on the settee feeding baby Luke. She smiled and said hello, popping the bottle out of the chubby baby's mouth to gesture Hilary to a chair. Sheila apologised for not being able to stay and, after patting Sarah's arm and kissing the baby's head, said she'd have to love them and leave them, but hoped to see the three of them in the pub before too long. With that, she left.

Hilary had seen Hector as soon as she walked in and was immediately taken with him. She wanted to say hello, but neither she nor Tom and Sarah seemed to know how to proceed. Hector broke the ice by bringing her one of his toys.

"He wants you to throw it for him," said Sarah, winding Luke over her shoulder.

Hilary gently threw the fluffy bone across the room and Hector shot under the table to retrieve it, bringing it back and putting it on her lap.

"He'll have you doing that for hours," said Tom. "Would you like a cup of tea or coffee? I'm not quite sure what I should be asking or telling you."

Hilary accepted a drink and chatted to Sarah about Luke and how she was getting on. She discovered that Sarah had worked in the kitchen of the bistro where Hilary had had her birthday party, and was able to reassure Hilary that the young waitress who had been so nervous that day was doing very well. Tom commuted to London every day but was now on extended paternity leave. As Sarah told Hilary all of this, Tom returned from the kitchen with a tray of tea and some delightful-looking cakes.

"It's just as well I have been off the last few weeks, with Hector being such a pain."

"What has he been doing?" asked Hilary.

"He is fine if we are both here, so that one can concentrate on Luke and the other on Hector, but if he is on his own with one of us, he growls at Luke, and you certainly don't feel you can put Luke down. Then, even if we are both here, if Luke cries, Hector barks. I feel so sorry for the neighbours. I've been around no end of times to apologise. They say they understand, but their patience will wear thin I'm sure. I feel torn, because I love Hector and it's our fault really because he was our baby before Luke. I suppose we've spoilt him, but he's a wonderful dog and I expect if we ever have another dog, we'll treat it exactly the same way."

Hector was sitting in front of Hilary's chair, his soft brown eyes looking at her and then at the toy, encouraging her to throw it yet again. She stroked his head and tickled him behind his ears. He leaned against her leg. It was love at first sight, but he was not to be put off by a bit of affection. He nudged the toy further onto her lap. "Come on, throw it," he seemed to be saying.

"Does he need a lot exercise?"

"What does he eat?"

"Where does he sleep?"

"Is he ever ill?"

Hilary's head was full of questions. Tom and Sarah answered as best they could and Tom went to the study to find Hector's paperwork.

While he was gone, Hilary, feeling relaxed and liking the people she had so recently met, felt brave enough to ask Sarah if she would be able to come to the charity coffee morning (with Luke, of course) and perhaps bake a cake or two.

Sarah was delighted to be asked. "I'd love to come and support the charity. Luke and I can come a bit early and help set up if you like. I can't see me getting any baking done though. My routines are all upside down – time just goes. I had no idea babies were so time consuming, and exhausting."

"Oh dear. How thoughtless of me. Of course you won't have time. Sorry. I should have thought before asking."

"Don't be daft – you didn't let me finish. In the later stages of pregnancy, when I wasn't working and I was bored waiting, I made loads of pies. Our freezer is full of them. Would any of those be any good?"

"Perfect, oh thank you, thank you."

Tom came back into the room. "Getting back to the tricky business of Hector – what are we going to do?"

"I love him already but I've never had a dog, and you don't know me. Are you willing to trust me with him?"

"I'm a great one for first impressions. I think ninety-nine times out of a hundred, your first impressions of someone are correct. I like you."

"I do too," said Sarah, smiling at Hilary.

"More importantly," continued Tom, "Hector likes you." They all looked at Hector, who was now lying down across Hilary's feet, his head resting on crossed front legs, a picture of relaxation.

"Can I suggest a week's trial period? If it's a disaster, perhaps we'll have to think again. It goes without saying that you can visit whenever you like. I'm not that far away."

Tom and Sarah agreed, both relieved that a solution had been found.

"Now, how much do you want for him?"

Tom and Sarah looked shocked. Although they had bought him as a puppy three years before, they couldn't sell their baby.

Without looking at each other, in unison they said, "Nothing."

Tom gave Hector's papers to Hilary and then gathered up his bowls, toys, lead, food and blankets. He wrote their phone number down in case Hilary had any problems.

With a surreal feeling, Hilary packed Hector's things into the boot of her car. With Luke safely out of the way in his cot upstairs, Sarah and Tom stood on the front step, looking lost. Hilary encouraged Hector onto the back seat of her car. He jumped in without a backward glance, sniffed around, did three quick turns and lay down. Hilary put her seat back into place, dropped the lead on the passenger seat and put one leg in the car.

"What have we forgotten?" said Sarah, as Hilary got out of the car and came back towards them.

"Nothing," replied Hilary. Sarah thought that she was going to give them a hug as she came back with her arms outstretched, but her left arm fell to her side and she formally shook hands, saying, "Thank you so much."

Hector had immediately made himself at home. His basket fitted into a corner of the kitchen that seemed to have been made for it. He followed Hilary around the house, but his favourite place was in Phyllis's recliner. Hilary had planned to get rid of it because it had always been too big for the room. She had managed to get as far as writing an advertisement to put in the newsagent's window, but the ad lay on the table in the hall for weeks, going no further. It was like getting rid of the final bit of her mum from the room and she couldn't do it yet. Now Hector had commandeered the chair, the seat protected by his bone-pattern blanket. Hilary didn't agree with animals on the furniture but this seemed right somehow, and he didn't try to get on any other chair.

On the day of the coffee morning, Sarah arrived early and on her own.

"Where's Luke?" asked Hilary, as she helped Sarah in with a tray of pies.

"Tom's mum is staying at the moment. She could have come too, but I could tell she wanted some time on her own with Luke, so they've gone for a walk in the park and she said she's happy to look after him as long as I'm here. So, unless I get a frantic phone call, I can help you clear up too. That way, she gets a bit of time with her two boys without me in the way. Don't get me wrong – we get on really well, but you know what it's like with mothers and sons."

Hilary put the pies in the fridge while they worked out how they would set everything out. Sarah bent down to fuss over Hector, who was running round trying to get her attention. As they went into the living room to plan their strategy, Hector jumped onto his chair and curled up contentedly.

"Right, down to business. What needs doing?"

Hilary had done most of the preparation the night before. Over the years, she and her mum had got the planning down to a fine art and all the necessary equipment was stored in a cupboard in the garage. The water heater had been rinsed and filled with water and was almost boiling, the big teapots were lined up, and milk jugs and sugar bowls were placed nearby. The coffee maker was gurgling and filling the house with a delicious aroma. Cups and saucers from various tea services were laid out in the kitchen. An array of cake plates and stands sat on the breakfast bar, waiting to be filled. The tombola prizes had been labelled and were set out on the sideboard and the old tombola drum, which Phyllis had picked up at a car-boot sale years before, was full of the raffle tickets, waiting for Suzanne to take charge, as she did each year. Some people who were unable come had already bought tickets, so someone had to be in charge of distributing the prizes.

"It's just really setting out the cakes, and when people arrive, I'll need more help, taking the money, serving the cakes and drinks, selling as much as we can. We raised £280 last year – I'd love to break the £300 mark this year. Your pies will go down well because we rarely have savouries. We're all lazy and, for lots of people, one of your pies will save on cooking dinner tonight. I love the way you've wrapped and labelled them, very professional."

"They were all in the freezer and to tell the truth Tom is getting a bit fed up with them. He'd sooner go and get a takeaway if we're too tired to cook. And it gives him an excuse to call in at the pub when he goes to pick it up. It was a good idea but I got a bit carried away, obviously thought I was baking for hundreds. I do miss work. I'm not at all sure how I'll manage with Luke when I want to go back, but I can't stay at home for ever. For one thing, we can't afford it. Oh, listen to me waffling on. What do you want me to do?"

"OK. Let's get the cakes set out and organise where to put the reserves to keep the plates full. Will you meet and greet at the door to start with? Hopefully not too many will have coats on a nice day like this, but if they do, direct them to the hooks in the downstairs toilet. I'll take up my usual place behind the urn to get the tea served. If you come back into the kitchen once a few people have arrived, that would be really helpful. Then you can start helping me with serving and taking the money for the tea and cakes. There's some bags and boxes to put cakes and pies in if people want to take them home. What usually happens is that everyone has their first drink before buying anything to take away, but we need to be ready. In previous years, it's been very noisy and chaotic, but great fun. Let's just get going – the cakes are all here."

Hilary started opening tins and plastic boxes to reveal the tempting contents. The plates and cake stands were soon full and Sarah's pies were laid out on a tray raised at one end to show them off properly. They filled jugs with milk, straightened the pile of serviettes, put teaspoons and cake forks in dishes and finally stood back from the laden breakfast bar admiring their efforts just as the doorbell rang for the first time.

"Help. It's not eleven yet," said Hilary, anxiously going to the door. She opened the door and smiled when she saw Suzanne standing on the door step with two cash boxes and a large pink rabbit under her arm.

"A late entry for the tombola," she said, as she kissed Hilary on the cheek and walked past her into the hall.

"This is Sarah. She's been helping me set out. She's Hector's mum," Hilary explained, smiling.

Hector chose this moment to come skidding out of the living room to say hello to Suzanne, skittering round her legs until she put the things down and said hello to him.

"You were out early this morning, weren't you?" she said to Hector, tickling his tummy. "Sorry, Sarah, hello, nice to meet you. I've heard all about you. Where's your baby?"

"Hello, nice to meet you too. Luke's with his nan, being spoilt probably. I thought it best to keep him out of Hector's way for a bit longer. I can't believe how well Hector has settled in here." To prove it, Hector returned to his chair after being gently redirected from the kitchen by Hilary.

"Phew, have they all gone?" Hilary flopped onto the settee and took the coffee that Sarah put in her hand, smiling her thanks. It was one thirty and the last of the guests had finally left. Suzanne was sitting on the floor counting the money. Carol and Liz were stacking the dishwasher and wiping surfaces. Hector was trailing hopefully after Sarah as she cleared the plates from the living room.

"It felt as though there were a hundred people here, and I know I did more than fifty drinks because I ran out of cups and had to use those horrible polystyrene ones. Everyone was eating and buying. The noise at one stage was enough to raise the roof. I can't believe that nothing got broken or spilt. They're a tidy lot around here, aren't they?"

"They were a really nice crowd and everyone seemed to have brought a friend, which was great. How much have we made, Suzanne?" asked Sarah.

"I'm not there yet, but I've counted more than £300 already."

Sarah went into the hall to phone home and check on Luke.

"Isn't she lovely?" said Hilary and the others agreed. "You know the bistro where we went for my birthday. She works there."

"Yes, she was telling me," said Carol, coming in, drying her hands on a tea towel. "She's already planning menus for when she goes back after her maternity leave and her baby is only a few weeks old."

"He's a delight. It was such a shame they had the problem with Hector. But what good fortune for me. Hasn't he been good today?" she said proudly.

"He kept following me when I was passing cakes around but he wasn't too much of a nuisance and everyone loved him. You know, I still can't believe you've got a dog, Hilary. I always thought you were anti-dog," observed Liz.

"No, it was mum who didn't want a dog. I always did. As I told Janet, Dad once brought a puppy home but Mum made him take it to the animal shelter."

"Did someone say my name?" asked Janet as she came into the room having let herself in through the open front door.

She went around to greet everyone. "Sorry I couldn't make it to the main event. Did I win a prize with my tombola ticket?"

"Oh, yes." Suzanne eased herself up from the floor and went to the table, which now held the last five prizes waiting to be claimed. She took the ticket from the pink rabbit and presented it to Janet, laughing.

"Oh, he's cute and, actually, I know a good home for him. Mum loves soft toys. She was always so scathing of people making a fuss of stuffed animals but now she is surrounded by them."

"How are your parents?" asked Suzanne.

"Coping at the moment, thank you. We are always waiting for the next disaster but all is calm at the moment. Dad has been able to get into the garden a bit, which I think has helped keep him sane. He puts Mum in a deck chair with a sun hat on and a blanket over her knees and just potters about, keeping her in sight. I've only just got back, that's why I couldn't come today. There was a meeting this morning with the social worker and carers to reassess Mum's needs and so I needed to be there. I stayed overnight last night as they were supposed to be there at nine – though it was actually nearer ten. It's really strange staying in the room I slept in as a child. In fact, just being in the house is strange. I feel about fourteen again. It's not unpleasant, just strange."

"I can imagine," said Carol. "My parents moved about so much there wasn't one house that had any particular meaning for me. But your parents have always lived there, haven't they?"

"Yes, and nothing much has changed except that all the neighbours have got older or died," replied Janet ruefully. "Anyway, the meeting was a bit of a waste of time. The social worker looked as though she hadn't slept for a week and was very harassed and disorganised but, fortunately, the outcome was that nothing will change. Not sure why we needed a meeting for that, but at least the care package, which is working well, will continue. I don't know why she didn't just phone me or Dad and ask how things were going. Did she actually think that Mum had been putting it on and was suddenly going to be better? Oh, I'm sorry, I'm going on again, but so much time is wasted by people who are supposed to be helping us get through this. Ageing isn't new. Why is it suddenly so difficult to deal with?"

"Come on, sit down – here's a coffee. I saved you a bit of lemon drizzle cake, and Sarah hid one of her pies so that you wouldn't miss out." Hilary pushed her gently onto the settee. "Meet Sarah, Hector's mum."

"You'll have to stop introducing me like that," laughed Sarah. "Hello, Janet. It sounds as though you've had a terrible day so far. Sit down and relax. I think we all need a break. I've just checked on Luke and he's fine, so I'm free as long as you need me for clearing up duties. I know we've all had cake but I put some bits and pieces together for lunch. I'll go and get them out of the car."

Sarah came back with two foil plates of sandwiches and, after finding the remaining serviettes, passed them around.

"How on earth did you manage to make these with a young baby to look after?" asked Liz. "I know when Lisa was tiny, all I could do was sleep when she didn't need feeding or changing."

"I find it relaxing, and there's nothing clever in any of these sandwiches. The most complicated bit was shopping for all the ingredients, and Tom did that," Sarah replied. "Hilary tells me you look after your granddaughter now. Luke's with Tom's mum today. She loves having him. I don't think she can wait for me to go back to work."

"I enjoy looking after Siobhan, but she wears me out. She came to these coffee mornings with me when she was tiny but, last year, she was a bit of a handful, wasn't she? She ate too many cakes, got under everyone's feet and hid under the table with the star prize from the tombola. She was very sweet but a bit annoying, so I got Lisa to swap her day off this year. John thinks I do too much for Lisa but she's had such a hard time. I want to do what I can. Siobhan's dad has nothing to do with her and certainly doesn't give them any money. Siobhan will be starting school soon so I won't be needed as much – although you do lots of the school runs for your grandchildren, don't you, Carol?"

"It's great, I walk or go on my bike and I can't believe the number of people I've chatted to since I started taking the grandchildren to school. I can't say I cycle or walk every day. I'm not going to get drenched for anyone and the children wouldn't stand for it, especially the older ones. They are beyond the age when jumping in puddles is fun!"

"Yes, I've found the same with walking Hector. He's such a sociable dog, I often get into conversations with other owners."

"Three hundred and twenty-four pounds and sixteen pence," announced Suzanne, surveying the piles of coins and notes in front of her. "Not bad for a couple of hours' work."

"That's wonderful. Thank you so much for all your help. Mum would be so proud – and annoyed that we'd beaten her best total." Hilary beamed round the group.

Carol got up to reload the dishwasher and Janet refilled everyone's cup. Sarah did a final round with the sandwiches and the few left-over cakes. Hector lounged in his chair, overseeing the proceedings, as they relaxed and chatted into the afternoon.

When the next cycle of the dishwasher was complete, Sarah reluctantly got up and said that she ought to make a move. She gathered together her trays and containers and said goodbye to everyone, tickling Hector behind his ears. Tired but happy, she made her way to her car to go back to take up the reins at home once again.

The others finished tidying up. Hilary had to stop Carol getting the vacuum cleaner out.

"I can do it later, or even tomorrow. You lot have done enough. I know we've just raised loads for charity, but would any of you like to join me for a charity ten mile walk along the canal in October? You can get sponsors, but I was just going to pay the entrance fee and add a bit of a donation."

"Love to," said Liz, Carol and Janet almost at the same time.

"I'll persuade Richard to come too. He could do with a bit of exercise. What about John and Jonathan?"

"John might if Richard's going," said Liz.

"And I bet Jonathan won't want to be left out," added Carol. "What about you and David?"

"We're off to the Seychelles for three weeks in October."

"Fantastic," enthused the others. "Lucky things."

"Well, there's a bit of a sting in the tail. I'm being buttered up because David's mum is moving into the flat over the garage in November. I'm sure it'll be fine. We get on OK, but I'm not sure I want her that near. We'll see."

"At least she'll have her own space and she's pretty fit at the moment, isn't she? And if she does become ill, you won't have all the travelling that I have. It's never easy, is it? But, wow, the Seychelles will be wonderful, and David will spoil you rotten."

"He will. To be fair, he always does. I can't wait."

The final cups had been washed and put away for the next event, the water heater emptied and the coffee machine cleaned.

Hilary saw them out, fed Hector, put the telly on, and fell asleep.

Chapter Twelve

October Walk

"It wasn't supposed to be a race," said Liz, plonking herself down next to Richard in the window seat, unwinding her scarf and taking off her hat.

"No, but we won though, didn't we?" beamed Jonathan.

Carol cuffed him on the arm as she pulled her arm out of her coat. "I must look like the wreck of the Hesperus," she said, dragging her fingers through her hair, which, to everyone else, looked as good as ever.

"Well, as we are one drink ahead, I'll go to the bar. What does everyone want? I'll get some menus too – I'm starving," said John, getting up and squeezing past the legs of the others to get out from the big round table in the bay window.

The pub was busy, as the charity walk had ended and begun in the car park. Hilary had taken the precaution of booking a table, but it looked as though it would be a long wait for any food. It's nice to be sitting down though, Hilary thought. She must have become fitter walking Hector twice a day, but it hadn't prepared her for the ten miles they had just walked. She thought she wasn't going to make the last bit from the canal to the car park. Fortunately, Hector had come to the rescue, back on the lead, pulling her those last difficult yards.

"We should have got sponsorship for Hector. He must have run twenty miles." Janet looked at him as he stretched out in front of the fire.

He'd had a wonderful time, running ahead to catch up with the leaders and then dashing back to chivvy the stragglers, skilfully negotiating all the legs and walking poles along the tow path. He'd stop at intervals to lean precariously over the canal bank to take long noisy drinks. He got up as John came back from the bar with a tray of drinks and a pile of menus.

"Yes, I've got your crisps, Hector." John pulled the packet from his pocket and handed it to Hilary as he put the tray down.

There was a flurry of organisation as drinks and menus were distributed, drinks tasted and swapped until everyone had what they had ordered.

They shuffled round so that John could sit and toasted each other's success at walking the ten miles.

"I bet Suzanne and David haven't had to walk ten miles to get a drink. Did you see where they are staying? It looks like paradise," said Liz enviously, taking a long drink of her white wine.

"Actually, I'm not sure it would be my kind of holiday. I need something to do and things to see. Let's face it – I'm no good at relaxing and doing nothing." To prove her point, Janet rummaged in her rucksack for a pen and paper and proceeded to take the food order. "Aargh, I'm not sure I can get up. I hate this business of getting old."

She struggled to her feet, leaning on the table, the others providing counterbalance. But once up, she walked easily to the bar to order the food.

"I wish Janet would relax more," said Richard, as she walked off. "But even if I booked the sort of holiday Suzanne and David have gone on, it wouldn't do any good. As she says, she needs to be doing something. That weekend you went on did her the world of good and this couple of hours out will help, but I know even now she is thinking of her parents and waiting for the next problem. I wish, in a way, that we had some grandchildren to fuss over. I know she'd be even busier," – he stopped Liz interrupting – "but at least it would be something positive for her to think about. There is only one outcome with her parents and that's not a very jolly one."

"It's great getting close to the grandchildren but it's very temporary. Just when you are getting close, they either move away or circumstances change so they don't need you as much. You have to make the most of whatever chances you get," said Carol wistfully.

"I thought you hated all the bother of the grandchildren. That's why I've done so much," replied Jonathan.

"So did I," replied Carol. "But I've realised lately that I'm afraid of getting too involved with them because of the wrench when they go." A look passed between them, a look of understanding and revelation.

"You know, I'm not looking forward to next year when Siobhan goes to school. It's funny how we all need to be needed. Talking of needing, does anyone want another drink? I'm going to catch Janet at the bar before she finishes the order and get another glass of wine." Liz got up to go to the bar, wincing as she twisted to get past the others. "I'm going to be stiff in the morning."

"I'm surprised how many people turned out on a day like this for the walk. I hope they make a lot of money."

"Whenever I do anything like this, I always think that it'll be the start of a new fitness regime. But life takes over and I never get round to it."

"Doesn't your golf keep you fit, Richard?"

"Well, it would if I walked the whole course every time, or carried my clubs. We are just all so lazy these days."

"I really enjoyed the swimming at the spa and thought I'd go every week, but I haven't been since," admitted Carol. "Has David said why his mum is suddenly moving into theirs?" she asked, changing the subject. All this talk of exercise was making her feel guilty and she wanted to wallow in the good feelings engendered by the walk.

"I think that David is looking to develop the site that his mum's house stands on. It's such a big plot he can build several houses. He's always looking for money-making schemes. I think he gets it from his mum. They were in the pub, plotting, a few weeks ago. She's just as keen as him to secure some money for a comfortable old age. I know Suzanne is a bit worried about it, but the flat over the garage is far enough away from their house to ensure that they don't get under each other's feet."

"I know I'm a bit cynical," started John, "but I got the impression he wanted to get hold of that plot in case his mum met someone and got married again.

"I know she's nearly eighty but she's still pretty good for her age and certainly very lively," he continued over the protests and laughter. "OK, so it's unlikely, but not impossible."

"What's not impossible?" asked Janet, coming back after finally getting her food order in at the bar.

"John thinks David is worried about his inheritance if his mum gets married again," explained Carol.

"There was a couple at mum's 'Over 55 Club'. That's a laugh in itself – there's no-one under seventy in that club," put in Liz. "Anyway, there was a couple who got married last year. It caused no end of upset in the family. There seem to be lots of people our age who are planning how to spend their parents' money even before they 'go'. So I think David is quite sensible, really, and if he and his mum do it together, it means she has an income too and can be independent a bit longer."

"I would like to think that if anything happened to Mum, Dad would still be able to get out and enjoy himself, but I don't think he would marry again. He and Mum were childhood sweethearts. They have only ever had each other. No, I don't think he would marry again, but then again, I didn't actually ever imagine that my healthy, bright, organised Mum would get dementia. So I suppose we never know what's around the corner," mused Janet. "Sorry, I'm being maudlin again. Let's change the subject. Oh, here's the food – that was quick."

Talk turned to food, drink, plans for Christmas, and the afternoon passed pleasantly. Hilary was the first to leave to get Hector home for his dinner, but the others followed soon after.

*

Jonathan and Carol had come in Richard and Janet's car. Richard manoeuvred out of the still full car park and headed back towards town.

"I wonder how Suzanne and David are getting on. At least the weather will be better," said Jonathan. The weather had been dry but cold when they started the walk, but it had started drizzling when they got near the end and now it was raining insistently.

"I never really thought their relationship would last," admitted Carol. "David is so loud and Suzanne so quiet. But they seem to be very close. They look after each other. Their opposite natures seem to compliment rather than clash."

"David is very shy and unsure of himself, believe it or not. I think he overcompensates with his loud brashness," explained Richard. "I have seen him very anxious sometimes, particularly about money. I like them both, but David does sometimes get a bit hung up on material possessions. He loves his designer labels."

"I wonder what they'd think if they knew we were talking about them," said Janet, as ever worrying what others thought.

"They'd love it, and we haven't said one bad thing, have we?" said Carol. "I hope people think of me when I'm not here."

The others agreed and talk turned to immediate plans for soaking in the bath and washing clothes.

John and Liz also talked about Suzanne and David as they drove home, both expressing mild envy at the freedom they had. But then John said, "We could have exactly what they have, but I'm afraid to take risks. Richard said that David gets anxious about money. I'd be a nervous wreck if I took some of the risks he does. Anyway, we can't have long holidays while you are looking after Siobhan. They don't have children, so they haven't had all the stress that we've had with Lisa. Yes, I have been stressed too," he said, as Liz tried to contradict him. "But one of us has to stay calm and, if I'm honest, the biggest stress for me was the effect that it was all having on you. You perhaps don't realise, but when it all blew up with Lisa and that horrible lad, I spent a lot of time on the phone to Edward, for someone to talk to, to keep him in the loop and to reassure him that he was important too. I think in a way he felt responsible because he thought that if he'd been around, being the protective big brother, Lisa wouldn't have met the mad Irish man and got into trouble. Of course, that's rubbish, but our thoughts and feelings aren't always logical."

"You know, I had no idea," said Liz quietly. "I'm sorry, really selfish, aren't I?"

"I could never describe you as selfish, Liz, but some of us have felt a bit neglected. I just knew if I was patient, you'd come back, although I was beginning to wonder whether I'd be waiting until Siobhan went to university." He laughed and Liz joined him. They were both thoughtful as they pulled onto their drive.

Chapter Thirteen

Back to Reality

"You had good weather, then?" Hilary called, as she passed Suzanne getting out of her car on the drive.

"It was unbelievably wonderful. Photos don't do it justice. I think it was because I was feeling so well that it seemed so wonderful," Suzanne said, looking uncharacteristically dreamy eyed. "Even another resident dying couldn't spoil our trip."

Suzanne bent down to pet Hector, who had pulled Hilary down the drive. Hilary pushed her hood off her head. "What did you say? Someone died? Oh no, how awful. Oh dear, I am sorry."

"Are you on your way out or back in?"

"Out," replied Hilary.

"Right. Can you wait while I put the frozen stuff in the freezer and get a coat and I'll join you. Then I can tell you all about it and you can fill me in on all the news from here. Hector certainly seems to be thriving."

Hilary picked up one of the shopping bags and followed Suzanne down the side of the house to the back door, remonstrating with Hector as he pulled on the lead, eager to explore a new house.

The shopping safely stowed and both wrapped up in warm coats, scarves and hoods, the two women set out across the edge of the golf course.

"So, what happened?" Hilary asked eagerly.

As they walked briskly towards the woods where Hilary could let Hector off his lead, Suzanne described the fateful day, reliving her feelings of helplessness. She and David had been sunbathing on the beach when the peace was suddenly shattered by a commotion nearby. They both jumped up and ran to the water's edge to find a man and a woman struggling to pull another man from the water. David rushed forward to help, his strong arms taking the leaden weight from them and laying him on the wet sand. Suzanne was right behind him and immediately took charge, sending the shaken-looking man to get help. She shouted to rouse the inert man, checking for a pulse at the same time. The man was not breathing. After checking his airway, she started cardiac massage, as she had been taught. A mouthful of water came out of his mouth as she rhythmically pressed on his chest. People from the hotel arrived then, the first-aider running in front, carrying what Suzanne was pleased to see was a defibrillator. They dried his chest and applied the pads, while Suzanne kept up the pressure. The screen showed a flat line. They continued cardiac massage. After what seemed like hours, they heard the sirens approaching. Then paramedics arrived, heaving all their equipment across the beach. Suzanne moved to let them take over, filling them in on what had happened, suddenly self-conscious that she was wearing only her bikini. Another fifteen minutes passed and the man was pronounced dead. It was all over.

"It was awful. I felt such a failure. His wife was so stoic though, accepting and calm. A lovely lady, Esmee – she's Dutch. We spent some time with her before she went back home to be with her family. You'll like her."

"Will I meet her?"

"We've already exchanged emails. I've invited her for New Year and I think she might come."

Hilary bent down to let Hector off his lead and wiped a tear away. "I wish I could be as strong as Esmee sounds. I still miss Mum. I do feel silly really, but there it is…" she trailed off.

"I think, reading between the lines, Esmee had already been through all that when her husband nearly died the year before. It was still horrible for her but she was half prepared for it to happen. She's a much stronger person than I am, though. I was a wreck after the failed resuscitation. I still felt bad even after I found out that it had, in effect, been too late before we even started trying. Anyway, enough about that. I'll show you the photos when we get back and you can be jealous. It was a fabulous trip. I've never known David to be so relaxed. But you must tell me how the charity walk went. I'm not sure I was sorry to miss that one. The coffee morning was more my scene and we raised an amazing amount, didn't we?"

"The coffee morning was the best yet, but I really enjoyed the walk too, even though the weather was awful. We raised… GET BACK HERE!" shouted Hilary at the top of her voice, as Hector shot off after a rabbit.

"HECTOR, COME HERE!" she uncharacteristically screeched. He responded to this tone, realising that she meant it. He stopped and, losing impetus and sight of the rabbit, ran back towards Hilary, who was flapping her arm to her side, calling him back. He stopped within inches of her feet, looking immensely pleased with himself, wagging his tail madly. Seeing she wasn't overjoyed to see him, he turned his attention to Suzanne, who automatically rubbed him behind his ears.

"Don't be nice to him. He's got to learn not to run off and chase everything. You can't believe how liberating it's been having someone to boss about," she continued, as she struggled to get Hector back on his lead. "I know I'm in charge at work, but everything has to be negotiated, discussed, changes have to be made tentatively and, in reality, most changes come from the top. I have very little freedom. And, of course, when Mum was alive, quite rightly, she was in charge and it was her house. I didn't realise how much I had had to toe the line until she'd gone. I didn't realise that I constantly bowed to her wishes. I didn't resent it. In fact, it suited me. I think I got a bit lazy, having someone else make all the decisions. She was a very strong lady, but I think I'm finding a new strength in myself since she's gone and, as I said, it's great to have this rascal to boss about because he loves to please. I probably spoil him and treat him like a child, but I try not to stand any nonsense. He'll try it on, but he knows when I mean 'no'. I can honestly say he's the best thing that's happened to me in a long time."

Suzanne walked quietly beside them, thinking back across those short months to the time just after Phyllis's death and how different Hilary was now. She seemed like a different person, so much more sure of herself.

"You're not going to become one of these batty old women who take in stray animals and forget how to relate to people, are you?" she joked.

Hilary let Hector off his lead again and he went scurrying off into the undergrowth, sniffing intently, running along with his nose to the ground. She laughed, "Oh dear, no, I don't think so. I love him to bits, but I don't want a house full. We've got it sorted just fine. What he has done though is the opposite really, because since I've been walking him, I've talked to so many more people around here than I ever have in the past. There's a sort of camaraderie amongst dog walkers and there are very few who don't say something. Unfortunately, there haven't been any story-book moments with attractive men sweeping Hector and me off our feet! I think that moment may have passed."

"It's never too late," countered Suzanne, thinking that this new Hilary was so much more attractive than the mouse of old.

"Wait for us," came a breathless shout from behind them. They both turned to see Liz and Siobhan, both bundled up in thick coats, scarves and hats, hurrying towards them, Siobhan pulling on Liz's hand to hurry her up.

"My welly came off in the mud," announced Siobhan. "It sank right down and Nanny had to pull it out while I hopped."

They all looked down obediently to examine her pink spotted welly and then Siobhan was almost swept off her feet as Hector came charging back from his recent explorations. She yelped and giggled and then put her arms round his neck as he licked her all over her face.

"Ugh, stop it Hector," said Hilary, as she tried to pull them apart.

"I like it – it tickles."

Siobhan stood up, wiping her face with the back of her gloved hand. Hector shot off after real or imaginary prey and Siobhan galloped after him.

"Stay where we can see you," Liz shouted after her.

"You look great," said Liz to Suzanne as they sauntered, keeping an eye on dog and child scampering in the wet leaves.

"I feel like a different person. What started out as a sweetener to get me to accept what was happening with his mum ended as the most wonderful trip that has brought us closer together."

"Tell her what happened," interjected Hilary. "It ended up a bit of a busman's holiday."

Suzanne told her tale again with no embellishment or exaggeration and spoke fondly of Esmee. "But," she concluded, "that was really only a few hours. The rest of the time was like living on a film set, surrounded by perfection, being pampered by the staff and spoilt by David."

"I wish John was as thoughtful. Our relationship seems to have gone a bit stale. Although I'd probably be bored on an island paradise. I'm hopeless…"

There was a high-pitched squeal, and they turned to see that Siobhan had tripped over a tree root and fallen headlong onto the muddy path.

They all fussed round her, with Hector trying to help, and she was soon upright and laughing as they cleaned her up.

"Let's walk quietly for a little way," said Liz, taking her hand, as Hilary put Hector back on his lead.

"Can I hold him?" asked Siobhan.

"You can try, but if he pulls, I'll have him back. I don't want you to fall over again. Nanny will shout at me," replied Hilary.

"She won't," said Siobhan, seriously. "She doesn't shout, but she looks like this when she's cross." She stopped in her tracks, faced them, then pulled her eyebrows together, narrowed her eyes and with her mouth in a very thin straight line, looked just like Liz when she was upset.

Hilary, Suzanne and Liz roared with laughter and Hector didn't quite know what was happening as Siobhan was pulled into their arms. He barked and tried to untangle himself from all the bodies. After a moment or two of chaos, they were all on their way again, Hector in front with Siobhan proudly holding the lead, Suzanne with her arm through Liz's and Hilary holding Siobhan's other hand.

"Paradise was great but this is much more fun," laughed Suzanne.

After a short distance, Hilary said, "I'll tell you the other benefit of having a dog. I've lost weight. I bet I could get into that costume that had to be cut off me. I tried on the polka-dot swimsuit the other day and I think it looks great."

"We go swimming on Mondays," piped up Siobhan. "Swimming Monday, great grandma Tuesday, shopping Wednesday, Mummy Thursday, ballet Friday," she chanted.

"What a busy week," said Suzanne. "How is your mum?" she asked, squeezing Liz's arm.

"She's really well, looking forward to turning eighty next month. It's funny how getting older is such an issue when you are younger, not wanting to reach forty or fifty, but then when you reach eighty, I suppose it is an achievement, something to be proud of."

"We made biscuits last week," put in Siobhan, "and then we ate them. Mine had chocolate bits in."

"She is amazing really, completely independent, and she still likes to cook, and although she was upset and disappointed when Lisa got pregnant, she adores Siobhan. I don't remember her being like this with either of my children but I suppose she was still working and then looking after Dad. She probably didn't have the time or the energy. I know I'm enjoying looking after a grandchild much more than I ever enjoyed the children."

"You could come swimming with us in your dotty costume," Siobhan was saying seriously to Hilary.

"Definitely," added Liz. "We could all go. Are you around on a Monday morning?" she asked, turning to Suzanne.

"I've altered my hours, so I'm working less. So yes, I'm off on Mondays now."

"We could have a swim then have coffee or even lunch. The salads in the coffee bar at the leisure centre look great, although I've never tried them. And they do other things too."

"Shall I contact Janet? We could make an occasion of it. Oh dear, I'm not sure what day she goes to her parents. I'll check."

"That's set then, next Monday. We'd better get back now so I can clean madam up before delivering her back to Lisa. We don't want a cross Mummy, do we?" she asked, turning to Siobhan.

"Will Mummy still be crying when we get home?"

"I don't know, sweetheart, but we can make her better, can't we?"

"This is why we are out today, Thursday – Mummy's day. The latest disaster left last night, leaving Lisa with a broken heart and a load of debt. I certainly had my cross face on when I heard," she said ruefully.

She took Siobhan's hand, Hector was handed back to Hilary and, with hugs and waves and goodbyes, they separated at a fork in the path.

"Shall we go and get a gingerbread man for Mummy on the way home? You can choose a nice smiley one and that will cheer her up, and you can show her the ballet steps you have been practising for tomorrow."

Siobhan pirouetted elegantly in her wellies, put her hand back in Liz's and set off purposefully on a mission to cheer up Mummy.

"See you Monday," Liz shouted over her shoulder.

Hilary, Suzanne and Hector continued their walk back towards home.

"Oh dear, children are such a worry, whatever their age. Do you have any regrets not having children?"

"Not now," replied Suzanne. "I've had such a good life. I suppose I regret not having that experience, but there are so many things I couldn't have done if I'd had children. I think my life has been pretty useful anyway. No, I don't have regrets. What about you?"

"No, I'm too selfish for children. I love little babies and toddlers, but I don't think I'm grown up enough to deal with a teenager. I'll stick with my life. I suppose I do regret not having a dog earlier but I think everything has a right time. Fate… Nothing to do with that, but shall I ask Sarah if she wants to bring Luke swimming Monday? He's old enough now. I do like her. If I had a daughter, I'd like to think she'd be like Sarah."

Suzanne and Hilary continued to muse on friends and life as they walked home. Hector, tired now, trotted at Hilary's side.

"Come in and see the photos. I'll put the coffee on."

"I'd love to. I'll just put Hector in the house and put his dinner out. See you in a minute." Hilary hurried across the road to sort Hector out and then spent a pleasant hour with Suzanne admiring the photos and chatting over coffee before returning to the comfort of her own home and Hector's quiet company.

Chapter Fourteen

An Energetic Morning

"I can't think why we don't do this more often," said Hilary, towelling her hair as she came towards the mirrors, shouting over the noise of the hairdryers.

"Nanny and I come every week," piped up Siobhan, sitting on the side next to the basin, combing her hair and trying to get the bobble to hold up her top knot.

"Well, I must admit, I nearly cried off first thing when I looked at the weather," said Suzanne. "The thought of getting into a swimming costume was the last thing on my mind in the gloom at seven o'clock this morning. I looked out and it was tipping it down. If you hadn't phoned to check what time we'd arranged, I'd have chickened out. Oh no, I've forgotten my moisturiser," she moaned, as she rummaged in her capacious white leather hold-all.

"Oh dear. Here, borrow some of mine," said Hilary, pushing a large pot towards her. "I'm sure it's not your usual cream but it was on offer and I can't resist a bargain."

Suzanne looked suspiciously at the label, but took her up on the offer nonetheless, smoothing the cream into her flawless skin before leaning towards the mirror to reapply her make-up.

Liz lifted Siobhan down, took her hand and, gathering their bags together, said over her shoulder, "We'll see you in the café."

As they left, Janet joined the other two at the mirrors. "I don't know how you are all so quick at getting dressed and ready. You will wait while I make myself presentable, won't you?"

"Of course we will," reassured Hilary, as she made space for Janet at the mirrors.

"I really enjoyed that. Thank you so much for inviting me. I heard you saying," she said, turning to Suzanne, "how you nearly didn't come. Actually, I nearly said no when Hilary phoned. I am so tied up and fixated on my self-imposed treadmill, I'm forgetting how to live. I'm surprised Richard stays. He and Claire creep around me, scared to say anything in case they upset me. At least I am reassured that they have each other and they can look after themselves while all my energies go on Mum and Dad. Do you fancy coming up to see them again, Hilary? It really helped me, and Dad enjoyed the break. We could arrange it so that he could go out again. I don't think he likes to if I am on my own. We spend our time trying to look after each other. I suppose the habits of being a dad are hard to break." She tugged a comb through her short hair, then ran her fingers through it so that it wasn't plastered to her head, absent-mindedly put some moisturiser on her face, took a lipstick out of her bag and put it back in without applying it.

"I'd love to come with you," replied Hilary. "I said I would last time. Sorry, life just takes over, doesn't it? I didn't intend to leave it so long."

Suzanne had put the finishing touches to her appearance. They gathered their belongings and headed towards the door.

"Hold on a minute," said Janet, as she reached the door. "I must go to the loo again. Oh dear, I do hate getting old. I'll catch you up."

Hilary took Janet's hold-all as she battled with the cubicle door. "We'll see you in the café. Shall I order you a coffee?"

"Oh yes, please," said a very flustered Janet.

"She is in a state, isn't she?" commented Suzanne, as the changing-room door shut behind them. "I wish there was something we could do to take some of the pressure off."

"She's her own worst enemy," replied Hilary. "She tries to be everything to everyone and her standards are so high she is never going to achieve everything she sets out to do."

They made their way up the stairs to the café area, the glass walls streaked with rain, the November half-light belying the fact that it was almost midday. The swimming pool had been upgraded over the last few years, taking over a large area of the park in which it sat. It was now a leisure centre with a gym that extended along one side of the pool so that people could cycle and run for hours without getting wet, cold or, indeed, going anywhere. The café had been upgraded too; the glass counter housing KitKats and Mars bars had been replaced by an extensive salad bar, and the choice of tea, coffee or squash had been replaced with a frightening number of alternatives.

"Do you remember when they first started doing toast in the café? I can still smell it now," said Hilary, with a dreamy look on her face. "Dad used to bring me swimming on a Saturday morning and we always had tea and toast afterwards. It was our guilty secret because it was dripping in butter." She licked her lips in remembrance of pleasures past.

"I only ever came with the school and it was a chore, not a joy," said Suzanne. "I didn't really start to enjoy swimming until we went abroad and I could swim in the sea or those outdoor pools on the camp sites we used to take the caravan to. I could never quite understand the point of swimming up and down, or those daft life-saving lessons when we had to swim in our pyjamas and rescue a brick. But I suppose it has turned me into quite a strong swimmer."

"Golly, I'd forgotten all about that," replied Hilary, as they queued for their coffees. "I had to borrow Dad's pyjamas because Mum insisted that it wasn't lady-like for me to wear pyjamas to bed. The legs and arms were miles too long. I can still remember the tangle I got in and the frustrated look on the teacher's face. If I'm ever shipwrecked in my pyjamas, I hope I'm wearing ones that fit."

"Hurry up you lot, we're over there. Nanny's got hot chocolate with cream on and she let me put my spoon in it and I got it on my nose." Siobhan's words tumbled out as if they were all joined together. Grabbing Hilary's hand, she pointed to the table in the corner where Liz was guiltily sitting behind her huge drink, which was overflowing with fluffy white cream.

"OK. We'll be there in a minute. Just let me order, sweetheart." Hilary extricated her hand and gave her order to the unfriendly teenage assistant, who looked as though she wanted to be anywhere but in front of a monster coffee machine.

They gathered chairs and settled down on either side of Liz and Siobhan, the rain still pouring down the streaky plate glass and making the car park look even more depressing.

"It'll be Christmas before we know it."

"That's enough, Hilary," interrupted Suzanne. "We've got six weeks yet. I haven't even thought about it. Oh, but what will you be doing?" she continued contritely. "You'd be very welcome to join us." After her initial difficulties when her mum died, Hilary seemed to have returned to her normal placid self. They saw her out and about more than before, because of Hector, but otherwise it was hard to remember that she had so recently lost her mum.

"I think Hector and I will have Christmas lunch in front of the telly, something I've never been allowed to do. I'm becoming a rebel in my old age," Hilary laughed ruefully. "But you are right, let's not talk about Christmas. It's just that, in the shops, it's forced upon us from August."

"STOP IT," shouted Liz, startling them all. Siobhan looked up guiltily, holding one end of her wet swimming costume, the other end posted through the loops of Suzanne's designer bag. "I'm so sorry," Liz said to Suzanne, extricating the costume and dabbing ineffectually at the bag. "Take your eye off her for one moment and she's up to mischief."

Siobhan's bottom lip went out and tears threatened to fall, but Suzanne scooped her up saying, "No harm done. Grown up talk is boring. Shall we try threading this scarf through instead?" She produced a scarf that, to Liz, looked worrying like Hermès and Siobhan happily helped her thread it through the loops.

"I wish I had grandchildren to look after," said Janet wistfully.

"How on earth would you find the time?" countered Liz.

"Oh, I think I would for something like that, the time and the energy. Old people are so draining, but babies and little ones imbue you with energy, they *make* you carry on."

"I don't think I thought like that when my own were young but, you are right, it's different with grandchildren." Liz looked thoughtful but then was suddenly alert again when she saw Siobhan trying to undo the tassels on Suzanne's bag. "Right, young lady. Time to go home for a nap. Upsadaisy." She picked Siobhan up off Suzanne's lap and gathered their bags together. "Sorry to break up the party." They said goodbye, making vague future plans, knowing they would see each other over the next few days and, if they didn't, someone would take the initiative and arrange something. The relationship between the women was fluid but solid in its foundations. They didn't have to be in constant contact for the ties to remain.

Janet, Suzanne and Hilary relaxed back in their chairs, Suzanne surreptitiously checking her bag for signs of damage before placing it on the chair next to her.

"Are you in a rush?" she asked the others. "I quite fancy some lunch and the salads did look lovely and fresh."

"Can we join you?" Sarah pushed Luke in his buggy up to their table. "Sorry I missed you in the pool. I still haven't got the hang of timing with a young baby, but we've just had a lovely time in the little pool. He loves it." She looked dotingly on her now sleeping son.

"Of course, you can join us. We were just thinking about lunch," said Hilary, moving a chair to one side to make room for the buggy, and putting Liz and Siobhan's dirty glasses on a neighbouring table.

They studied the menu on the table and then Sarah and Janet went to the counter to order.

"She's such a lovely girl," said Hilary, looking at Sarah's back as she queued at the counter. "I hope it all works out when she goes back to work. I thought of offering to babysit, but I don't really want to be tied. But, of course, she knows I'd help in an emergency. And this lovely lad," she touched Luke's hand, "has doting grandparents queuing up to look after him."

"I wouldn't mind babysitting either, just occasionally, but I don't want to turn my house into a crèche like Carol. Where is she today? I thought she was coming."

"I think it was one of her charity things today."

"Right, it's all sorted," said Janet, coming back with a tray of drinks and a wooden spoon with number 31 painted inexpertly on it. "Sarah's bringing the salads. My omelette and Hilary's bacon baguette will follow."

Lunch duly arrived and they all tucked in hungrily.

"When do you go back to work, Sarah?"

"Just after Christmas, although they could really do with me for the Christmas rush. I didn't think I could face it and I didn't want to be exhausted for his first Christmas." As if he knew they were talking about him, Luke stirred and looked around with enquiring eyes, checking out his new surroundings.

"He doesn't cry when he wakes up, does he?" said Janet. "He just seems pleased to be wherever he is. It must be very strange to wake up in a different place from where you went to sleep, but it doesn't seem to faze him."

"Believe me, he does cry sometimes. But you are right, he's very laid-back. He takes after his dad. I am so lucky to be blessed with such a good baby."

Sarah lifted him onto her lap and gave him a plastic giraffe to gnaw on gummily while they carried on chatting.

The table was cleared and they drank more coffee before finally getting up to leave.

Hilary kissed Luke and hugged Sarah, suggesting coffee or a dog walk or both in the week ahead.

Janet pinned Hilary down to a day for another visit to her parents and the three older women promised each other another trip to the pool in the weeks ahead.

They waved goodbye to each other as they left the car park.

Chapter Fifteen

Secrets

"Did you ever feel glad that your mum had gone?"

This startling question caught Suzanne by surprise. She and Hilary were enjoying a coffee in Hilary's living room. Hector was back in his chair after consuming his quota of biscuits. Controlled spoiling, Hilary called it.

"I loved Mum. How could I have stayed at home this long if I hadn't? But now she has gone, I realise how controlling she was. Look at this room. Apart from Hector's corner, the only thing I've managed to alter are the cushions. I work in Lewis's for heaven's sake, home of middle-class style, but the house still looks like something out of the 1970s."

"Well, Hector's a pretty major change," countered Suzanne. "Don't do anything too rash. I don't want the Hilary I know and love to change too much, and if you take a look around at the moment, 1970s fashions are all over the place."

They both took a swig of their coffee, looking around the room. The heavy well stuffed three-piece suite, upholstered in beige fabric with wide stripes of stylised pheasants and ferns, competed with the bold pattern on the brown carpet. A glass-fronted bookcase fitted snugly in between the sofa and Hector's chair. The shelves were loaded with books, ornaments and knick-knacks of all shapes and sizes; many years of acquisitions proudly displayed.

"Do you think David would come around and give me some ideas for updating the layout? I love this room, but Mum and I often talked about changing it."

"Of course, he would. He has some brilliant ideas. He can look at a space and rearrange it in his head. The only parts of our house that I don't think really work are the areas his internal designer friend had a hand in. And that's not the jealous wife talking – I just think David has better ideas."

Hilary looked thoughtful, glancing again around the familiar space. "Oh dear, I'm not sure I dare admit this." She paused and her eyes filled with tears. "We're talking about changing the structure of the house and I haven't even been able to clear Mum's room and her clothes yet. I didn't move her apron from the back of the kitchen door until the day of the funeral. I moved Hector in and he took over her chair. I didn't think about it. It happened. I was helping someone out. I used to be scornful of people who made a shrine of their loved ones' things, who wouldn't move on, but I can't seem to do it. I go into her bedroom full of good intentions. The number of times I've taken the black bags in… One day, I even made out labels – Rubbish, Charity, Keep. I threw them away. The black bags are waiting in the wardrobe." She looked sheepish and sad at the same time. "Sorry. I'm hopeless, aren't I?"

"No, you aren't hopeless at all. We all have to do it in our own time. It was a terrible shock when your mum died. I remember my mum taking ages to sort Dad's stuff. But when Mum died, we'd had loads of time to prepare. In a way, she helped me. We did it together. As she became ill, her needs changed and we cleared things as we went along. It gave us something to do together that wasn't directly related to her illness or her care. We were even able to joke about the fact that it would be easier when she had gone. We talked about what to give to charity and which charity. I found out which things meant something to her and what she was happy just to throw away. We had a great time doing 'Do you remember when?' Your mum was very practical and down to earth. She knew she wouldn't live forever but she departed before any of us were ready. I'd be happy to help when you are ready to go through your mum's things. Just ask."

"What about now? I do want to do it. It'll be easier with two. You'll stop me being morbid and sentimental. Let's finish our coffee. There's no time like the present. Can you stay a big longer?"

"Of course, I can. Anything to put off the ironing."

With that, they gulped the last of their now lukewarm coffee and got up. Hector glanced up at them but, realising that neither a walk nor food was on offer, settled back into the cushions of his chair.

Phyllis's room was very neat, and as dated in decoration and style as Suzanne had expected. The apron that Hilary had moved from the kitchen door was neatly folded on a stool in front of the square plain dressing table, a stool that Hilary said her mum hadn't been able to sit on for years because of her arthritis, but had insisted on keeping because it was part of the set. She used to move a chair behind it whenever she wanted to see herself in the triple mirror. The room was exactly as it had been when her dad was alive and yet Hilary knew that her mum would have been scathing of her reticence to start clearing things away.

"Oh dear, where shall we start?" Hilary looked a bit unsure, now that they were in the room.

"Well. Let's start with underwear. I know it's very personal but, oddly enough, it's the easiest thing to clear away as, unless your family is very odd, there is no sentiment attached." They smirked at the innuendo. It helped Hilary to distance herself from what she was doing. "It's impossible to be sentimental about an old lady's underwear. Most of it will have to just go, unless, like my mum, she kept new sets just in case. I was never sure what the just-in-case circumstance was but…"

Hilary opened the top drawer of the tall dark chest of drawers, out of kilter with the other 1970s pieces. It had come from her dad's family home and, therefore, its place was secured.

Underwear, piled high, came above the top of the drawer as she opened it. She took her hands off the metal drawer handles and they clattered onto the wood. She put her hand on top of the soft piles of clothes as if to press them back in again but, ever practical, Suzanne took charge and took the drawer by its sides and placed it on top of the bed. The soft smell of lavender wafted up to them, from the sachets tucked into the corners.

"Where are those bags?" asked Suzanne quickly, as she saw Hilary's face start to crumple. Hilary retrieved the roll of black bags and a pack of labels from the wardrobe. Glancing at the tightly packed dresses, skirts, blouses and coats hanging above piles of neatly stacked shoe boxes, she shut the door quickly. She looked at her mother's room reflected in the dusty mirror before turning the key in the lock and taking a deep breath, putting her shoulders back, mentally pulling herself together, as if her mother was watching her. She stepped over to the bed to help Suzanne. One thing at a time.

"Right," said Suzanne, taking charge. "Let's put it in piles first – bin, charity or sell, keep."

She took three embarrassingly grey pairs of knickers and placed them at the top of the bed. Two rather grey bras followed, their elastic straps pulled and twisted, and laid them on the pillow. Hilary added some more dubious-looking knickers and a slip with a tear in the seam. "Rubbish, I think."

A new pile was started for bras, vests and slips that one of them would take to the local charity shop or put in a clothes bin for the Salvation Army.

The top drawer was soon empty, save for the flowered wallpaper lining the base and the lacy lavender bags tied with mauve ribbon – a reminder to Hilary of a holiday in Provence not long after her father had died. She hadn't wanted to leave her mum, in case she died too, but Phyllis had persuaded her to go. She still thought the gift inadequate, but her mum had appreciated the thought and she must have refilled them over the years, as the fragrance couldn't have lasted that long. Could it?

They placed the neatly folded piles of clothes in the black bags and lined them up against the wall by the door, before replacing the drawer and getting to work on the next one, laying it on the now crumpled mustard-coloured candlewick bedspread.

The second drawer contained neatly folded jumpers, three piles of soft pastel knitwear wrapped in tissue and interspersed with cedar balls and moth balls, the camphor smell assailing their nostrils as Suzanne lifted it out. Hilary gently lifted the tissue from the top sweater and gently stroked it.

"She was constantly at war with the moths. They always won."

"I want to know why they always choose your best or favourite clothes, leaving the everyday jumpers intact," countered Suzanne. She looked at Hilary, who obviously wasn't just thinking of moths. A tear was running down her cheek.

"Are you OK to carry on?"

"Of course. It's got to be done. Sorry, I'm just a sentimental old fool and she hated this jumper anyway. She only wore it because I bought it for her last year. I heard her telling one of her friends that it was too thick and it scratched at the neck. Just another example of us looking after each other's feelings. Funny, isn't it, how even after living together so long, we still crept around each other."

"I'm just the same with David. This watch is far too big for my wrist but he chose it. I couldn't bear to hurt his feelings when he gave it to me – he was so pleased with himself. I'm used to it now, though, and when I put my old one on, I can't see the time. He was so smug the first time he saw me peering at the dainty gold face of the watch that I thought was more suited to my wrist." Suzanne laughed ruefully. "He's much more honest. He's very quick to tell me if he doesn't like something, but I daren't admit how much it hurts, especially if I've taken ages choosing it. We women are too eager to please and prevent hurt. It must be bred into us. Your mum looked lovely in this twin set," she continued, pulling pale blue cashmere from the bottom of the drawer.

"Would it suit me, do you think? I've always loved it."

Hilary pulled her top off and drew the soft short-sleeved jumper over her head. Her mum had been bigger than Hilary, but the jumper looked just right and the cardigan didn't look too big.

"Beautiful, you should wear that colour more often."

"I know it suits me, but Mum had so much of it, I always avoided it. We didn't want to look like a bizarre set of twins. I suppose I'm free to wear it now. It's another thing that I can inherit from her."

She took the twinset off and folded it carefully, starting a new pile of things to keep.

The drawers of jumpers and then blouses were soon sorted, and they moved on to the bottom drawer. It was full of scarves of every colour and hue and every material from silk to hand-knitted. At the bottom of the drawer they found two turbans, made of what felt like nylon, softly padded with crumbling foam. They put them on and were transported back to their childhoods when their mothers and grandmothers would never go out without a hat or a head scarf, sometimes covering curlers, sometimes protecting a new perm from going frizzy. They looked into the mirrors and saw their mothers, causing them to dissolve into fits of childish giggles. They rolled about the room with legs crossed, tears streamed down their faces and then, in the midst of all this hilarity the doorbell rang.

Hector barked and ran to the door. Hilary tugged the turban off her head, leaving her hair a mess, flecked with bits of foam. She left Suzanne mopping her eyes and went to the door with a silly grin on her face, to be greeted by a distraught Liz, who pushed past her, ignoring Hector's desperate pleas for attention.

Liz's momentum took them to the kitchen. Suzanne came through from the bedroom dabbing her eyes with a tissue.

"You should have seen…" Suzanne tailed off as she saw the tragedy etched on Liz's face.

"Is it your mum?"

"Lisa?"

"Siobhan?"

Liz shook her head at each of these. Her head hung down, her hair like closed curtains shielding her face.

"John," she muttered. "He's gone." She quietly dissolved into tears. Hilary placed the kitchen roll in front of her and she tore a piece off, blowing her nose messily on the incongruously patterned paper, covered with line drawings of manic dogs.

"A letter came this morning. He's gone to find himself." Hilary and Suzanne looked at each other over Liz's head as she sat down on the kitchen chair. Suzanne felt another giggle well up inside, left over from the turban episode, and she saw the same in Hilary's eyes. But Liz's distress was real, even if John's reason for leaving was an old cliché.

"He didn't come in Monday night. Nothing new really, he often goes to the pub. I suppose I've got used to him being there when I want him, but I'm so wrapped up with Mum, Siobhan, Lisa and you lot, I hadn't taken much notice of him recently. He was just there, like the settee, the mirror above the basin, the kettle – things you never think about until they've gone. I thought of going to the pub to find him, but didn't bother. I assumed he'd just come home as usual. Then he didn't come home last night. I phoned Richard, Jonathan, David this morning. None of them had seen him. Richard was in the pub, but none of the others, and definitely not John. They were as surprised and shocked as me. Well, they seemed to be. I don't know what to think any more."

Hilary placed a coffee in front of her. Liz absentmindedly took a sip and put the cup down again, looking around her as if she wasn't sure where she was.

Hilary and Suzanne said nothing. What could that say? Platitudes weren't going to help and they were just as shocked as Liz. This was something you read about in magazines or watched on TV. Where had he gone?

"Do I have to just sit and wait until he decides to come back? What do I tell the children? Mum? The one good thing is that this week Lisa is on holiday so she's got Siobhan and I haven't had to explain anything. I'm too embarrassed, ashamed. What have I done wrong? Why hasn't he said something? Perhaps he has and I was too busy to hear. Perhaps he's ill. Perhaps he's dying and afraid to tell me. I feel a fool. I'm humiliated. Should I have seen it coming?"

"I wish I could think of something to say that would help," said Suzanne, as she and Hilary pulled kitchen chairs up to sit protectively on either side of Liz. "I'm sure there's some logical explanation. It can't be your fault. Perhaps something has happened at work."

Hilary voiced a thought they'd all had. "Oh dear. Do you think that there's someone else?"

Liz's head dropped further. She sobbed quietly, her hand coming up at intervals to tear off sheets from the rapidly depleting kitchen roll. Hilary reached behind her and felt for the tissues on the windowsill, discreetly swapping the roll for the box. Liz didn't notice. Hilary started to say, "Sor…" but Suzanne put her hand up behind Liz's back. The distress had to come out, interrupting wouldn't help. Liz didn't need an apology from Hilary for saying the words that had been going around her own mind since she realised John had gone.

Liz didn't dare admit that she had spent all night convinced that John had found someone else. She had searched his cupboards, examined his computer, delved into pockets, wallets, drawers. She even found herself feeling in the pockets of the old tweed jacket he wore when gardening and laughed at herself humourlessly. He was no-one's idea of Mellors. She had tortured herself imagining him in bed with another woman, sharing coffee at the breakfast table, fingers touching and lingering, holding each other's eyes. She found emails signed off 'love', notes with indecipherable initials and numbers, receipts from restaurants she had never heard of. She had sorted and filed as rigorously as if she was doing a PhD on the subject.

She hadn't wanted to tell anyone what had happened, fearful of being disloyal to John, not wanting anyone to feel sorry for her, to laugh at her, to think, 'Serves her right'. Time seemed to stand still, minutes took hours to pass, then this morning she had just been wondering whether to call the police when the letter had come through the letter box. She had known that she had to talk to someone. The letter said there was no-one else, but she didn't believe it. Why else would he go? And look at all the evidence she had found. She wouldn't admit to herself that what she had 'uncovered' amounted to nothing, nothing more than a misinterpreted normal life.

So here she was in Hilary's kitchen with two people who could have no idea what she was going through, but who were surrounding her with comforting empathy.

None of them noticed when Hector joined them. He sat on Hilary's foot and rested his head on Liz's knee. She felt the pressure of his head; tears dripped on him as she moved her hand from her face to stroke his ears. She felt calmed, the air in the kitchen seemed to lighten, and they all relaxed an inch. Hilary and Suzanne straightened up, stretched slightly, and grimaced as they realised how still and tense they had been, leaning towards Liz as if to catch her if she fell further. Liz lifted her head, her hair parting to reveal her tear-stained, blotchy face. Suzanne silently chided herself for thinking that it was just as well Liz hadn't put make-up on. Streaked mascara and smeared lipstick would have added to the general devastation of her appearance. As if to make up for her mean thoughts, Suzanne suggested they move through to the living room and more comfortable seats, but Liz shook her head and shakily stood up, saying that she must go home. However, this only brought on a fresh wave of crying and she slumped back in the chair.

Oh dear. What a year, thought Hilary. One by one we are falling apart.

"This is my punishment for not taking enough notice of him," wailed Liz. She gulped. "Over the last few weeks he just wanted to stay in. I moaned at him for getting old before his time, for not being fun any more. I got cross with him for not helping with Siobhan, for leaving all the arrangements for Mum to me, for not taking his shoes upstairs, for leaving the Sunday papers scattered about until Tuesday." She took another gulping breath, wiped her eyes on the sodden ball of tissue. "I've become an old nag. I vowed when I heard Mum go on at Dad that I'd never get like that. Look what's happened to me. What if I've made him really depressed and not even been sensitive enough to notice? Ooooh, what if he doesn't come back? What if he's suicidal? We've talked about how we'd end it all rather than become dependent and decrepit. What if I've driven him over the edge?" She looked from one to the other, her eyes wild with fear, her hand twisting Hector's ear round and round.

Hilary held Liz's other hand. Suzanne had her arm across her shoulder. They sat in silence for a few moments, fearing the worst, and then Suzanne asked, "What did the letter actually say?"

Liz took her hand from Hilary's and fumbled in the pocket of her cardigan. "Here," she said, taking the letter out of its envelope and placing it on the table in front of them.

My darling Liz,

I will be gone when you read this. Please don't blame yourself. I'm sorry I've been such a misery and a bore lately. I'm not sure if I'm depressed or just sad, old and in a muddle. I even went to the doctor last week. It was a locum. I think he'd qualified last week. He looked about 12. He said he could give me some tablets for depression but he didn't seem very convinced that they would help and the list of side effects was alarming.

I'm going away for a bit "to find myself" although I have a horrible feeling that I won't like what I find.

I haven't stopped loving you. I just don't like myself any longer.

I plan to come back, but don't put pressure on me, just give me time. There isn't anyone else. Who would put up with me? Bear with me.

Signing this with a heavy heart. I'm sorry I'm not even brave enough to say it to your face.

Love,
John xx

"Read it again," said Suzanne, putting it back in Liz's hand. "I am a bit worried that he does sound a bit depressed, but really he sounds more confused, a middle-aged man who's lost his way. Look at all the positives in the letter – he loves you, there isn't anyone else, he plans to come back. What he's done is incredibly selfish, but he has thought it through by the sound of it."

Liz folded the paper up after reading it through again.

"I didn't see any of that. The words in inverted commas leapt out at me. Even the darling at the beginning seemed mocking. I think you're right. Reading it with John's voice, it just sounds a bit hopeless, sad. You're right, he does imply that he hasn't gone forever. I was so shocked, angry, upset. I didn't want to see things from his point of view. I'm still angry. Why couldn't he say any of this to my face? Going over the last few months in the last two days, I've realised how much I have taken him for granted. But he must have let me do it," she said defiantly. "What annoys me is that he must have planned it. I tried to get him to take some time off, to do something together on a Thursday, my one clear day. He didn't seem keen. He said I needed time for myself, which I do, too, but perhaps we wouldn't be in this mess if I'd given up just a few Thursdays for him. Oh, I don't know what to think. The person I need to talk it through with isn't here."

Liz seemed calmer again and suddenly appeared to notice that when she had come around to Hilary's, Suzanne was already here. She had been so wrapped up in her distress she hadn't thought about it.

"Did I interrupt something? Were you busy when I got here? Sorry, how selfish of me, bursting in like that. I just knew you'd be in, Hilary, and I had to talk to someone"

"Don't worry," replied Hilary. She couldn't help feeling pleased that Liz had chosen to come to her, whatever the reason. She got up to put the kettle on again. "Suzanne had persuaded me to start clearing Mum's stuff and was helping me with her clothes. She's going to ask David to come and give me some ideas for the bungalow."

"Have you finished? Can I help? It might help to take my mind off things. Whatever happens, I've got to get through. I don't suppose I've finished crying, but all this weeping and wailing isn't getting me anywhere, is it?"

"How about I take the bags we've already filled to the hospice shop?" said Suzanne. "I'll pick up some sandwiches on the way back. You and Hilary can get on with the sorting while I'm out and then we can have a spot of lunch and decide where we go from there. Do we need anything else while I'm out?"

"More bin bags, I think. And could you pick up some milk, please? I'll give you the money when you get back."

"I think I can run to that," said Suzanne, as she felt in her handbag for her keys. "I'll just pick up a coat from home. It might be easier if I pull onto the drive to save carrying these bags too far."

Hilary and Liz took the full bags out to the porch while she was gone, Hilary quickly tying the tops of the bags so that she couldn't change her mind as she glimpsed her mother's favourite blouse.

"Are you up to doing the wardrobe or do you want to call it a day?" Liz asked, having seen Hilary's face as she tied the bag.

"Let's do the ottoman and the other chest of drawers. I'll tackle the wardrobe another day," Hilary replied. "There are so many other things to sort through, apart from the clothes. It's a bit daunting, really."

"Right, let's get to it."

Without further ado, Liz opened the ottoman at the end of Phyllis's bed and lifted out clothes that Hilary recognised from years ago.

"Golly, I had no idea that she had kept all these. I think she last wore this for a speech day at school." She pulled a mauve Crimplene two-piece out of the pile. "And it was out of date then."

There wasn't the hilarity that there had been with Suzanne, but Liz was surprisingly sensitive to Hilary's mood and didn't rush any of her decisions. The clothes were soon in neatly folded piles, waiting for Suzanne to return with the black bags.

They went into the kitchen and put the kettle on. Hilary got out plates, knives and serviettes and they sat in the living room waiting for their sandwiches. Hector, as ever, sat in Phyllis's chair. He looked up to see if Hilary had food or the lead but, seeing she had neither, tucked his head back under his front leg.

"Do you think I should do anything or just wait for him to see sense? I'd be happy to have counselling if I thought it would help. I don't like feeling helpless like this. I daren't tell Mum. She'll say it's because we're not married. She's never really approved, although she loves John to bits. I sometimes think that she thinks more of him than of me. She'll certainly side with him. She's always saying that I neglect him. Dad was so spoilt.

She thinks every man should have his washing done, clothes ironed, meals prepared, house cleaned. She didn't expect Dad to do anything and, if he ever did try to help, it was never good enough for her. But I shall have to tell her. I'd hate for her to hear from someone else. Siobhan will be upset. I have no idea how Lisa will react. She'll probably blame me too." Liz was crying sad slow tears as Suzanne came back through the front door with the sandwiches.

They all ignored the tears and none of Liz's questions were answered as Hilary and Suzanne put the lunch on plates and carried it through to the living room. Hilary went to get the coffee and serviettes, and when she returned, Hector was nudging Liz's damp hand, asking for some sandwich.

"No," she said to him, pointing at the chair, and he obediently trotted back, secure in the knowledge that there would be treats later. There was no way they would finish all those sandwiches and crisps.

"The trouble is," continued Liz, as if there had been no interruption, "John is the person I would have asked. He has been my friend for so long, he is always the first one I'd go to. What a fool I am," she wailed. More tears led to more tissues and more hugs.

Chapter Sixteen

Revelations

When Liz and Suzanne finally left, Hilary felt unsettled. The television held no allure, she couldn't concentrate on her book, and the clues to the crossword eluded her. She found herself back in her mother's room, in front of the wardrobe.

Parting the tightly packed clothes, she took out the pairs of sensible broad-toed shoes. The painful memory of fitting the leather around her mother's deformed joints nearly sent her back to the safety of her own room but, instead, she laid them gently aside.

Kneeling down, she pushed her head between the skirts of her mother's dresses. She could see that the back of the wardrobe was lined with piles of shoe boxes. Old shoe boxes. The line drawings on the box-ends showed stilettos, peep toes with kitten heels, sandals with ankle straps, elegant court shoes. She pulled out the first box from the pile in the middle. The price, 69/11d, was clearly marked on the top. Lifting the lid, Hilary found not the red pointed court shoes depicted on the end, but a box full of familiar Basildon Bond paper.

Taking the box to the bed, she took out the first page. She saw the same neat, carefully formed handwriting that had filled the letters written to her at boarding school, the very round Os, the tall and upright up-strokes, the words in perfectly straight lines on the unlined page.

She lifted her glasses to her eyes and began to read. She felt her colour rising. Her skin became as red as the promised shoes. She felt an awakening 'down there' in that place never to be talked about, not even allowed a name. She fidgeted on the edge of the bed, unused to the sensations she was feeling. She felt hot and uncomfortable, but read to the last pages in the box. Her mother's writing, that had exhorted her to wear a vest and be a good girl for the teachers, was describing activities that she had difficulty imagining.

The shame deepened when she couldn't stop reading. Each box contained a chapter, a whole book taking the place of shoes she couldn't imagine her mother wearing. She lined them up on the floor, carefully replacing the lids, hiding the words away.

She felt shocked, as dirty as her mother had told her sex was.

Unable to take any more, she carefully replaced the boxes at the back of the wardrobe. She pushed the wardrobe door closed and locked it, avoiding her face in the long mirror as she scuttled out of the room.

"Come on Hector, let's go for a walk." She pulled on her coat, wound a scarf around her neck, and collected wellingtons, lead, keys, hat and gloves from the porch. Absentmindedly, she slipped Hector's lead on and went out into the cold, pulling the door shut behind her.

She walked through the wet streets, Hector for once walking at her side, not pulling, not eager to be off, sensing her distance, not wanting to leave her. Her mind couldn't grasp what she had found, couldn't tie the writing to the mother she had known. She walked. Cars drove past, splashing through the puddles. Shops were closing, electric shutters clattering down. People walked past, some smiling at the well behaved, handsome dog. She walked. She tried to think, but her thoughts wouldn't form properly. She tried to remember some of the words she had read. The ones that came made her blush. She tried to imagine her mother wearing those shoes. She tried to remember her mum. She came to her senses when she reached the crematorium – the site of her last contact with her mother. She stopped. Hector stopped at her side. Waiting. She sat down on the bench, sheltered from the rain by the pillared portico. She absently twisted Hector's ear. "What am I going to do? I wish we hadn't started to clear her room. I can't tell anyone. Can I? What will people think? I bet she planned to destroy it. I'll shred it. I hope Dad never knew about it. What shall I do? Oh Mum… What shall I do? Oh Mum…"

Fearing that someone would find her talking to herself, she stood up. "Come on Hector, let's get home."

She slept fitfully and, the next morning, woke feeling heavy-headed. She'd felt silly the night before, creeping into her mother's bedroom and checking in the wardrobe, just to make sure that she hadn't imagined it. She hadn't.

On automatic pilot, she showered, dressed, had breakfast and, putting on all her layers, took Hector out for a walk.

She was so lost in her thoughts that she almost walked into Liz as she reached the top of her drive.

"Whoops, sorry."

"I just wanted to say…"

They both spoke at the same time.

"…thank you for yesterday," finished Liz.

Liz looked much calmer, more together, more like Liz. Her face still showed signs of all of yesterday's crying. Her eyes were swollen, but now made up and cared for.

"Would you come for a walk with me? I can lend you some boots," Hilary said, looking down at Liz's feet clad in brown leather loafers.

"I'd love to come. These shoes are ancient. Unless we're planning on fording streams, I'll be fine. Have you got any gloves though? I came out without mine."

Hands and feet sorted, they made their way across to the woods running along the edge of the golf course, waving to David as he pulled into his drive.

They walked in silence, the muddy path and fallen leaves making it slippery underfoot. Hector pulled on his lead, exploring the sights and smells around him as if he had never been on this path before. As the sounds of the road receded, Hilary let him off his lead and he scampered off, running in and out of the trees, gleefully chasing squirrels, sending them fleeing up the tree trunks, putting birds to flight, but all the time keeping Hilary and Liz in sight, coming back frequently to run around their legs or to touch Hilary's hand.

"No, I haven't got a ball today," she told him. "I'm not sure whether he comes back looking for a treat, for me to throw the ball or just to check that I'm still here. But it reassures us both. So…"

Hilary's voice seemed flat.

"Are you OK? Has clearing your mum's clothes upset you?"

"Not the clothes." She hesitated. "I found something last night. It's turned my whole head upside down."

She looked uncomfortable and, almost with relief, went off to clear up after Hector, hiding her red face as she bent down.

Thoughts went through Liz's head.

Was Hilary's dad not her real father?

Did she have a half-sister or brother?

Was there a bigamous marriage?

Or no marriage at all?

Had her mum re-mortgaged the house, leaving mountains of debt?

Joining Liz again, Hilary blurted out, "I found a manuscript for a book that Mum must have written years ago. In the back of the wardrobe. In shoe boxes. Each chapter in a different box."

"That's brilliant…"

"No," interrupted Hilary. "No, it's not. It's really rude, explicit." Hilary blushed just thinking about it. "Even the shoes that the boxes had contained were sexy." Liz was shocked to hear that word on Hilary's lips; she felt embarrassed for her. She could not imagine a life as barren as Hilary's. She had missed out on so much.

"But sex sells. You'll make a fortune," said Liz, getting carried away.

"But it was written by my mum," wailed Hilary, almost in tears.

"I lived with her all my life. The mum I knew couldn't have written something like that, you have no idea. She hated sex. You should have heard her on the dangers. She made out it was dirty. She tutted when sex scenes were shown on telly. She made me turn it off sometimes. That's why I got a TV in the bedroom, something I hate, because otherwise even someone like Jane Austen could be off limits. The mum I knew couldn't have written this stuff."

Hector chose that moment to come flying back and jump up excitedly, planting muddy paws on her coat. She pushed him down crossly and then felt awful as he put on his sorry face. It wasn't his fault.

"Sorry. Can we talk about something else?" She felt irritable, almost angry. What could they talk about? Both their lives were ruined.

Hector saved the day by finding a tennis ball (possibly one he'd lost on a previous walk). He dropped it at Hilary's feet, waiting for her to throw it. They walked in silence for a time, Hilary throwing the ball for a seemingly tireless Hector, both women deep in their own thoughts. Hilary pocketed the ball as they neared the road and put a tired, dirty Hector on the lead. They parted company at the end of the path, with plans to meet at Hilary's the following day after she had finished work.

In the event, Hilary didn't go to work the next day. She did something she had never done before: she phoned in sick. It wasn't a lie. She felt awful; her head felt heavy and jumbled. She hadn't slept at all the night before. In fact, she hadn't been to bed. She'd taken the boxes out of the wardrobe again. Like a tongue probing a painful tooth, she couldn't leave it alone. Then, under the final chapter, she found something that knocked the stuffing out of her. She didn't know how to feel – ashamed, embarrassed or proud.

The creased black and white photograph at the bottom of the box was of her mother – a long-legged beauty in six-inch stiletto heels, a halter bikini made of feathers, her hair piled high on her head, and topped with a headdress of jewels and ostrich feathers. Her smiling eyes were framed by impossibly long eyelashes. On the back, written in pencil, was 'REVUDEVILLE 1952'.

Hilary went straight to the computer and Googled the word. It referred to the Windmill Theatre and she avidly read its history. Her mother had been part of all this. She couldn't believe it; it didn't match the mum she knew. It all looked so beautiful and exciting. What had happened? Why had she ended up so ashamed that she buried this entire side of herself? There was a photo of a reunion of the Windmill girls in 2011; they all looked so happy and proud to have been part of it, but her mum wasn't there.

Her parents had married in 1954. Her father had been a quiet, gentle man (a gentleman in the truest sense of the word). Her childhood had been happy, no arguments, no upheavals – but now that she thought about it, no excitement either. Granny lived with them for a time before she died. Without a murmur, Dad had simply accepted his mother-in-law occupying the front room of the house for three years. He tinkered with the car, mowed the lawn, went to work. He was always interested in what she was doing if she volunteered information, but he never asked. It was always Mum who wrote to her while she was away at school and, she'd have to check, but she didn't think that Dad was mentioned very often in the letters. She'd look later.

She found her parents' wedding album on the bookshelf in her mother's room. Without opening it, she took it into the living room where all the other albums were neatly displayed on shelves at the side of the gas fire. She compared the woman in the photograph with the picture of her parents on their wedding day. She was in no doubt that it was her mother in the feathery finery. Then she looked at more recent photos, after she had appeared on the scene. Even in Hilary's baby photos, Phyllis looked like her sensible mum. None of the photos showed too much leg or cleavage. On the beach she wore a swimming costume, never a bikini. Her skirts were always respectably knee length, her shoes were always sensible.

Hilary sat in the living room surrounded by the photograph albums that she had pulled from the shelves. Her mother's life, as Hilary knew it, seemed to start when they got married. Looking carefully at the wedding photographs, she saw that, although her mother looked virginal in white, very pointed silver shoes peeped from under her dress. Hilary had never

162

noticed this before and realised that the heels must have been very high for her parents to be the same height in the photo. Her mum had told her that her family didn't have a camera and that was why there were no pictures of her before she got married. In fact, apart from a few from his army days and a large framed baby photo, there were no photos of her father either, so she never thought to question it.

She had loved her father but in a distant, dutiful sort of way and so when he died, she and her mother had arranged an appropriate funeral and continued their shared life with few changes. Hilary had felt ashamed from time to time that she had never got around to leaving home. At first, she was waiting for Prince Charming to come along and take her away on his white charger. When he didn't materialise, it was just easier to stay put. By the time she could afford to buy somewhere, her mother needed help. Where had the time gone?

Realising that it was daylight, Hilary let Hector out into the garden, gathered the albums together and filed them back on the shelves, exactly as they had been before. She went into her mum's bedroom and tidied away the shoe boxes. She carefully put the photo of her mum from 1952 in the front of the wedding album and put the album back on the shelf. Her home looked normal again, but her insides were churning. She felt sick with tiredness and anxiety. She needed someone to talk to. She had never felt like this before. She had always been able to sort things out for herself. Mum dying had been a shock that had thrown her off balance but, in the end, even though she knew there had been lots of support around, she had come through the worst of it on her own. Now she needed someone to talk to. This was too big to untangle on her own.

She had a shower and put the kettle on, and then phoned Liz to see if she could come round a bit earlier. She wasn't sure if Liz was the right person to talk to. She had her own troubles, but she'd start with her. Then, perhaps, when she felt a bit more human, she'd see what the others thought.

Hilary was sitting in the kitchen having her second cup of coffee when Liz knocked on the front door and walked in, leaving her dripping coat and wet shoes in the porch.

"Hiya," she shouted, walking through to the kitchen. "What a horrible morning."

Hilary looked out of the window; she hadn't even noticed it was raining. "Did you walk in this?" she asked.

"I thought it would do me good. I was wrong. I'll probably catch pneumonia." She plonked herself down opposite Hilary and poured herself a cup of coffee, her purple mohair cardigan clashing with the orange blind at the kitchen window.

"Well, did you finish the book? Have we got a blockbuster on our hands? Have you been up all night? You look as though you haven't slept, but at least you don't look as though the end of the world, as we know it, has come." Pushing her hair behind her ears, she looked quizzically at Hilary. Her hair sprang forward again before she got to the end of the sentence.

"Yes, I don't know and I was – to answer all three of your questions. I hope we have got a blockbuster because I might lose my job. I've never phoned in sick before, but I couldn't have worked. I felt – and feel – awful. I just wish I didn't feel so guilty."

"Too late now, anyway. We're halfway through the day, so stop feeling guilty and let me into the secret. I'll have to go in a couple of hours – I've got to pick Siobhan up from playschool."

Hilary took her through to the living room and, taking the wedding album down from the shelf, showed her the picture from the Windmill Theatre, putting it alongside the picture taken at her parents' wedding.

"Wow." Liz was rendered speechless. She immediately knew the relevance of the wording on the back of the photograph. She kept looking between the two and then up to the mantelpiece to a more recent picture of Phyllis and Hilary on one of their trips.

"She was beautiful. And what fabulous legs!"

"Yes, why did I have to inherit my father's physique and not hers?"

Hilary smiled ruefully. For the first time since she had discovered the manuscript, she felt proud of her mum. Everyone had liked her but, like Hilary, they'd also been a little afraid of her. She had been larger than life, bossy and opinionated. This history gave her a new dimension, somehow softened her memory.

"Will you let me read her book?"

"Oh dear, I'm not sure I want it to leave the house just yet. You could come here and read it. If I'm not working, I could take Siobhan out to the park for an hour or so, or the shops or something, or you could come on a day when you don't have her. It has been hidden for I don't know how long, so there is no rush. Looking at the writing, I think she may have written it while I was away at school. Dad was very kind and good, but I think life was a bit boring and routine. Now we know what she did before she was married, her married years must have been really dull. I think she and I had more outings and more fun than she and Dad ever did. I wonder why she married him."

"Mmmmmm."

Hilary stood up and put the cups in the sink. "While you're here, I don't suppose you'd help me box some of her books to go to the charity shop? She's got loads of Mills & Boon and Catherine Cookson."

"Of course, I will. She obviously wasn't copying their style when she wrote. I can't wait to read it."

With the books boxed and neatly stacked by the front door to take to the charity shop on a less rainy day, Liz set out on the walk back home with a borrowed umbrella and a date arranged to start her reading. Hilary zipped herself into her anorak, shoved her feet into her wellies and took a very patient Hector out for his walk.

Chapter Seventeen

Admissions

Hilary phoned Suzanne as soon as she saw her car pull into the drive. She hadn't been able to settle after Liz left and the walk with Hector had done nothing to calm her nerves. She'd come home, tidied up, vacuumed and cleaned the bathroom. She even thought of making a cake, but she didn't have enough flour, so she abandoned the idea. She put the telly on but switched it off again. She couldn't yet face *Countdown* without her mum. In her mind, her mum seemed to have become two people. Just when she was coming to terms with losing her, she had found a whole new person, who she never knew existed.

"Just give me time to get out of my uniform and then I'll put some coffee on," Suzanne said, putting the receiver back in its stand.

Within fifteen minutes, Hilary was on her doorstep, with a plastic carrier bag carefully shielded from the rain under her umbrella. She shook herself like a dog as she stepped into the tiled hall; she was drenched from the fifty-yard dash across the road.

Hilary took a thoughtful sip of the delicious, strong coffee. How did Suzanne do everything so well? Even her coffee seemed better than anyone else's.

She and Suzanne were sitting in the conservatory, the darkness outside only pierced by the distant lights of the golf club. The rain battered the glass roof. The earth in the potted ferns smelt loamy, the sharp scent of the lemon verbena competing with Suzanne's exotic perfume. Hilary repeated her story. Suzanne didn't say that she already knew; that Liz had phoned her at work, all excited, full of Hilary's news, and not a word about John. She quickly realised that Hilary wasn't interested in the commercial possibilities of the find. She was grappling with the new mother she had unearthed.

"She had such definite ideas about how I should look and behave. She told me I looked like a painted lady once when I tried wearing make-up in my teens. I hardly ever wear it even now. My underwear had to be practical – nothing remotely sexy, no skirt too short, no neckline too low. It's so ingrained. I never questioned any of it. Not only do I look like my dad, I'm just as passive and boring as he was. Why didn't I rebel? I feel cheated now, angry that I can't ask her about it but knowing that if she was here now, I wouldn't be able to. Oh, I'm in such a mess." Hilary pulled the wedding album out of the carrier bag. She placed the photograph of her mum on the table in front of Suzanne and opened the album at the formal picture of her parents.

"She was such a beautiful, sexy, confident-looking woman." Suzanne stared at the photograph as if trying to get it to answer. "Your mum was a lovely lady, but in all the years I've known her, I couldn't describe her as any of those things. This photo was 1952. When did they get married?"

"1954."

"I wonder what happened in those two years to make her change. Something made her want to hide her past. An abortion, perhaps? They were illegal then, so it would have been a backstreet abortion. I talked to a patient once who'd been through one. It sounded horrific – it's amazing anyone survived. Or perhaps she was raped, or had an abusive boyfriend." Hilary was looking more and more horrified at these possibilities. "Or perhaps it was just that her parents didn't know, found out and dragged her back home. Parents have great influence, as you well know. We'll never know. If your mum had wanted you to know, she would have told you, and maybe in time she would have done. She was taken so suddenly. We all thought she had years to go, including her. For whatever reason, she was ashamed of her past. Perhaps she met your dad and he didn't like that side of her life and she loved him so much that she bent to his wishes. We could go on speculating forever."

"I suppose what upsets me most is how whatever happened to her has had such a profound effect on me and left me this dried-up old prune. She put such fear into me that I've always been a bit afraid of sex," Hilary admitted, looking down at her coffee, her hair hiding her blushes. Suzanne was wondering if they'd be better sitting in the kitchen when Hilary's words brought her back to the conversation with a jolt.

Suzanne glossed over the last few words, feeling that now wasn't the time for an in-depth discussion. David would be in from the pub soon and she wanted to relax a bit before work tomorrow. "Can we go into the kitchen so that I can start preparing supper?" she asked, as a way of escape. "Bring your cup and I'll top you up. And don't be ridiculous – you're not old. You're planning on a makeover for your house. Why not a makeover for you too?"

The move through to the kitchen broke the air of confidences and David came home while they were talking about possible changes for both the bungalow and Hilary herself. He poured wine for all three of them and Suzanne shooed them out of the kitchen while she finished cooking, with instructions to David to give Hilary some ideas about updating the bungalow. He needed no second bidding and, his tongue loosened by two pints of lager at the pub, he bombarded Hilary with ideas and schemes.

Hilary left them to their meal, carefully protecting her bag of photographs as she pushed against the wet hedge, squeezing past David's car. Hector greeted her as if she had been gone for a week as she let herself into the warmth of her home.

Later in bed, Hilary lay on her front, her arms folded under her, the fingers of her right hand resting against her lips as if to silence her thoughts. But they wouldn't be silenced; they went around and around, preventing sleep.

When she finally drifted off, she fell into a dream. Her mother was at the kitchen sink, dressed as she was in the photograph. But she wasn't the young beautiful woman of the photograph; she was the old stiff woman that she had become. The image was both grotesque and sad. Hilary floated above her, watching as the kitchen changed to the stage and Phyllis tried to move her fat arthritic limbs in a macabre dance, her stage make-up leaking into her wrinkles, her smile false and sneering. Hilary found herself in the folds of the stage curtains and she could feel herself straining to catch her mother's eye, willing her to come off the stage and stop embarrassing them all. The stage was rising and falling, changing shape. Beautiful young dancers came and went, seemingly oblivious to the spectacle of the octogenarian taking the lead.

As the stage took another turn, Hilary caught sight of the audience made up of hundreds of images of her father, as a young man, in uniform, in his wedding suit, in the suit they had buried him in, complete with the old-school tie. All the faces had the same besotted look, mesmerised by the vision on the stage, their eyes following her every move.

Hilary stepped out from the wings. There was a collective gasp from the audience as Phyllis, turning to see what was happening, fell forwards. Hilary flung out her arms to catch her. She missed.

Hilary woke with a start. She was drenched in sweat, her heart beating rapidly, with the feeling that she had let her mother down again. She felt anxious and frightened, trying to grab hold of the images in her dream but not really wanting to remember them. The sheets were damp and crumpled. She got out of bed and pulled her old dressing gown around her. The bungalow was cold and felt unfriendly and unfamiliar. As she came out of the bedroom, she heard the reassuring sound of Hector padding towards her. Ever sensitive to her moods and movements, he gently touched her hand with his nose and walked with her to the kitchen.

He knew it wasn't time to get up but, if Hilary was up, he was willing to fit in with whatever she was planning and, after all, the treats were in the kitchen, so you never knew. Hilary poured herself a small sherry to steady her nerves. The slightly sticky almond smell reassured her and reminded her of happy times with the more familiar version of her mum. She remembered the guilty giggles when they had a glass of sherry before her father got home, if their day had been trying, the glass of sherry with mince pies on Christmas morning, the sherry before dinner on rare holidays together. She absentmindedly stroked Hector's ears, their silky feeling reminding her of the fringe on the embroidered silk shawl her mother had worn around her shoulders over the long black dress reserved for formal dinners, when Hilary was left with babysitters. The fringe would brush against her face as her mother bent to kiss her goodnight. Hector, enjoying the attention, leant heavily against Hilary's leg. Both were now completely relaxed.

Hilary sent Hector back to bed and, taking the bedspread off her mother's bed, settled down on the settee, too tired to think about changing her damp sheets. She quickly fell asleep with Hector snuffling and fidgeting nearby. No disturbing dreams came this time or, if they did, she didn't remember them.

Chapter Eighteen

Coming to Terms

"Who'd have thought, after all my adventures and experiments before marriage, that I'd enjoy sex most with a sixty-year-old man?"

"He's not sixty, is he?" Hilary was more amazed at Richard's age and too concerned that she'd failed to send a card for a significant birthday to be worried about Janet's revelations.

"Well, he's in his sixtieth year. Five years older than me. Mum and Dad were so relieved when I found someone decent. I think they were on tenterhooks all through my first marriage to James. They loved Claire when she came along and I can see now that she was the only good thing that came out of the marriage. Thank goodness he's on the other side of the world now. I must have been blinded by lust or something."

"How did you meet him? I never knew him. It's really odd to think that you were once David's sister-in-law."

"I forget sometimes, it was so long ago, but David has been a good friend all the way through and he was a lovely uncle when Claire was little. Mum never said anything but I know she thought I married the wrong brother. James was a post-grad when I started university. To me it was karma that we had ended up in the same place. He took his studies seriously while I was making the most of my liberty after eighteen years within the constraints of the Forster family home. The total freedom was scary but so intoxicating. Like a good girl, I phoned home every week, Sunday evening at six, and gave Mum an edited version of my week, concentrating on lectures and tutorials, professors and tutors, what I had read, not what I had done."

Janet pulled out into the outside lane to overtake a lorry, the spray almost blinding her. They were on their way to her mum and dad's now. He'd said not to bother, the weather was too bad, but she couldn't not go. Hilary had offered to come with her; Hector was sitting curled up on a blanket on the back seat, his head on Hilary's handbag. Talking took her mind off the anxiety induced by driving; it made her feel safer to have Hilary in the car, but she was still glad to pull in past the lorry and be able to see more clearly. The early-morning November fog had cleared as they drove but the spray kept visibility and her speed down. It was going to be a long journey.

"James and I met at a rather debauched party," she continued. "A toga party where everyone went wrapped in bed sheets. There were none of the expensive fancy-dress outfits you can hire or buy now. People like Suzanne or Chahna would look elegant in a bed sheet – most of us looked as though we had just got up. The boys had sheets tied at the waist with a dressing gown or pyjama cord. I had my chain belt around my waist. I remember being reassured by the fact that most of the guests had clothes on underneath their sheets, although there were one or two of the beautiful people dancing in the front room who certainly had nothing on underneath, nothing left to the imagination. He was one of those beautiful people the first time I saw him."

"So were you dancing?"

"No, we met in the kitchen, looking for a drink. It was a typical student house, small terrace with the kitchen at the back, pantry at the top of the cellar steps, front room leading straight off the street, one bedroom and bathroom upstairs, second bedroom in the loft. The whole space seemed full of these white-clad, ghost-like figures. I'd pushed past James to try to get to the bottle of red wine that I could see by the side of the cooker, but when I picked it up, I realised that he was holding the only corkscrew in the place. A perfect match. He looked like a Greek god with his curly black hair, muscly shoulders." Janet shivered a little thinking of the vision. "We took the bottle outside and shared it in the back yard, leaning against the cold, dirty brick wall, the metal dustbin smelling rank, weeds between the cracked concrete tickling my bare legs. I've no idea why it seemed so romantic but I was smitten. Lost. No advice from Mum, Dad, my friends could sway me – this was the one. Oh, I wish I'd listened. Oh, we did have some wonderful, fun times and I did get my degree, a 2.1, a fluke because my head was in the clouds the whole time – but I suppose it helped me understand those romantic poets I was studying. We married – you should see Mum's disapproving face on those photos. Oh dear. She was cross but she came, bless her. Then Claire came along. I had to give up work, not that it was much of a job, but it meant that I was at home all day and James had a free rein. Somewhere along the line the studious man I had first met had disappeared. I was at home looking after Claire. He was always out and about somewhere, cooking up deals, seeing other women, who knew. He was a real charmer. It still took four years for me to see sense – I just kept hoping it would all be all right. I was so besotted, so stupid."

Hilary had sat quietly through this monologue. She had never seen this side of Janet before. The good thing was that the reminiscing was stopping Janet anxiously overthinking every manoeuvre as she drove.

"So when is Richard sixty?" Hilary like a terrier with a rabbit it wouldn't let go of.

"February, just after yours."

"Brilliant – that's something else to plan for. So how did you meet Richard? You've been together ages haven't you?"

"We've been married twenty-three years now, but I've known him twenty-seven. I'm not sure where the time went. We met at work. After James and I split up, Mum took charge, looked after Claire and packed me off on a secretarial course. I'd have liked to have gone into teaching but I was feeling a bit battered and, realising that every decision I had made up until then had been wrong, I let her take charge. I did rebel a bit though, because I stayed on and got an extra diploma to be a legal secretary and got myself a job in a family law firm. Richard was visiting the firm for something and I just fell for him. Will I never learn? He was the exact opposite of my Greek god. He was skinny, pale ginger hair, suit that looked as though he'd borrowed it from his dad, too big, a bit crumpled, just looking as though he needed looking after. We got chatting. He took me for a coffee and the rest, as they say, is history."

"Was he really thin?" Hilary asked, thinking of Richard's rounded frame now, topped with faded, almost white hair, thinning at the crown.

"All skin and bones. I didn't realise how thin until he took me to the coast a few weeks after we met and I saw him in swimming trunks. He looked like a pale Lowry figure, his legs like the tines of a carving fork poking down from his trunks."

Hilary laughed.

"I'd never have guessed anything like this about you. I suppose I didn't know you before Richard. You seem as though you were born together, if you see what I mean."

"Oh yes, Richard was the best thing that could have happened to me. A true friend, the first person I could really talk to and just be me. In Mum's eyes, it was the one thing I ever did right. You wouldn't believe some of the battles we had over the years. Julia could do no wrong and I was such a disappointment. At least Dad thought…thinks…I'm worth something."

"She seemed very proud of you when I met her last year."

"Oh, she was – married to the right man, a grandchild. I'm finally a good girl, but now she doesn't know. She hardly knows who I am, let alone what I am doing." Her eyes filled with tears but she brushed them away quickly, not wanting to lose sight of the road.

"I can't imagine ever going against my mum as you did against yours. I was such a scaredy-cat. A goody-two-shoes. I suppose not going to university…"

"How come you didn't? Funnily enough, I always assumed you had."

"I couldn't face the thought of it. I'd been at boarding school. I wasn't very popular. Head in a book too much, probably – no good at sports. I imagined university would be more of the same. I just couldn't face it."

"I didn't go to boarding school but I should think there's loads of rules and restrictions, whereas university is complete freedom. For the first time in my life I was in charge of what I did, no school rules, no parental constraints. Actually, not everybody loved it though. Some couldn't cope with the freedom and, without someone telling them to get down to work, they didn't."

"Oh, I'd have enjoyed the studying, but I think I'd have been just as lonely as I was at school. Work was the right thing for me. And I know I haven't reached any dizzy heights, but I've enjoyed my job and I know I'm appreciated, which is enough for me."

"Don't put yourself down," Janet said, as she pulled off the motorway, indicating left at the approaching roundabout. They'd soon be there.

"I wish there was some of my old Mum left," said Janet wistfully. "I don't want her to approve or disapprove of me. I just want her to be aware. I'm not even sure she knows who I am any longer."

They were silent as they pulled into the drive, each with her own thoughts. Their entrance was a little frenetic, with Hector making his presence felt, but after seeing George off in a taxi, they had a peaceful day. They took it in turns to sit with Beryl, watching daytime TV, making cups of tea and coffee. Janet did some cleaning, but wouldn't let Hilary help. The day passed amicably enough, but there were no more revelations, and no more reminiscing. Hector spent most of the day either curled up on Beryl's feet or staring out of the patio window, watching for squirrels and cats, dashing for the back door if he saw one, scrabbling to be let out. They took it in turns to let him out, watching him hurtling down the garden after the now disappeared squirrel or cat. Janet seemed lost in her thoughts, remembering the mother she once had, the one who would have spoiled Hector with treats and attention, who would have laughed at his antics, but who now barely seemed to know he was there.

They left soon after George returned from his lunch, not wanting to have too much of the drive in the dark.

Waving goodbye, George, leaning on his stick, stood at the door and watched them go. He shut the door as they turned the corner.

Janet turned the heater up and put the windscreen wipers on as it started to rain.

"So, have you decided what to do with the manuscript?"

"Oh dear, no. My mind, which I thought I'd sorted, is completely in a jumble again. I feel as though I've got to come to terms with Mum's death all over again. I'm not as cross with her as I was, but I do feel as though I've been deceived, cheated, made a fool of. Why couldn't she trust me? Liz is very keen that I publish it and she might be right, but it will probably have to be typed up first. I don't suppose publishers want boxes of handwritten stuff. I haven't seen her for a day or two. She came last week for two days and read the manuscript. I was probably being a bit over-cautious. It wasn't as if she was likely to lose it."

"Or copy it," put in Janet.

"No, but it gave me the opportunity to play with Siobhan. What fun that was. Hector and I had a wonderful time in the park with her. I had no idea how easy and how rewarding it is to make a child chuckle. I tied Hector up outside the play park and she had a go on everything – no tears, no tantrums. She kept going over to check that he was all right, stroking his nose through the fence. The only hairy moment for me was when she tried to twist round to check on him while she was on the swing. My heart was in my mouth, but she did as she was told and sat around again. The temptation to scream at her was very great. I'm glad I didn't – she would have fallen off in fright."

"Oh yes, children have a habit of scaring you like that."

"I desperately wanted a go on the swings but I thought the other mothers there would disapprove. So many of them looked so bored, texting and talking while little Henry or Henrietta tore around the park. I'd hate to get like that, but I suppose I was just having the fun bit. We fed the ducks. Siobhan was very brave until the swan came and hissed at Hector. She hid behind me, her little fingers digging into my legs like bulldog clips. It took a while to prise her off, but we were soon laughing again as Hector picked up a stick and dropped it at her feet to throw. We had a lovely time. We had ice creams in the café, in November! Must be potty. Then, the second day, I took her on the bus into town. We sat at the front on the top. I think she enjoyed that more than the Disney shop. She's such a sweetheart. I can see why she's so good for Liz – simple pleasures. It did me the world of good and when we got back, Liz was sitting in Mum's seat with Hector on her lap, looking more relaxed than I'd seen her in days. She thinks the book's great – the plot's a bit weak, but she said it certainly keeps your attention. I must read it again with less jaundiced eyes."

"Liz has heard from John."

"Oh, brilliant. She didn't say."

"No, it was only yesterday. I saw her with Siobhan at the pool. She had to wait until Siobhan had told me all about Hector before she could give me the news." Hilary smiled. "He sent her a postcard from Brussels. She seemed quite excited. She said it was just like the cards he used to send when they first met. She seemed all gooey, not like Liz at all. I don't know what he's done about work while he's been away. Perhaps he can stay in control via the internet or perhaps he just took holiday. It did all seem rather pre-planned."

"Yes, it all seemed so cruel. She was so upset that first day. I was worried about her."

"Me too, but yesterday she was just like the old Liz."

"Watch this space for the next instalment." They were both thoughtful for a moment. Then Janet said, "Talking of instalments, I could help you with the book. If I take my laptop to Mum and Dad's then I could type it when I'm with Mum. You saw today how boring it can be. She needs someone there, but most of the time she is asleep or just staring at the TV. I could do with something to occupy my time."

"That's a thought. I might take you up on that. Although it is a bit racy – I wouldn't want to shock you."

Janet laughed. "Oh, it takes quite a bit to shock me, but I definitely would be happy to help. The more I think about it, the more I think it would help both of us. Heaven forbid, I was thinking of taking up tapestry or something to fill my time. This would be a life saver."

"Brilliant. We'll get it organised."

"Oh, I've just thought. Do you know how are things going with David's mum moving in with them?"

"It's all arranged for next Wednesday. Suzanne has been dashing about like a mad thing. She was a bit distracted when I went over to tell her about the book and Mum and everything. Very kind, as ever, but not listening with her full attention. I thought it was just because of work, but with everything with my mum, I had completely forgotten about David's. I talked to him as well and he didn't mention it, but I expect he's left all the organising to Suzanne. She's been dashing about getting everything ready. She and Betty had a trip into town to choose new curtains. Apparently, she's not keen on the ones in the bedroom in the flat. I saw them on their way out. I think it went OK. They came back together and I haven't heard of any disasters."

"I'm not sure I'd like my mother-in-law on my door step, but Betty is very independent. I should think she'll be out and about with her own friends and she and David have grand schemes planned for her old house. It's a massive plot – they'll get loads of houses on it. I suppose James will get a share of any profit. I hope he doesn't have to come back. It always upsets Claire when he's around."

"I hope David leaves enough time for my little project."

"You'll have to make sure he does. I think Suzanne is a bit afraid that she may be left out, but I'm sure it will all work out. I wonder if she'll do her usual New Year party this year?"

Talk turned to Christmas preparations and plans for the intervening weeks. The journey passed quickly and without incident.

Janet dropped Hilary and Hector home, feeling sad that they were going into an empty house, looking forward to seeing Richard, smiling as she remembered again when they had first met and how he had changed her life so much.

Hilary went to bed early, tired after her day, thinking of what she had learned about Janet, another dark horse. Perhaps everyone except her had a secret past life.

She woke with a start. Another dream disappeared as she tried to grab hold of it. She thought about what Janet had been telling her. Beryl sounded just as strict as Phyllis, but Janet hadn't become a recluse, hiding herself away from men, pretending she didn't care or want any of that.

Pulling the duvet tightly round her, Hilary allowed herself to think back to her first boyfriend. She felt cold shivers come over her as she remembered her mother sitting her down and showing her a cutting from an unfamiliar local newspaper. Her skin bristled in goose pimples, the disbelief as real as it had been forty years before.

It had been in the Easter holidays.

She and Brian had met at the Christmas disco. They were confined to separate boarding schools in Hurlford, but at the Christmas disco the boys and girls were officially allowed to mix. They'd talked and talked, sitting on the hard chairs arranged around the hall, teachers looking ill at ease, trying not to look like undercover policemen, the beautiful teens dancing with grace and elegance to the rock music blaring out, the rest of the pupils standing around in sullen groups or dancing self-consciously. It was such a relief to find someone who thought as she did. They discussed the people around them without the cattiness that came out when she tried to do the same with the girls in her year.

"I thought I'd found my soulmate," she said to the bedroom, looking through the darkness to the shelf that held the album with her only photograph of him.

She remembered arranging to meet when they could during the term, the excitement and intrigue of it all. They had sent each other letters and postcards using stamps she should have used to write to her parents. They compared notes on everything, from homesickness to homework.

They'd made plans to meet up in the summer holidays, at each other's houses; parents had been consulted, arrangements made. It was something lovely to look forward to.

They couldn't meet in the Easter holidays because her family always went to Devon at Easter. Her father preferred Devon at that time of year, before all the other visitors got there. The beaches were peaceful and wild at the same time. They went as a family in the Morris Marina but her dad always went off bird watching for hours on end, leaving Hilary and her mum to explore the countryside and towns on their own, travelling on local buses, walking miles, buying postcards and trinkets to be filed away when they got home.

That year, when they returned home, Hilary was unpacking and setting out her shells and tiny bottles of Devon Violets on the shelf above her bed, putting the postcards on her desk ready to be glued into her scrapbook, when Phyllis came in and, looking grave, said, "Sit down, Hilary." Hilary sat down on the bed and her mother sat down close to her.

Hilary rubbed her thigh as she remembered, as if she could feel the material of her mother's Crimplene dress against her skin.

Her mother only used her name when she was telling her off. Somehow, the rest of the time, Hilary knew when things were directed at her or perhaps, being an only child, she just responded when her mother spoke. But her mother didn't sound as though she was telling her off; her voice sounded soft and kind, not like her usual strident tones.

She was holding a pale blue envelope in her left hand and, in her right, thin blue paper covered in tiny neat writing, a folded newspaper cutting behind it. As she unfolded the newspaper cutting, the first thing Hilary saw was an advert for a garage in Tersingham.

"That's where Brian lives," she said, excitedly.

She remembered wondering if he'd sent her something and then it dawned on her that the letter couldn't have been addressed to her. Her mother would never have opened it; never opening other people's mail was a strict code that was always observed in their house. It even crossed her mind that Mum and Dad might know someone else in Tersingham but Phyllis put paid to the wondering by putting the cutting into her hands.

The crease was right across his mouth. The headline screamed *DEATH OF A BRIGHT STAR*.

It was a copy of the picture he had given to her, the one in her suitcase waiting to be put back in its place next to her bed, a school picture taken on a sports day. The sun was shining. Even in the grainy black and white she could see his blond hair against the blue sky, his nervous toothy smile, his red school football shirt. She felt herself falling into a hole, involuting, disappearing into her mother's arms. Time stood still. Her mother said, "He was on his way back from his paper round. A car came out of nowhere. There were witnesses. It wasn't his fault. He wouldn't have suffered…"

"Of course, he suffered," Hilary remembered screaming at the top of her voice. "He wanted to live. He wanted to carry on being. He didn't want to die." Tears came then. Tears that hardly stopped for the rest of the holiday but that had to be dried up at the start of the term so that she could go back to school and "Be a good, brave girl."

Hilary put the light on and, taking a tissue to wipe her streaming eyes, walked across to the shelf of photograph albums and pulled out the one for 1974. As she opened it, the newspaper cutting floated to the floor. Bending stiffly to pick it up, she smoothed it out and read it again.

DEATH OF A BRIGHT STAR

Star pupil Brian Thompson (14) was killed when he was knocked from his bicycle at the junction of High Street and Mill Road. First aid was administered at the scene but he was pronounced dead upon arrival at the hospital.

The writer carried on for four paragraphs about the danger of the junction and action to be taken to make it safer, as if Brian's only purpose was to highlight the danger.

Hilary folded the brittle paper back up and slipped it in the cover of the album, and then turned to the page with the picture of Brian, a bright goofy child staring at her from the page. She hardly remembered him, but she remembered the intense feeling of belonging that she'd had when they were together.

Her mother had been right to pack her off to school at the end of the holiday. She had no recollection of her father at that time. He must have been there, but he hated fuss and would have stayed out of the way. She had written a letter to Brian's parents at her mother's insistence and it had been put inside a condolence card with a white lily on the front. She knew that Brian would have hated the card; he could never understand the appeal of white flowers. He loved bright colours. "White is the absence of colour," he had told her once. She had thought him very profound.

It was half past five, hardly worth going back to sleep. She had to go into work today, so she got up, put the kettle on and had her shower, wondering how those few months over forty years ago had had such a profound effect on her.

She dressed carefully after her leisurely shower. She was only going to work but she had decided, as the water cascaded around her, that things were going to be different. For some reason, she felt different.

She put on the white underwear that she had bought for the holiday that she and her mother had never taken. She sprayed perfume behind her ears, between her breasts, on her wrists. She slipped on her straight navy skirt but instead of her usual white polyester work blouse, she shrugged her shoulders into a white silk blouse, relishing the feel of the material as she fastened the buttons and tied the floppy bow at the neck. She looped her pearls under the bow and fitted her pearl earrings into her ears, smelling her perfume as her wrist passed her nose. She applied a little face powder and reddened her lips. Looking in the mirror, a more confident, grown-up person looked back her. She smiled.

Going through to the kitchen, she put on her flat boots and old duffel coat and took Hector around the block, the air crisp and cold on her face, making her feel even more alive.

She had decided she was going to see her manager today and ask for a cut in her hours. She'd manage with less money. If Liz was right about the book, she might not have to. She wanted to try new things. There must be more to life than working for someone else and doing as you are told. She felt energised, fizzing. "Thank you, Mum," she said to the air, not quite sure what she was thanking her for. She almost did a little skip on the pavement but her boots wouldn't let her, and Hector was already looking at her as if she had gone mad. She took him back inside, made sure he had enough water, picked up her handbag, her keys and the bag with her work shoes in and set off to work. She decided to walk; perhaps getting slimmer and fitter could be one of the first changes.

She felt as though her life was changing. It was an unsettling but not unpleasant feeling. The goofy teenager who had haunted her subconscious all these years was being laid to rest. In her mind, he had taken an undeserved precedence and had coloured her judgement in a nebulous way ever since.

She stopped at the bus stop. It had started raining and she didn't want to go to work looking like a drowned rat. Perhaps getting fitter and slimmer could wait. Perhaps she should allow herself more fun, she thought, waving to David as he roared past in his four-by-four. The days with Siobhan went through her mind and she smiled as she thought of the joy that Hector brought her. Things were already different and were looking good. She could think of her mother with warmth and pride. But she wished that she had known all about it before. She wished that she could have known the real woman that her mother had been. She would read the book again tonight and then put it all together for Janet to type. She arrived at work with a spring in her step and, being early, went to the canteen and treated herself to a cappuccino and Danish pastry, smiling at other early birds, receiving smiles in return, tinged with mild surprise at her demeanour.

The meeting with her manager went well. Together they made plans to reduce her hours. He was secretly pleased that she had come to him, as, since her mother had died, she had been less reliable; all that sick time and then another day at the end of the previous week, and she had not been as efficient when she was at work. He'd always been able to rely on her to be aware of customers' needs and keep other members of staff in order, but her heart no longer seemed to be in it and her head seemed elsewhere. At least now he wouldn't have to say anything to her. Hopefully she would cope better with fewer hours.

The plan was that she would begin to work reduced hours in the new year. She knew he was secretly relieved, but he was too polite and too professional to say anything.

She was still on a high at the prospect of cutting back on work when she went for her lunch break. She chose to go to the coffee shop next door, rather than the staff canteen.

As she opened the door to the coffee shop, she faltered. She saw a woman her own age helping an elderly woman to a seat, placing a cushion on the chair, moving her walker out of the way, and putting her handbag over the arm of the chair before joining the queue. She imagined they must be mother and daughter.

A lump came into Hilary's throat; tears filled her eyes and threatened to spill as she turned to walk out the door. She got tangled up with a buggy being pushed by a young girl who scowled at her as she muttered her apology. She looked through the window and smiled briefly towards the old lady. Turning away, she felt lost, unsure of what to do. Mentally pulling herself together, she slipped into M&S and bought a bottle of water and a sandwich and went and sat in the locker room to eat her lunch, feeling unsettled and off balance. She'd thought her course was set, but she wasn't there yet. Her mum hadn't yet settled to rest.

Chapter Nineteen

Back in the Pub

"Is your mum settled now?"

"Just about. It went more smoothly than anticipated. I thought there'd be lots of angst, leaving all those memories behind. I think I was more sentimental than she was. I found myself fishing things out of the charity bags and when she asked me to take Dad's desk to the tip, I couldn't. It's in my lock-up. It's really battered and the leather on the top is all scuffed – worth nothing, but I couldn't let it go." David took a long drink from his pint to hide his embarrassment. "She's been into town with Suzanne a couple of times in the last week and she's ordered all sorts of new furniture. I thought she loved all the traditional dark stuff and all the knick-knacks. How wrong can a person be? When I think of all the ornaments I've bought her for birthdays and Christmases; she probably felt she had to display them so as not to hurt me. What an idiot! Even Suzanne was surprised. It's been ten days of revelations for all of us. They've realised they've got loads in common. Mum never really got to know Suzanne. When we met, she was too busy looking after Dad and then getting over him, being strong, not showing any weakness. She came to the wedding but was quite distant. Her way of coping I suppose."

"We all react differently. I remember... Oh, here's Richard – I didn't think he was coming out tonight." Jonathan lifted his arm to attract Richard's attention.

"Do you want another?" asked Richard as he came over. They put in their orders. Richard came back with the three pints, and took a packet of peanuts out of one pocket and a packet of crisps out of the other. He took off his damp overcoat and unwound the woollen scarf from around his neck before settling on the stool nearest the fire. He opened the peanuts and crisps, took a handful, and with his mouth full, gestured to the others to take some.

"I'm trying to cut down at the moment. We were very self-indulgent on the holiday, in all sorts of ways," David smirked, "and all my clothes are getting tighter." He patted his bulging stomach. "Suzanne never says anything, but I see her frowning at the straining buttons." He sat up, trying to take the pressure off the lower buttons of his shirt.

"You're OK – you never seem any different. Look at me. I can't believe how much weight I've put on in the last few years. I was under eleven stone when I met Janet. I daren't get on the scales now."

"I was twelve stone three pounds when I left university. Don't ask why I remember," said Jonathan. "I know I thought I was overweight then. I was twelve stone four pounds yesterday. Not bad, eh?"

"I don't know how you do it. You seem to eat and drink the same as the rest of us."

"Luck, I suppose," Jonathan said, looking smug. "Also, I don't go to any of those fancy lunches that you two get invited to. And Carol will tell you I'm miserable and boring. I can't remember the last time we ate out. Then, of course, I get all that exercise looking after the grandkids and digging the allotment – you should try it. I don't know really. Just one of those things," he finished lamely.

"I'm just greedy," said Richard. "Open a packet of biscuits, I eat the whole packet. Janet daren't make cakes any more. I just eat them all. Upbringing I suppose – finish what's on your plate. Think of all the children starving in Africa. Waste not, want not. Do you think we're made of money?" Richard collected up the last of the crisps and popped them in his mouth and flattened the peanut packet, extracting the last nut and dropping it into his mouth too. Realising what he was doing, he laughed ruefully at himself and finished his pint.

"Janet is going to be typing up Hilary's manuscript," he said, quickly changing the subject. "Anyone want another?" he added, looking around at the glasses.

"What manuscript?" said Jonathan, looking puzzled.

"My round," said David, getting up. "You fill Jonathan in on all the gory details while I'm at the bar."

Jonathan turned to Richard, absentmindedly rolling up the crisp packet and putting it in his empty glass.

"I haven't seen Hilary in ages. She's a funny old stick, isn't she, old fashioned, old maidish. Carol gets on well with her though. I think she's seen her from time to time. So, has she written a book?"

"No, but her mother has."

"I thought she died? Carol said something about her dropping dead in Tesco."

"She did, terrible shock, so undignified. No, Hilary found it in the back of the wardrobe, all in shoe boxes apparently, and a photo of her mother as a dancer in one of those risqué shows from the fifties or sixties. According to Janet, the book is really sexy. She hasn't read it all yet, just little bits, but Liz has. She thinks it should be published. That's why Janet is going to type it up for her. Do you remember Phyllis? Talked a lot, grey perm, big 1980s glasses. What I'd describe as a tweedy woman. Can't imagine her in a swimming costume, never mind ostrich feathers. Used to drive that battered old dark blue Fiat."

"I remember. I'm not sure I'd recognise her but I do remember the car. She went on driving a long time after she should have been stopped, didn't she?"

"Well, she must have been quite different when she was younger, by all accounts."

David returned with the drinks.

187

"Must have been," he said, holding the beer up to check which one was which. "She was really strict with Hilary though, probably why she is as she is. Suzanne thinks it must have been a reaction to her life before she was married, but she can't have thought it all bad if she managed to write a book about it."

"I don't think it's about her life. I think it's just a novel, but she must have had some experience to write about such stuff."

"Suzanne hasn't read it yet either. She felt a bit guilty because she didn't really let Hilary talk about it all when she first found it. It all coincided with Mum moving in and Suzanne had too much on her mind. Still, it looks like I'll get another job out of it all. Nothing to do with the book, but Hilary wants to have some major changes in the bungalow and she's more or less given me a free rein. That can be a curse though – people who don't know what they want until you do what they know they don't want, if you see what I mean."

Richard and Jonathan nodded as they untangled this logic.

"So, will we get to read it or do we have to wait for publication?"

"Don't know. I don't think Hilary knows what she wants to do yet. It must be really strange to find out something about someone you thought that you knew so well. I hope my mum hasn't got any secrets. Although I think we'd have found them helping her to clear her house. Next time I'm in the lock-up, I'll have to have a good look through Dad's old desk for a secret drawer."

"There're no secrets in our family," said Jonathan. "Although look at what's happened with John. You never really know people, do you?"

"Liz has heard from him now though, hasn't she?" said Richard. "I think they've arranged a meeting."

"Think so. He's been in Belgium, of all places." David smirked. "I wonder what possessed him to go there? He must have gone by train – his car is still here."

"Perhaps he just got on a train and ended up there," said Richard, laughing.

"There must have been a bit of planning," countered Jonathan. "He must have had his passport with him."

"True," agreed Richard.

"It's going down well again tonight. One more?"

They had a final round before wrapping themselves up for the journey home.

Chapter Twenty

A Reconciliation

"Can I come and see you? I'll be going back to work soon and then my time won't be my own. Luke's been to nursery a couple of times. He loves it. I hated leaving him there, but he was fine."

"Of course you can, Sarah. I'm in a bit of a mess because I've finally started sorting Mum's things. But I'd love to see you. Are you bringing Luke or will one of the grannies have him?"

"No, he'll be coming. He's trying to crawl now, but he doesn't get very far, sort of crawling on the spot. Will that be OK? I can sort out a babysitter if you think it will be a problem."

"It'll be interesting to see how Hector reacts. If there's a problem, we'll go out for coffee. We'll sort something out. Are you coming straight around?"

"If that's OK."

"See you in a few minutes then. I'll get the coffee on, or are you still on herbal tea?"

"Oh no, coffee please, that phase soon passed."

Hilary quickly washed her breakfast things, then picked up the packing box that she'd put next to the display cabinet, ready to take the many ornaments. She put the newspapers, bubble wrap and tissue inside the box and carried it through to her mum's bedroom, then shut the door on all the disorder. She put Hector's treats close at hand and popped some in her cardigan pocket in case rapid distraction was called for. Back in the kitchen she spooned coffee into the cafetière, put out cups and saucers, filled the milk jug and put it in the microwave to warm, and took shortbread biscuits from the tin and placed them on a plate. She took a tray from the side of the dresser and set out morning coffee as her mother had shown her when she was a little girl. The only difference between Hilary's and Phyllis's morning coffee was that Hilary used a cafetière instead of the stove-top percolator that her mother had been so proud of. When Phyllis's friends visited, Hilary's job had been to watch the milk on the stove and turn the gas off as it started to rise. She dared not take her eyes off it in case it boiled over. Then she was allowed to serve the biscuits, listening to the conversations about recent purchases, garments knitted, recipes tried on unsuspecting husbands ("If you don't tell him, he won't realise you've put garlic in, like Keith Floyd says"), their stiff hair unmoving on bobbing heads, the cloying vapour of hair spray vying for attention with the scent of face powder and cheap perfume, all competing with the aroma of coffee. The noise would increase and Hilary, sitting unnoticed on the tapestry footstool, would drink it all in with her glass of orange juice. Then, all too soon, the powdery faces would be bending down to kiss her goodbye and she would help her mother to clear everything away until it was their turn again.

The doorbell made her jump. She checked her pocket, told Hector to stay. He hadn't even thought of moving and, with seeming absolute obedience, he remained on his chair, watching her put her hand to the treat in her pocket.

Sarah and Luke were on the doorstep, both grinning, Luke holding his multi-coloured dog tightly in his hand. Sarah shifted his weight on her hip as she leaned towards Hilary to give her a kiss.

"Hasn't he grown? You are a big boy now. Is it still raining?"

191

Hilary ushered them in, holding Luke while Sarah took off her coat. She made no attempt to undo Luke's coat; it was all she could do to hold him – what a weight. Hector had come out to see who was visiting. He was delighted to see Sarah and barked excitedly. Luke clung to Hilary, then cried for his mum, realising that it wasn't she who was holding him. There was a moment of chaos, as Sarah patted Hector and took Luke back in her arms. Hilary pushed Hector down and shepherded them all into the living room.

She directed Sarah to the settee and Hector to his chair and gave him his treat. Taking Luke's cup from Sarah, she went to the kitchen to get drinks.

Luke became quiet as soon as he was back with his mother. When Hilary returned, he was sitting next to her, playing with his noisy dog, beeps and bells and crackles coming from various parts of the toy, interspersed with Luke's delightful chuckles. Hector looked a bit unsure. Putting the tray of coffee on the table, Hilary sat next to it, at the opposite end of the settee to Sarah and Luke. She put up a warning hand to Hector as she saw him finish his treat and think about getting down from his chair.

Luke kept looking over at Hector who was busy eyeing up the brightly coloured dog. Sarah and Hilary watched both with bated breath.

"It's a bit of a test. Probably best to try now before Luke is really on the move. Hector looks great, really fit and happy."

Hilary played peekaboo behind one of the pheasant-adorned cushions, enjoying even more of Luke's chuckles.

Hector had crept across the room unnoticed and now put his nose on Hilary's knee, as if to say, "I'm here, don't forget me."

She put her hand down and stroked his ear between her fingers, not noticing that Luke had pushed his toy dog to the edge of the settee.

Hector saw his opportunity and grabbed it. The squeak made them all jump, and Luke let out a long wail of surprise and distress as he saw his treasured toy being kidnapped.

Sarah pulled Luke onto her lap and Hilary called Hector back.

"Bring it here." Hector jumped onto his chair and looked at Hilary.

"Bring it here," she said, more firmly.

Luke was now watching his dog from the safety of his mother's arms. He reached out as if asking Hector to give the toy back.

"BRING IT HERE."

This was the voice Hector knew he must obey. He jumped down from the chair, looked balefully at Hilary, then dropped the dog on the settee at Luke's feet.

Hilary and Sarah looked at each other and burst out laughing. Hilary pulled a treat from her pocket and gave it to Hector, giving his ears a friendly twist. Luke pulled forward in his mother's arms, rescued his toy dog, and started to chew its ear. Thoughts of germs, dirt and dogs' mouths flitted through Sarah's mind, but then she thought of the bits he picked up off the floor at home that went straight into his mouth. After all, Hector had held the toy by its tail. She gave the toy a quick wipe with her sleeve and patted Hector as he went back to his chair.

"Will you get rid of that chair when you update the bungalow?"

"I'm not sure I can now. I'll wait until the time comes. We'll sort something out." She looked fondly at Hector.

"I saw Liz at the swimming pool the other day. She told me about your mum's book. How exciting. I couldn't believe it when she told me. I thought it was some sort of joke."

"No, it's no joke," said Hilary a little stiffly. "Oh dear. I'll be the talk of the town. I don't know whether to be embarrassed or proud. Me, the prude." She put her hand up as Sarah started to interrupt. "No, I know what people say about me, old fashioned, old maid, blah de blah."

"Oh Hilary, don't be like that. Everyone loves you. I've never heard you sound so bitter before."

"Sorry, I'm not bitter, just upset and in a muddle. The mum I knew isn't my mum."

"Of course, she was your mum. Whatever happened in her past doesn't or shouldn't affect the way you think about her. She was still your mum. We all go through different phases in our lives. There are some we hope other people don't find out about, some we are not so proud of, but all these little things make up, shape or whatever the word is, who we are, what we become. I should think you feel a bit let down by her altogether.

193

She died before either of you were ready, in a distressing, undignified way. She had a secret life. Who knows, she may have been planning to tell you the day she died. We just don't know. You are angry with her for all these things, but the anger is only going to make you feel worse."

"Oh Sarah, you are so wise. You have such an old head on those young shoulders. You are so right, and a couple of days ago I was getting used to it all and feeling very positive. I'd decided to make changes in my life. I'd almost decided to look into trying to get her book published. But then something...just seeing a daughter helping an old lady in a café, made me cry. It's so embarrassing. It reminded me so much of the mother I had lost and made me realise I hadn't finished grieving for the woman I knew. So how could I grieve for this new character? It's all so difficult and I hate the fact that it makes my life feel so out of control. Sorry."

Hilary suddenly realised she hadn't poured the coffee, which was now cold on the carefully laid tray. She got up to make some more, stepping over Hector who had abandoned his chair and was lying at their feet.

"It will all be OK," Sarah said, shifting the now sleeping Luke in her arms. "Go and get that coffee. Could you put some water in Luke's cup for when he wakes, please?"

Happy to have something to do, Hilary went to the kitchen, pondering Sarah's words about feeling let down by her mother. She had thought she felt so awful because she had let her mother down, but perhaps Sarah was right.

Oh, when did life get so complicated, she thought to herself, pushing the switch down on the kettle.

They enjoyed a quiet coffee before Luke woke. As soon as he stirred, Hector went back to his chair, guard duties over.

"It's getting dark and it's hardly three o'clock. I hate these short days, although it'll make me finish clearing out Mum's stuff. There's no garden to tempt me out and walks with Hector tend to be just functional."

"I can help if you'd like."

"Do you need any crockery? I have so much, and apart from a few special items like grandma's tea set, I'm tempted to have a great big clear out and get all modern stuff."

They went through to the kitchen, Hilary pulling down the orange blind. "And I so want to get rid of this," she said, as she turned on the fluorescent light. "I love the down-lights Suzanne has, so much more stylish. Oh, I think I'm going to have fun."

She opened the cupboard and Sarah raved about the 1970s coffee set in mud brown. She took a cup and turned it in her hand, feeling the weight, marvelling at the chunky feel and rough texture. "Oh, wow, these are beautiful," she said, taking one of the Royal Worcester vegetable dishes, the painted fruit vibrant and incongruous.

"Mum collected Royal Worcester. I think, at one stage, she knew one of the artists who did the painting on the crockery, before it was all done by machine. There's some very special pieces all wrapped up at the back of the pantry."

"You have a pantry? Oh, after a utility room, that is what I would love the most, with a marble shelf for cooling my desserts and rows of jars of home-made jam. Oh, and, of course, I would love a linen cupboard. I think I should have been someone's housekeeper."

"They call me old fashioned – you are pure vintage. Come with me a minute." They walked along the hall. Sarah picked up Luke from the floor where he'd been happily playing with a fish slice and plastic bowl. Neither woman dared say anything, but both were thinking how amazing it was that Hector had stayed on his chair. Fingers crossed, all would stay calm.

Turning a corner towards the bathroom, Hilary stopped in front of a tall cream-painted cupboard.

"Would this do?"

"It's wonderful," enthused Sarah. "Perfect." She turned to Hilary. "Can I open it?"

"Of course," laughed Hilary. "There aren't any secrets in there."

The little key was a bit stiff in the lock, its fine filigree end feeling insubstantial in Sarah's fingers. Inside there were evenly spaced, painted, slatted shelves piled with neatly folded sheets, towels and table cloths.

"Oh, it's perfect," repeated Sarah.

"Dad bought it in France in a flea market on one of our caravanning holidays in the early seventies. He insisted on wedging it between the seats in the caravan. When we stopped on the way back, we had to unpack it and stand it in the awning. I remember Mum being furious, but I think it was more because we had to put the awning up, not because she didn't like it. She put stencils all over it – flowers and swirls in the eighties, then painted over them again a few years later. I need to sort all the bedding – some of this is ancient and I certainly don't need all these table cloths. I think the towels in here will only be good as cleaning cloths."

Sarah was fingering the fine lace edging on one of the cloths. Luke was sitting on the floor and had succeeded in pulling out a towel from the bottom shelf before they realised what he was doing. Hector, finally getting up from his seat, came to see what they were up to and, as Sarah crouched down to prise the corner of the towel from Luke's fingers, Hector grabbed the fringe on the other end. They all ended up on the floor in the confined space of the hall, Hilary pulling Hector's jaws apart and untangling the fringe from his teeth, Sarah moving along the towel; as fast as she loosened Luke's grip on it, he got hold of the next bit up. Chuckling away, he'd found a good game. The towel would certainly only be any good for cleaning now. Hilary pulled herself up, keeping hold of Hector's collar, just in case, but he didn't seem interested in Luke any more. He'd smelt the final treat in Hilary's pocket as she'd got down next to him and was now nudging at her cardigan, trying to sit at the same time but still restrained by her hand on his collar and the restricted space he found himself in. He was showing his teeth as if he was grinning at her. Sarah had lithely stood up holding Luke (and, Hilary noticed, not holding onto anything. How she wished her own body still worked like that), the ochre and orange striped towel trailing after him. Hilary let go of Hector. He sat down and she gave him the treat. He trotted up the hall to eat it in peace, where he was in no danger of Hilary taking it from him or the little human coming to investigate.

With calm restored, Luke fiddled with the beads around Sarah's neck as they looked again at the cupboard.

"You can have it if you've got somewhere to put it. I'm not keen on it, but I wouldn't like to think of it on the scrap heap."

"I'll have to measure, but I'm sure it would go in the alcove on our landing. It's just perfect," she said for the third time, looking dreamily at it.

"If you want any of the table cloths, take them. Otherwise I'll give them to the charity shop."

"Oh, you can't, they are beautiful. It must have taken you hours to iron them."

"I never have. Mum will have done it years ago and they've sat there folded up ever since. You might find that when you open them out, they disintegrate in the creases."

Sarah took one from the top of the pile, the stiff cotton sharply creased, slightly yellowed along the creases, but intact, the lace around the edge scratchy and discoloured.

"It's beautiful. I'm sure it would wash. Oh, and this next one has embroidery all over it." She carefully took it off the pile and they saw that the round damask cloth was covered in embroidered signatures.

"It's from their wedding. Mum told me that it was her mother's idea, something they did in her family. But Mum was no good at sewing, so I think Nan had to do all the embroidery in the end. Everyone at the wedding breakfast signed the cloth and then she went over it in chain stitch. Look at the tiny stitches, what patience. And look, she's done some flowers too, pansies and forget-me-nots I think. Nan wasn't the greatest needlewoman either," she finished, ruefully.

"What a lovely idea. You'll have to keep that one."

"I suppose so. But I've got no-one to pass it on to, so, if you'd like it, you can have it. It's a talking point, if nothing else. Now I've started clearing, I've realised that it was Mum who was the sentimental one, not me. I'm happy just with my memories. I don't need so many things. Please take all of them if you want and any of the towels you can use. I'll put the sheets in the drawers under my bed and then you can have the cupboard if you want it. You'll have to collect it, though. I don't think it will fit in my car."

Sarah touched the table cloth reverently. "Are you sure you don't want it? It's a family heirloom."

"I don't have any family left and I haven't seen it since I was about twenty, when Mum thought I might get married. But she'd made me so wary of men, they couldn't get anywhere near me. She must have had something terrible in her past. Suzanne suggested perhaps an abortion or an assault or something. The only positive thought is that there can't be any half-sisters or brothers out there. I would have found some evidence by now."

"I didn't know your mum but you were obviously very close. I'd love to read her book," said Sarah. "I can wait until it's published," she added quickly.

"Oh, she must have had such an exciting life then, dancing at the Windmill…"

"Is the book about the theatre and dancing?"

"No, it's about a young couple meeting and exploring the world and at the same time exploring each other." Hilary blushed and busied herself refolding towels.

"How romantic."

"To me, it's more rude than romantic, but you know what I'm like. She must have done lots of research because I'm sure she's never been to most of the places mentioned. But just thinking about that, I do remember when we went to the library when I was little, she'd always get travel books out with wonderful pictures in and we had a massive atlas that was almost as big as me. I wonder what happened to that? She must have lived lots of her life in her imagination. Dad was lovely, but he was pretty boring. He liked to read his newspaper – no word was left unread. He'd tinker with the car or wash and polish it until it shone. He loved to polish shoes too and then, once a year, he'd get all the silver out of the cabinet in the front room and lay it out on newspaper in the kitchen and polish it till you could see your face in it, before placing it all carefully back in the cupboard behind the glass doors. I was allowed to watch and then, with cotton gloves on, carefully put some of the pieces back. We hardly talked, but it was such a special time with him." Tears sprung to her eyes and she brushed them away impatiently. "Oh, listen to me going on. I hadn't thought about any of this for years."

"That's what things can do sometimes – they evoke memories. Perhaps you shouldn't be too hasty about getting rid of everything."

"No-one could accuse me of being hasty, and no, I think I need a clean sweep, start again, get my thoughts in order. Have you ever thought of being a therapist instead of a cook? I think it's you that's made all this come to the surface, not a few towels and a tablecloth."

Luke, who'd been sitting contentedly in Sarah's arms, decided he was bored with the conversation and wriggled to get down.

"Let's go back to the kitchen and put the kettle on."

"Thank you, but I think we had better get going. Can I come around Saturday with some boxes, before you change your mind?" Sarah was collecting her belongings. She handed Luke to Hilary, who sat him on the kitchen table. He entertained himself with the fruit in the fruit bowl, taking it out as fast as Hilary could put it back again, his chuckles making Hilary feel like hugging him.

"It must exhaust you looking after him all day."

"It's pretty tiring, but he's quite self-sufficient really. A lot of the time I can leave him in his playpen and he occupies himself, and, of course, he still has two long sleeps a day. I certainly make the most of that time. Tom's mum is very good. She loves having him."

"What about your mum?"

"She's too far away and she's too busy." Sarah's face seemed to close. Hilary didn't pry any further and Hector, as if sensing that Sarah wasn't happy, nuzzled her hand with his nose. She stroked him absentmindedly. "Life is never straightforward. We just have to make the best of what we have, and not get upset about things that aren't right."

"I wish I was as wise and philosophical as you."

"Huh, I'm not wise," Sarah said, as she put Luke in his coat, gathering him up from the table. "I can't be bitter and miserable with Luke, and Tom's family have done more for me than mine ever did. Anyway, that's enough of all that. We'd better go. See you Saturday. Thank you, thank you, bye, bye, bye." She waved and then lifted Luke's arm in a wave before strapping him in his car seat. Hilary called Hector back into the house and shut the door against the cold and wet day.

She walked through the bungalow, straightening the mat in the hall that Hector had rucked up in his eagerness to get back in before she shut the door. She continued along the hall to the linen cupboard and pushed the door shut. She would move bed linen out later and Sarah could sort out what she wanted on Saturday. The rest would go to charity. Looking around as she walked back to the living room, she realised how little of her there was in the house. Her bedroom was the only place that showed any of her personality and that was very bland and functional. I must have a personality, she thought. All these years I've just been whatever others want me to be. Who am I? After this thought passed through her mind, she smiled to herself. How daft I am, going mad in my old age, all these silly thoughts. "Hector, what are we going to do? We'll make some changes here though, won't we?"

Hector looked up at her, wondering if she was talking about his dinner, which was a bit late in being served. He'd had a good day playing with that small human, so he didn't mind. He put on his best understanding face and sat listening attentively, as Hilary spoke to him.

"I like the kitchen. David suggested updating it, but I like it as it is. Maybe later. But the living room and the bedrooms need changing, and I like David's idea of turning the whole house around, extending outwards from Mum's room with the lovely view across the garden towards the woods and using that as the living or dining room, perhaps. Then what is now the living room could be my bedroom. But then we'd have to move the bathroom. I don't want to have to walk half a mile in the middle of the night."

Hector's ears pricked up at the word 'walk' and he sat up straighter, but lay down when Hilary didn't make a move to get his lead or her coat.

"I want all modern furniture – perhaps Suzanne or Liz could advise me on that. Perhaps I could have a patio, too, then we could sit outside for dinner in the summer."

That was too much for Hector. He'd listened for long enough and yes, please, he would like his dinner.

He sprang up and jumped around Hilary's legs, trying to grab her hand to show her where his dinner was. She took the hint and fondled his ears before following him to the cupboard to get his food.

"I know, I know, give me a chance," she said, as she filled his bowl and put it down next to his basket.

While he ate, she walked from room to room. When she got to her mum's room, she hesitated outside the door. Don't be silly, she said to herself, pushing the door open. As always, her mother's perfume overlaid with that indefinable powdery old lady smell assailed her nostrils. The room looked bare and much bigger now, the furniture showing the knocks of numerous years now that the ornaments and tranklements of daily life had been removed. She pulled the curtains across the window. It was too dark to see anything out there. In her mind's eye, she could see bifold doors opening onto a patio, the room extended into the hallway, opening up the entire back of the house. It occurred to her that it was more likely to be breakfast outside in the sunshine, and not dinner as she had told Hector. As if knowing he was in Hilary's mind, he trotted into the room, having finished eating. He lay stretched out by the radiator, keeping one eye on her.

She sat down on the edge of the mattress. The bedding had been stripped and removed from the room. She had only the furniture to dispose of now. As she looked around, she couldn't see anything that she wanted to keep. The 1970s dressing table was at odds with the tall dark wardrobe; the bed had a hideous pale pink, padded headboard, over-sewn with gold thread between frayed gold-covered buttons. The dark scuffed lacquer of the bedside cabinets had cupboards that would originally have held a chamber pot. The room was a real hotchpotch of things that had always been there and new items added without thought for design. Her mum had always been so particular about her clothes and appearance, it struck Hilary as odd that her room had so little appeal. Perhaps she had decided that after Dad died no-one else would see it. But the entire bungalow was the same. It contained lots of nice things, but without pattern or style. She would ask Sarah if she and Tom could use any of the other furniture.

"I'm going to start again," she said aloud, pushing herself up off the mattress. "Thank you, Mum. I thought you'd messed everything up, but you've opened up a whole new life for me." She stroked the silky wood of the wardrobe door. "I certainly had no idea what secrets lay in here, but perhaps now I can find out who I am. Come on Hector. Let's go and see what's on telly and I suppose I'd better feed myself too. What a funny day."

Chapter Twenty-One

Changes

"Hello Carol."

"Yes, I'm fine thanks. I'm phoning for a favour really. Is Jonathan there?"

"Oh, OK, I was just wondering if he could help with some furniture removal if he's still got his big van."

"Oh, great, thank you. Yes, Saturday morning, please. Why don't you come around for coffee while they get on with it? Sarah and Tom are taking several pieces and they have arranged with the charity shop to deliver the rest there. Then their friend with a van let them down. They were going to hire, but I thought I'd ask Jonathan first."

"Oh, that's great. Ten o'clock Saturday then. We can take Hector out if the weather's not too terrible."

"OK, see you Saturday."

Carol turned to Jonathan, who was sitting on the settee next to her, dozing in front of a wildlife programme on the TV.

"Well, that's a first. Hilary never asks for anything. She always gets everything done herself. I hope you don't mind, but I've offered your services Saturday morning."

Jonathan sat up, "What?"

"I've offered your services Saturday."

"Yes, I heard. What am I doing?"

"Hilary is getting rid of some furniture and Sarah, who I think is the girl she got Hector from, is having some of it, then there's some to go to the charity shop in town."

"Aren't we supposed to be going to see Dad?"

"No, I told you, that's Sunday."

"OK, I'd better make sure there's some petrol in the van before the weekend then." With that, he settled back into the sofa and his eyes turned back to the screen, just in time to see the hyenas attack the remains of the zebra carcass left by the lions.

Carol continued to think about Hilary. She'd heard all about the book that Hilary's mum was supposed to have written and how she had been a dancer at the Windmill. But she found the change in Hilary more amazing than any of that. She thought about how she had been when they went on that weekend, much livelier and quite good fun. She felt that of all her group of friends, Hilary was the one she knew least. She was just there. In discussions, her opinion seemed to be that of the last person who'd spoken. She always seemed to say what others wanted to hear. Kind, yes, helpful, yes – she'd do anything for anyone. Generous to a fault. A good listener. But, really, a bit boring. Thinking about it, she had been completely overshadowed and controlled by her mother.

"What do you think of Hilary?"

"What?"

The lion cubs were lying around their parents like a photograph of the royal family.

"What do you think of Hilary?"

"Oh, she's all right. A bit boring, but nice enough. She's just there really, isn't she?"

His eyes were glued to the screen as one of the cubs dared to climb on his father's back and was unceremoniously knocked off for his trouble.

"Mmmmm, I think she's changed since her mum died. Do you want a coffee?" Carol asked, pushing on the arm of the settee to get up. "We're going to have to get a higher sofa. My knees don't like getting up off here."

"Do you want me to make the coffee?"

"No, I'm up now."

Hilary put the phone down and said to Hector, "I never knew how kind people were. I'd have never dared ask for help when Mum was around. It always felt like weakness, but Carol sounded really pleased to help. I thought it was just doormats like me who did things for other people, but I suppose we all need to be needed to a greater or lesser degree. It has to be two-way, doesn't it, for a proper friendship?"

Hector wagged his tail. He liked her soft and gentle voice. It caressed his ears, like her hands caressed his coat. It made him feel relaxed and he trotted after her back to the kitchen, happy just to be there. Hilary was opening and shutting cupboards and Hector sat in front of the cupboard where he knew his treats lived. Then, looking at her, he realised she was sad. He nudged her hand to remind her he was there. She seemed to come around and impatiently wiped her hand across her face.

"I mustn't dwell on what might have been. Mum and I made a good team and life has been good to me. I was happy with the way things were. Mum was still Mum whatever had happened in her past. She did everything for me with the best of intentions. I just wish I'd had the chance to talk to her about all of this. I realise now that she was my best friend. No wonder I feel so bereft. But perhaps if I let others in, I can have other friends, friends to do things for me as well as people that I can do things for."

Her thoughts were in danger of going around in circles again. She decided against sorting the kitchen cupboards. It could all wait until Saturday.

It wasn't raining, so she bundled herself up in her outer clothes, pulled on her boots, picked up her keys and Hector's lead, and set off across the road for a quick walk around the block to clear her head. The cold air bit into her face. The road was slightly slippery underfoot and the bare branches of the tall trees played with the light from the street lamps, making the pavement opposite look even more uneven than it actually was. Hector pulled on his lead, eager to be off and running but happy to be outside. As they reached the other side of the road, Hilary brought him back to her side.

"Heel," she said sharply. "You'll have me over."

"Are you all right, Hilary?" David made her jump, looming up in front of her, appearing from behind the beech hedge that edged the drive. He was carrying what smelt like a takeaway in a brown paper bag. He pressed the car key, locking the car with a clunk.

"You made me jump. I didn't see you pull into the drive."

"No, I was on the phone. Had to finish the call – but I'd better take our dinner in now." He lifted the bag higher, out of Hector's reach. "Any more thoughts on the renovation?"

"Loads. Go and have your dinner. I'm off round the block. Don't worry, I'll be in touch about the bungalow."

David went towards his front door, raising his hand to his mother's window above the garage. He wasn't sure if she'd see him, but the light was on and she had taken to sitting by the window to watch the comings and goings along the road. He still couldn't believe how lucky he was that she had settled in so well. Her few pieces of furniture had slotted in as if they belonged, and the curtains that Suzanne had helped her choose made the rooms cosy and homely. He liked to go and sit with her for a coffee for a few minutes each day and, while he knew James would always be the blue-eyed boy, he thought that his relationship with his mother had grown stronger. Their project on her old house was taking shape. It looked like the planning permission was going through and subcontractors were lined up waiting to get their tenders in. Things really were going well and if he could get the work on Hilary's house too, it brought everything closer to home. Less travel, less dashing about, less searching for work.

"Life's good," he said to himself as he walked into the bright, warm kitchen.

"What?" asked Suzanne, taking the plates from the warming drawer. She had heard the car come into the drive and, when he hadn't appeared, she had gone to look through the dining-room window. Seeing him in the car on the phone as usual, she went back to the kitchen to wait for him. The call could be anything from one to twenty minutes, so she settled down on one of the leather-covered bar stools at the breakfast bar and leafed through the local paper. She paused on the page listing the deaths and noted with sadness the name of a patient who had crossed her mind only that day because she hadn't been in for her dressing for a couple of weeks. Suzanne hadn't worried because Ethel often went to stay with her daughter. This time, though, she had 'died peacefully after a brief illness'. She'd have to check her records tomorrow to see if there was any more information.

She was brought out of her reverie by half hearing David's muttered "Life's good."

"Just thinking how lucky we are," he said, putting his arms around her waist and kissing the back of her neck. "Just seen Hilary, off on a walk with that dog of hers," he continued. "She certainly seems to have more life these days, less down-trodden, less of a dogsbody. I think I might get to do the renovation, upgrading or whatever you want to call it on her bungalow. Anything will improve it. I must admit they've kept it up well, she and her mother, but it's a bit soulless, isn't it, bit of a throwback? She has loads of scope for extension. I bet I could even get planning permission to make it two storey..."

"Hang on, there's only one of her. She doesn't need a mansion and I don't know how she is for money now her mum has gone."

"She could extend, do it up, sell and find somewhere more suitable."

"Perhaps she doesn't want to move and I like having her for a neighbour. I can think of a lot worse. Anyway, let's have this Chinese before it goes cold." They collected the cutlery and went to sit in front of the giant TV, the lions on the wildlife programme almost larger than life.

"I can't imagine her mother as a dancer, even though I've seen the photo. As long as I've lived here, any movement has seemed difficult for her, but perhaps it was all that dancing that caused the damage," Suzanne mused.

"What a stunner though! I'd like to have known her all those years ago. Those legs…"

Suzanne lifted her own leg and waggled it in front of him as he put a forkful of bean sprouts into his mouth.

"Better than mine?" she challenged.

"Of course not, darling," he replied after a millisecond's hesitation, and then ducked as she threw her napkin at him.

"She was lovely though, wasn't she? How age changes some people. Mum looked pretty much the same as she grew older and your mum looks great, she looks better than ever. But Phyllis had got so fat, hadn't she? I shall have to look at the photo again. If I hadn't seen her wedding photo, I wouldn't have believed it was the same person." She jumped as the lion batted one of the cubs with his massive paw, sending him flying. "Corporal punishment obviously still exists in the wild."

"Should still exist full stop. Never did me any harm."

They both got back to their dinner, not wanting to start an old discussion on which they never could agree. David had never seen the effects of corporal punishment that had gone beyond a quick smack on the back of the legs; Suzanne had seen too much.

Chapter Twenty-Two

A Backward Step

"I want my mum back."

Carol and Hilary were sitting side by side on the settee, tears streaming down Hilary's face. Carol turned and waved Sarah away as she put her head around the door to ask yet another question about what she could and couldn't take.

"Is this all too much too soon? Should we stop? MIND THE LAMPSHADE," Carol shouted over Hilary's shoulder as she caught a glimpse of Tom and Jonathan manhandling the linen cupboard along the hallway.

"Stay there a minute," she said, pushing a tissue into Hilary's hand.

She slipped out of the living room and, shutting the door, beckoned Sarah to her.

"I think it's all getting a bit much for Hilary. Have you got everything you planned to take?"

Sarah's face fell, distressed that she had upset Hilary.

"I didn't want to rush her. She wanted to do it. We can put everything back."

Sarah looked as though she was going to burst into tears. Carol put her hand on her arm. "Don't be silly. She does want to do it but that doesn't mean it won't affect her."

Jonathan and Tom had come back in from loading the van and were standing in the hall waiting for further instructions, brushing the rain off their clothes and shaking their heads like dogs.

"We could have picked a better day to get this done," Jonathan grumbled.

"Right," said Carol, taking charge. "Is the van loaded? Have you much more to pack, Sarah?"

"I wanted to check about a couple of things in the kitchen, but we don't have to do it today."

"Right then, if you all go and deliver whatever you've packed to wherever it's got to go to, then you three go and have a drink or something. Then, Jonathan, you can come and pick me up in a couple of hours. It'll give me a chance to have a proper chat to Hilary without you lot clattering about."

"If we go to ours first, unload the stuff there and I can start sorting on my own before your mum brings Luke back."

"We're in time to go to the football if we get a move on. If I take the van back when it's empty, Tom could you follow in the car and drop me at the ground?"

"No bother, and I won't drop you, I'll come too, if that's OK."

"Will five o'clock be too late to pick you up?"

"Carol, I can take you home." Hilary had come out of the living room and had heard most of the negotiations. "Five certainly isn't too late, but I don't suppose you wanted to waste the whole day over here."

"It'll be five before we've decided what we're doing if we don't get a move on."

Sarah hugged Hilary, ignoring her blotchy, tear-stained face.

Hector tangled himself up in everyone's legs as they tried to get out the door. Ten minutes later, the bungalow was quiet, the kettle was on and Hilary had composed herself. Carol tidied away the bubble wrap and Hilary was getting the vacuum out to clean the carpet where the linen cupboard had stood.

"Leave that now, dear. Let's just sit down for a minute. You must feel drained."

Hilary ignored her and quickly vacuumed the hallway, wiped the accumulated dirt from the skirting board and marvelled at the bright pattern on the carpet where the cupboard had stood for all those years, the stark outline and indentations from the feet emphasising the faded, slightly shabby russet carpet covering the rest of the hall.

"Have I done the right thing?" she asked, finally sitting down next to Carol on the settee.

"Who knows?" said Carol, and then, looking round, "Yes, definitely, it's about time this house had a bit of Hilary stamped on it. Until now it's definitely been your parents' house. It's your turn now."

"Oh dear, what if it's too late?"

"Don't be ridiculous. It's never too late."

"You sounded just like Mum then."

"Sorry…"

"No, you're right, I am being ridiculous but I am in a bit of a muddle. Sorry. I miss Mum so much because she is the one I would have talked to about all this. She is the only person I could talk to, who I felt understood me, but I suppose I never gave anyone else a chance. She sheltered me… smothered me. You have all been so good to me. I wouldn't have got through the last few months on my own. I even considered ending it all you know, in my darkest moment, but then Mum definitely told me to pull myself together. I'd sit in her room, talking to her," she confided. "You must think I'm mad."

"Don't be so hard on yourself – I'm only glad we could help. The others were around much more than me and I'm so glad you came on that spa weekend."

"That came at just the right time, dragged me out of the depths. I don't know why you invited me. You probably all think I'm a silly old thing, hopelessly boring."

"Stop it, we don't think anything of the sort." Carol mentally crossed her fingers behind her back at this white lie. "You are a good, kind person and we all love you. We can't all be the same. Imagine if everyone was like

Liz – it would be exhausting." They laughed. "You could perhaps do with a little updating, like this bungalow. You've lived in your mother's shadow for too long, and you've put her and others first for too long. Your turn now, but there's no rush. Grief takes time and, in a way, you are having to go through it twice, for the mum you know and the mum you discovered. To everyone else, all that discovery of the manuscript and everything is exciting, a possible money spinner, a mystery to solve, glamour in an otherwise ordinary life, but it must have thrown you into a spin."

Hilary started crying again. "Oh, stop crying, you silly old thing," she chided herself. "I can't believe you understand. I thought I was going mad. Everyone else seemed to think that I should be happy about the discovery, but I was just furious with Mum on so many levels, not least for not trusting me enough tell me or wanting to share with me. Perhaps she didn't think I was old enough to understand." She laughed through her tears. "I'm struggling at the moment because I can't remember Mum as she was. I only visualise her on the floor in Tesco with all those people around her or as a cartoon or caricature of that photo at the Windmill Theatre. I can't bring her to mind. I want to remember my mum. If I can't have her back, why can't I just have a happy memory of her?"

"It'll come. You'll see. Remember that blue patterned dress she wore on your birthday and she had her brown coat with the fur on the collar. Remember what she wore and she will gradually become clearer to you. Consciously remember happy times, even just insignificant times, and then those memories will replace the memories of the last few minutes of her life and push them deeper inside."

Hilary looked doubtful but she didn't want to disagree with Carol. She hoped that what she said would happen. Only time would tell.

Chapter Twenty-Three

Life Goes On

The writing caressed her, enveloped her. Her mother's hand, which had written all those letters to her while she was at school, instructing, informing, guiding but never really loving. How could the hand that had written those belong to the same person who owned the mind that had created this beautiful manuscript? For it was beautiful. The descriptions and the depth of feeling touched Hilary as she read. The initial embarrassment and shock had dissolved, and she became immersed in the words, the places, the feelings.

She could hear her mother's voice, voicing the unfamiliar place names, body parts and sexual acts, places she had never visited and parts of her body she had never been able to explore without guilt. Pictures crossed her mind. Her first sexual encounter behind the village hall, after her 21st birthday party – the fear of discovery, the embarrassment of knickers around her ankles and a pain so intense that she left it a long time before trying again.

Then a trail of abandoned, confused boyfriends. She recalled with sadness relationships that ended before sex became a possibility and then the joy of finding someone patient enough to let her go at her own pace, just happy to enjoy her company until she was ready to allow him nearer. But just as life was opening up for her, his job was moved to another town. Their relationship wasn't strong enough to weather the vagaries of public transport and infrequent phone calls. He soon met someone else in his new office. Hilary couldn't compete. She'd had other boyfriends. They never met her mother's exacting standards and, if Hilary was truthful with herself, none of them were the Mr Right that she was hoping for. Twenty years of celibacy followed after her last boyfriend left, hurt and belittled, with accusations of frigidity and coldness.

"What a waste," she said to herself.

But it wasn't her mother's fault. It wasn't anyone's fault. She had chosen the life she had led. That last boyfriend had been a mean-spirited bully. She hadn't meant to let him put her off men; she had just taken the path of least resistance. It was easier not to try.

She picked up the last of the notepads, wondering why her mother had chosen to write on writing paper rather than an exercise book. Perhaps all the time she was writing the manuscript, she had pretended to her husband that she was writing to Hilary. Perhaps Phyllis had had years of celibacy too in spite of being married.

"Oh Mum, I wish you could tell me."

Finishing the manuscript, she placed it carefully back in the box ready to be delivered to Janet for typing. She was glad that she had read it again. Liz was right – there wasn't much of a story, but the language and places were of a bygone era. Hilary was left with a longing to visit all the towns and cities described. If she took the book with her, it would be as though her mum was still by her side.

"So, do I want to have it published? What do you think, Mum? What do you want me to do?"

The phone rang, breaking into her thoughts.

"Liz, how are you?"

"Pearl's 80th. Your mum? I thought that was next year.

It's all happening, isn't it? Will John be back?"

"Oh, he's already back? How lovely."

"Is everything all right with you two now? Does your mum know about all this? Just so I don't put my foot in it at the party."

Hilary went quiet as Liz filled her in with all the details.

"Oh, that's fabulous news. When are you getting married?"

"A June wedding? Perfect. Your mum will be pleased and she'll think you are doing it for her, not because everything nearly fell apart."

"Siobhan a bridesmaid. She'll love dressing up. Oh, how exciting."

"Well, yes, I'd love to come on the 30th. Is it just drinks or will there be food? Do you want me to bring anything?"

"No, OK."

"See you in a week."

"I still can't decide, but I've just put the manuscript together to go to Janet's for typing. Then we'll see…"

"See you next week. Oh, what about presents?"

"A donation. Which charity?"

"Oh, Age UK – very close to my heart. I'll get onto it straight away."

"Bye, bye, bye."

She put the phone down.

"Oh Hector, how lovely. What good news. John is back. He and Liz are getting married. It's what he wanted all along, but he'd gone with her wishes and not known how to go back on his word. We are all silly, not being honest with each other, but sometimes the moment doesn't arise, or it does and we miss it. Life is full of misunderstandings and we go about trying to protect each other's feelings, often just guessing what others are thinking or feeling. That's when it can all fall apart. It's going to take Liz a long time to phone around everyone with the invites to Pearl's do if she has to explain everything. She did sound excited though, not at all like her usual cynical self."

Hector looked at her as if he understood every word and then spoilt it by nudging her hand for a treat.

"Hello mate, congratulations."

John hated being the centre of attention and felt like turning tail and going straight home again, but Liz had sent him out with express instructions to see the lads and so, here he was, in the pub. The place was crowded with early evening drinkers. It was too late to back out now. He'd brought this on himself.

David was bearing down on him, his arm outstretched, and the others weren't far behind.

Oh well, in for a penny, in for a pound, he thought, as he took a deep breath, felt his hand grasped by David and said, "My round I think."

"No, no, we've already set up a kitty, our treat – prodigal returns and all that."

He was shaking hands with the others, trying to field their questions, as if he was the centre of a press conference. They moved back to the table they had commandeered and David went to get his drink.

"Belgian beer is it now?" he bellowed, embarrassing John further. People were turning round to see what all the commotion was about.

"Ignore him," said Richard, reassuringly. "He'll get over it. You know what he's like. Is everything really OK now? Janet told me you're getting married next year. Is that right? I thought you two were dead set against marriage?"

"Only one of us. I asked her not long after we met. She said it was too soon and I just let things slide. I tried asking her again recently but I couldn't get her to listen. She was too busy and everything else was too important. I feel a bit silly now running away like that, but I had to go away for her to notice me. A bit childish though."

"She was really distraught. Janet said she'd never seen her so upset."

"Yes, Suzanne said the same," added David, bringing John his drink. "Worried us all to death, you both did."

"Sorry. I thought I was going mad. I couldn't get my thoughts in order, didn't know what to do. I thought perhaps I just needed some tablets. Your locum was a very nice chap, Jag, but not much help. Although poor thing, I didn't know what I was asking for, so I've no idea how I expected him to know the answers."

Jag joined in the laughter, but they all realised how serious things had been; people don't just up sticks and disappear to another country unless they are really distressed.

"You could have talked to us," Jonathan put in.

"What would I have said? 'Liz won't listen to me,' 'I'm feeling left out,' 'I can't go on like this'? You'd have thought I was a right dipstick. I realised I just needed some space to think, to work out exactly what I wanted. I hadn't been away twenty-four hours when I realised that I just wanted Liz, but I wanted her to marry me, not just to carry on as we have been. So, when I got back, I sort of gave her an ultimatum. I didn't realise I was quite as brave as I am. Even when she was desperately relieved to have me back and really humble, she was still a bit scary. I do love her. Heaven knows why!"

He took a long drink from his pint. John was too embarrassed to tell his mates about the reception he had received when he got home with a diamond ring in his pocket. He didn't want them to think badly of Liz (or himself, he supposed). The unnatural passivity of Liz, the quiet, closed, hurt face, followed by shouting, arguments, accusations, evidence presented like an Agatha Christie denouement. Then his explanations, repeated with proof of innocence, repeated with pleas to accept that there was no-one else. It had been an exhausting rollercoaster of emotions. She had finally allowed him to explain why he had felt he had to go. And then he hurt her once again by saying that he hadn't really expected her to notice. Each had misjudged and misinterpreted the other's feelings. At last, he had felt calm enough to say what he had wanted to say as soon as he walked through the door. Her pleasure at his proposal was as electrifying as it was unexpected, her excitement infectious. The conversation was possibly not yet finished, but at least it had started.

"Anyway, can we talk about something else? There must have been something happening around here while I was away. I hope you are going to be there for Pearl's birthday bash. I shall need some moral support."

There was a general murmur of assent and then talk easily turned to golf, cars and the other things that occupied their minds when they weren't working.

"Hello Liz, lovely to hear from you again. Of course, I'll help if I can."

Hilary sat down with the phone pressed to her ear, listening to Liz's request.

"But it's not exactly a party house like David and Suzanne's…" She was interrupted by further explanations from Liz and she was surprised how much like pleading it sounded, so unlike Liz.

"Well, of course you can. I'm obviously free on the 30th because you'd already invited me. How many are you inviting? I can provide glasses but perhaps we'll need paper plates. Sarah has just taken my spare dinner services. Do you want me to do any food?"

"Oh yes, Marks & Spencer is very good. Will it all be delivered?"

"The morning of the 30th – that's fine. I can be in."

Hilary wondered if Liz had been so sure of her response that she had already booked the delivery but she pushed this uncharitable thought to the back of her mind.

"So, I'll see you Saturday lunchtime. How exciting."

She hung up the phone thoughtfully. "We're having a party, Hector." He wagged his tail appreciatively.

Hilary picked up her empty coffee cup and went through to the kitchen. Liz seemed different. Of course, it would be much easier to have the party here, everything on one level, grab rails in the bathroom for Pearl's less able friends. Pearl's flat would be far too small and Liz and John's house too awkward. In the past, Liz would have booked a restaurant, and not asked Hilary. Hilary realised that her standing in the group had changed since her mum had died. Perhaps she had changed, rather than Liz, or perhaps it was just because her mum wasn't around any more and it was easier to get around her than her mum. Hilary's thoughts went around and around. She felt very gratified that she could offer her house for Pearl's party, but upset that her mother wouldn't be there to join in.

The phone rang again, making her jump.

"Hello, Liz."

"Of course I don't think you are taking advantage. I was delighted to be asked. I was just thinking it's a shame Mum can't join in, but she will be there in spirit."

"No honestly, it's fine. You've had enough on your plate recently. I'm not surprised you didn't get around to organising anything."

"Don't listen to John or Pearl. I really don't mind, as long as I get some help with the clearing up. It won't be late finishing, will it?"

"Although it doesn't matter, I haven't got to get up on Sunday."

"Oh, is it going to be all right if Hector is around? I'll try and keep him under control. I can give him a good long walk in the morning and I'm sure one of the men will volunteer to walk him during the party if he's a nuisance."

"Oh yes. I bet John'll be glad to escape if there's too much talk of weddings. He can't be getting married to you without any fuss. I'm looking forward to it."

"You love a party, Liz, and that's what the wedding will be. A great big party, with you as honoured guest. He can't back out now."

"Well, he can't expect a wedding to be planned without a bit of ceremony. I can't believe we're having this conversation when not long ago you were worried to death that he wasn't coming back. It's been a bit of a rollercoaster year, hasn't it? I think I'd like it to end so that we can start afresh with a new year. That'll be another do. I presume Suzanne and David are having their usual thing."

"Anyway, let's get your mum's 80th over first. I'd better get some cleaning done."

"I'm joking. You concentrate on your own family. Everything'll be ready when you come on Saturday."

The morning of the party was dull and cold, with an incessant miserable, misty rain. The food delivery was prompt and was now safely stored in the fridge. Hilary had pushed all the furniture to the sides of the room and vacuumed the carpet where it had stood. She placed side tables with coasters near the chairs, plumped the cushions on the settee and, much to his dismay, washed the rug on Hector's chair. The glasses were washed and polished and lined up on trays in the kitchen. A pristine white sheet served as a table cloth on the dining table, waiting for the food to be laid out. Perhaps she had been a bit hasty giving all the cloths to Sarah; perhaps she should have kept one or two. But no, the sheet looked good and none of the cloths had been that white. She had bought some flowers and arranged them carefully to brighten up the windowsills and shelves. She'd looked at banners and balloons but thought she'd leave that to Liz. She knew what her own mother had thought of such nonsense.

Liz was due at any moment, so she put the kettle on for a cup of coffee before checking around the living room and dining room one final time. I haven't put any cutlery out, she thought, and started rummaging in the drawers of her sideboard. She was on her knees, dragging the wooden canteen from underneath the sideboard, when the doorbell rang. She pulled herself up off her knees with a groan and went to the door to find Liz laden with paper plates, serviettes, plastic cutlery and with a pink balloon that shouted '80 TODAY' floating above her head. Hilary relieved her of her burden and Liz followed through to the dining room, taking her coat off as she went, shaking droplets of water from her hair.

"Ugh, I hate this weather."

"Oh dear, you are all ready and I haven't showered, let alone changed."

"Don't worry, we'll get these bits organised and then you can get sorted while I put the food out. John is picking Lisa and Siobhan up on his way to collect Pearl and they'll be here at about two. I think then Pearl's got him picking up two of her friends to save them getting a taxi. She's got it all organised. Oh, the cake's on the back seat of the car. I hope it's travelled OK."

"I'll put some coffee on – we've got time for a cup, haven't we?"

"Of course," said Liz, going out to retrieve the cake from her car. She returned and proudly placed it in the centre of the table.

"Oh, that's beautiful. Did you do it?" Hilary held a cup of coffee out to Liz and took a sip of her own.

"I wish. I made the cake but a neighbour of Mum's iced it. Amazing lady. You'll meet her this afternoon."

Hilary felt more comfortable when Liz called her mother 'Mum'. She simply couldn't get used to her using her first name, although Pearl didn't seem to mind and, thinking about it, Lisa never called Liz 'Mum'. It seemed odd to Hilary.

They set about their preparations. Hector padded backwards and forwards after Liz as she unpacked the food, arranged it on plates and carried it into the dining room. He was disappointed that nothing fell to the floor but he kept following her, just in case. Hilary came through, showered and changed, and shooed him back to his chair.

"It's looking lovely, and doesn't the living room look big now that you've moved all the furniture to the sides."

"I'm going to have to decide what to do with this place now. I might even get a chance to ask David this afternoon. Oh, did you ask them about using their drive for parking? We'll never get all the cars on this one."

"Yes, I did. It's all sorted. Do you think you'll stay here? It's a big bungalow."

"I can't imagine living anywhere else. But you are right – it is a bit big for one." Hilary looked thoughtful. "It's probably a bit selfish, but I think even if it's only for a time, I would like to enjoy this great big space on my own."

"Not selfish at all. If I had this place, I'd never give it up. It just needs modernising and, dare I say, personalising."

"I've just got to work out who that person is, though," said Hilary quietly.

"Oh, I think she's emerging."

They looked at each other.

"All change, eh?"

"Tell you what, shall we have a glass of Prosecco before they arrive. We deserve it."

When the doorbell went, signalling the arrival of the rest of Liz's family, she and Hilary were almost at the bottom of their glasses, relaxed and happy, ready for the fun to begin.

"Well, that went well." John and Hilary were at the kitchen sink, John wiping glasses on a rather damp tea towel. "Thank you for letting us use your place. It was perfect and it meant several of Pearl's friends could come who would otherwise have missed out. I hope Jonathan has managed to deliver them home OK. That Daphne was a bit vague about where she lived."

It just shows how much like an old peoples' home this is, thought Hilary, but she replied brightly enough.

"It was lovely. I sort of felt part of the family, not a guest." (Or staff, she thought.) "Siobhan certainly treats me like an aunty, not a stranger. I can't get over how good Hector was with her, although I'm not sure how much food she gave him. I caught her feeding him sausages at one point."

"She's a little madam, but I do love her. Did you get chance to talk to David about alterations for this place?"

"No, he was commandeered by Ethel and Bert who need a bathroom downstairs, so I didn't have the heart after that. There's no rush."

"Pearl had a lovely time. She and Liz are not at all alike, thank goodness. It was good of Lisa to take her home in a taxi. It meant Liz and I could stay and help clear up."

John put the last of the smeared glasses down and laid the tea towel out on the countertop.

"Shall I put these away?"

"No," said Hilary, thinking that they would probably all need doing again before she restored them to their rightful home. "It'll be quicker if I do it. I know where they all go."

She let the water out of the sink, dried her hands on the towel and, in one swift movement, picked up the tea towel and hung both up on their hooks.

"Let's see how Liz is getting on in the other room. I think we are pretty well finished."

"All done in there," said Liz, joining them in the kitchen. "Shall we finish this bottle? Not you, John." Taking the glass out of his hand, she poured the final dregs of Prosecco into it and handed John the little bottle of lurid fizzy orange juice that Siobhan had been drinking.

"Here's to Hilary," said Liz, raising her glass, and John chinked his bottle with their glasses. "Thank you so much – you saved my life. Mum would have had my guts for garters if we'd failed to celebrate her 80th in style. The cake was a big success, wasn't it? I'm glad David and Suzanne came. They are always good company and it meant we could use their drive. Jonathan and Carol are worth their weight in gold, aren't they?

Helping with ferrying the oldies about. But you are the real star Hilary. What would we do without you?"

"Come on old girl, let's get home before you get too soppy. Hilary needs to reclaim her home." John winked at Hilary as he started to steer Liz towards her coat and the door.

She acquiesced surprisingly easily, snuggling under John's arm.

When Hilary finally shut the door after waving them off, she looked around. She was becoming more and more fond of Liz. She felt really comfortable with her – but one thing she would never take from her would be housekeeping tips! The dining room that Liz had 'finished' looked as though a bomb had hit it. To be fair, the rubbish was all in a black bag, but the now-stained sheet was crumpled into a ball on the table and crumbs littered the floor – altough Hector was making short work of hoovering them up.

"Come on, let's get your dinner, then I can get this sorted. Won't take long."

Picking up the black bag, she took it out to the dustbin. After feeding Hector, she took a clean, dry tea towel from the drawer and polished the glasses before putting them away. She was just putting the sheet and tea towels in the washing machine, thinking of leaving the vacuuming until the next morning, when the doorbell rang.

"Who's forgotten something?"

Suzanne was on the doorstep. "I saw Liz and John leave. Is all the clearing up done? Much as I love Liz, she is a bit slovenly and I know how beautifully clean and tidy your house usually is."

Hilary laughed. "It's OK, I've very nearly finished. I'll vacuum tomorrow and then put the furniture back. It went well and Liz was so grateful. This upset with John has really shaken her. I think I preferred the strident, bossy Liz. This humble grovelling one is a bit hard to take."

"I know what you mean. I'm sure the real Liz will re-emerge. Anyway, I'll leave you to it. Thank you for a lovely party. See you."

"Phew, let's see what's on the telly. I'm done in." Hector took his place on his chair and dutifully looked at the screen as she turned on the set.

*

The next morning, Hilary was up early. She dressed and was out of the house before seven, much to Hector's delight. She was thoughtful, as Hector pulled on his lead, eager to get to the spot where he knew she would let him off. She wished she could find out more about her mother's life before she had come along.

If only she had family who would have known what had happened, but Hilary was the only one left. She felt a stab of loneliness. After her mother died, she had tried to push to the back of her mind how alone in the world she was. Both her parents had been only children. They'd had friends, of course, or her mum did; her father had never seemed to need them. There had been second cousins and cousins once removed, attached to her parents' parents, but they had long since died and Hilary had no idea if any of them had had family. Growing up, she had 'aunties' and 'uncles', but they were her parents' friends and people from neighbouring houses. It came back to her that, as a child, she had made up relatives when doing a family-tree project at school, using those pretend aunts and uncles to give herself some cousins. Her grandparents had been from small families too.

Hilary let Hector off his lead and, tucking the lead in her pocket, tramped purposefully along the muddy path. She shivered, thinking how totally alone she was. At her mother's funeral there had been friends and neighbours, but she had been the only family and now she was the only one. The family tree held only bare branches, devoid of twigs.

After her mother died, Hilary had sent a letter to everyone in her mother's address book and two of them turned out to be old school friends. She had received a nice letter from one in spidery old-lady's writing, talking about shared experiences and reunions. Hilary had written again after finding the book and the photograph, and asked the woman if she knew anything about her mother working as a dancer, but she had received a rather curt note from the woman's son saying that his mother had recently died. It was another blind alley. A letter from a distraught-sounding daughter had informed Hilary that Phyllis's other school friend now had Alzheimer's, so she wasn't going to be any help either. All of her mother's friends at the funeral were more recent, people she'd known from her committees and groups. None of them would have known her when she was younger.

Hilary's eyes filled with tears of self-pity, but she ignored them. It was better that way. She treated the unwanted tears like Hector's bad behaviour – if she ignored them, they went away sooner.

Hector chose that moment to distract her by dashing up with a ball in his mouth, dropping it at her feet to throw. She obliged, sending him scampering off into the bushes.

Throwing the ball again, she thought to herself that if she had been cleverer, she could have done some in-depth research and unearthed some distant family member who knew something, or a piece in the newspaper if there had been a scandal. But, realistically, she knew that her mother's life was likely to remain a mystery.

She felt so alone. She had always enjoyed her own company, had actively sought solitude, but that was when it had been an active choice, not inflicted upon her, as it was now. She hated the silence. She realised how much she missed the sounds around her mother – the television, the phone, the unsteady clumping steps, the unconscious grunts of pain as she moved around the house, her voice. She missed her voice. Hilary shuddered as she remembered the downward spiral in those days after her mother died, trying to fill the silence with the television, trying to escape the loneliness with sleep. It had taken her back to the despair of her childhood when she had first gone away to school – the feeling of being completely alone, surrounded by people, but feeling lost, afraid to join in, afraid of what others thought of her, the overwhelming feeling of being different and not fitting in. She had learned to playact, to put on a brave face, to pretend that everything was OK. To a certain extent, things were OK and she got through. One of her reports had even said, 'a popular member of the class'. She had never really recovered from that feeling at school and her mother's death made her feel that she had been left at the school gate permanently. Suzanne, Janet, Liz and Carol had coaxed her back from the brink, first by accepting her as she was and then by encouraging her to join them and come back to life. When they were all busy with their own lives, she still felt very lonely, but Hector had helped and, of course, Sarah was another blessing.

Hilary smiled to herself as she pocketed Hector's ball and got his lead out.

She must nurture these deepening friendships. She had her mother to thank for that, in an odd sort of way; the book and her exciting secret history had given Hilary a freedom that she had never experienced before.

Chapter Twenty-Four

A Get-Together

The restaurant was half full as Suzanne and Chahna were shown to the table in the window set for six. Christmas decorations adorned the room, all white and silver, but the luminous cherubs around the window looked more embarrassed than elegant and the bearded silver Father Christmas looked decidedly sinister. The table looked out onto the garden, the sodden wooden furniture dotted across the grass, the borders brown with the bedraggled remains of the Michaelmas daisies.

"I'm sorry we won't be able to come to your New Year do this year."

"I just couldn't believe it when Jag announced at work that you two were going away for twelve months. A complete bolt from the blue. What about his mum? You must have been planning it for months."

"We have been, but we weren't sure whether it was going to come off. Jag got the agreement of the other partners to take a sabbatical ages ago, but actually arranging it was more complicated than we thought. Believe it or not, his mother is coming with us, staying with family in Mumbai. She can't wait. She won't be travelling around with us, but there are already loads of plans for her. The girls are looking after the house."

"I didn't get around to asking Jag what he is going to be doing – or are you both just having a break?"

"You know Jag, conscientious to the last, takes everything very seriously. He's going to be studying Ayurveda – a really ancient form of medicine, the original holistic medicine, treating the whole person, not the disease, and it relies a lot on diet I think, particular foods for particular symptoms, very specific. It all sounds very interesting, nothing like conventional medicine. He might come back thinking it's a load of mumbo jumbo, but I'm sure he'll get loads from the experience. It will add to his knowledge and that can only help his patients here when he gets back. Me, though, I'm just having a break and exploring India. I can't wait."

"Well, that's brave. I can't believe you are giving up work. What if there isn't a job to come back to."

"I have to do it. I seem to flit all over the place, never settle. Look at everything you've invited me to that I've had to miss. I need to re evaluate my life, as they say. Take stock." She paused, looking thoughtful. Then, looking towards the door, she said, "Here's Liz and Carol. I wonder if they came in the same car."

They waved, calling them over to the table. With greetings out of the way, Chahna repeated her news.

"You are so brave," Carol said admiringly.

"You are so lucky," said Liz. "Such an exciting prospect. Shall we order a bottle of wine while we're waiting for the others? Have you driven or did you get a lift?"

As they were giving their order to the waitress, Liz exclaimed, "Is that Hilary?"

It was Hilary, coming towards them a little unsteadily, unaccustomed to wearing high heels. Her grey bob had been replaced by a short, tousled platinum blond hairdo; her make-up was perfect, understated, her eyebrows neat arcs. She was wearing a fur-trimmed camel coat over what was revealed to be a fine, knitted shift dress coming to just above her knees.

She smiled sheepishly as she sat down.

"Wow!"

"You look fabulous!"

"I love your hair!"

"What a transformation!"

Their voices clamoured around her; she coloured under her make-up.

"Oh dear. Have I overdone it?"

"Heck no, you look stunning!"

"I nearly didn't come. I nearly chickened out. But the old Hilary can't let people down so the new Hilary just had to come along. Do you recognise the coat, Liz? It was one of Mum's we found in the wardrobe. I've had it cleaned and the sleeves shortened. I love it. I don't remember her ever wearing it."

"Who did your hair? It looks great. And where did you get that gorgeous dress from. Is that one of your mum's too?"

She felt bombarded by the questions but fortunately the wine and the menus arrived, giving her a little breathing space.

Gradually the story came out – the appointment with the personal stylist at work, being persuaded to have a make-up lesson and finally being taken to the hairdresser. The whole adventure had been free. She'd planned to pay, but her colleagues had clubbed together when word got around about her proposed makeover.

"What do you really think, Hilary?" Carol asked her quietly.

"I love it. I feel a bit as though I'm playacting but I really love my hair. I had to slink about with my hood up when I took the dog out because I didn't want Suzanne to see and spoil today's surprise. I bought the dress and a couple of other things and got lots of really good advice on colours and styles. The only things that will have to go are the shoes. I love the way they look but they are far too high. I don't know how I was persuaded to buy them. I think I just got a bit carried away. I'm frightened I'll break my neck. There must be something stylish that's not quite so high."

"Looking at you, I think I'm going to get my hair coloured or highlighted or something. I can't believe how much it's changed you. Makes you look ten years younger. Do they do consultations?"

The talk flowed with the wine, and finally Janet arrived, flushed and rushed. Taking her coat off, she took the final chair and accepted a glass of wine.

"Sorry I'm late. Wow, Hilary you look great. And Liz, I love your hair tied back like that."

Liz's wild locks had been pulled back into a plait, a few curls breaking free from the diamanté-tipped clips that secured it.

"Well, I love your dress. Where did you get that?"

Janet was wearing a bottle-green shirt-waister with a cream square collar and big round buttons. She laughed. "It came out of Mum's wardrobe. Dad found me holding it against myself and he encouraged me to take it. We'll never get Mum in it again and he bought it for her on a trip to London in about 1960. He was really touched that I wanted it."

Her eyes filled with tears.

"Well it's great, very à la mode, certainly suits and fits perfectly."

The waitress came to take their order, and then Chahna repeated her news to the latest arrivals.

Hilary sat quietly, taking in the moment, surprised at how different she felt, wondering what on earth her mum would have said about her hair.

Janet broke in on her reverie. "I've brought the manuscript," she said, taking a purple file from the carrier she had placed by the side of her chair.

Hilary took it, opened it and touched the pages reverently, studying the neat double-spaced lines bordered by wide margins. She turned the pages and read a few lines. The words flowed easily towards her, no longer offensive or embarrassing now that they weren't in her mother's hand. It was her turn for her eyes to fill with tears. Then she looked up, realising the others had all gone quiet.

"I'm so proud of her."

"Come on, don't spoil that perfect make-up by crying. There's nothing to cry about," said Liz.

"I haven't read it yet," said Chahna.

"Neither have I," added Carol. "I know it's a bit erotic, but what's the story?"

"It's about a couple's exploration of each other's bodies, while at the same time exploring the world," explained Hilary.

"What I found amazing," interjected Liz, "was that the two characters in the book – and there are only two, apart from the odd incidental waiter or hotel receptionist, but they don't count – anyway, the two main characters don't have names. They don't have jobs or lives outside the story and we know them intimately, very intimately, but I didn't notice until a long way into the manuscript that we don't know their names."

"I know. And not only that, all the places are described exquisitely and in detail but never named, and the couple just appear in the places. There are no details of the journeys, they are just there. It's very cleverly written."

"Yes, Janet," agreed Hilary. "When I first read it, I just thought it was a book about sex, almost a 'How to' manual, but it's so much more. It's beautiful."

"I'd love to read it," said Carol.

"You must," chorused the others.

"I'll wait till it's published. I haven't got time to read it before we go," said Chahna.

Hilary carefully put the file back in its bag.

Their meals arrived. As they ate, each chatted to the woman sitting closest to her. Janet brought them all back together, saying, "There's something else that no-one else seems to have noticed about Hilary's mum's book. It doesn't have a title."

"We'll have to think of something before getting an agent or publisher or whatever we have to do. Any suggestions? I had thought of *The Journey* but I'm not sure that does it justice."

"What about *Explorations* or *The Awakening*?" Janet piped up, putting down her knife and fork and wiping her lips on her napkin.

Suggestions then came hard and fast from around the table.

"*Discoveries.*"

"*Exploring the Unknown.*"

"*Secret Journeys.*"

"*Contours and Continents.*"

"More like *Contortions and Continents,*" added Hilary to much laughter.

"What about *Around the World in Eighty Positions* or *Travels with My Arse.*"

"*Liz,*" they remonstrated, laughing uncontrollably, but she was unstoppable.

"*A Tale of Two Titties…*

"*Potholing for Beginners…*

"*Titty Titty Bang Bang…*

The Rise and Fall of…" She couldn't continue for laughing.

Their raucous laughter attracted the stares of other diners and, when Hilary, with tears of laughter smearing her make-up, was tapped on the shoulder, she turned guiltily, expecting to be told off, but instead saw a smiling Sarah standing behind her.

"I thought it was you, but Tom said it couldn't be. 'Too young,' he said. You look lovely."

Hilary stood up to give her a hug, almost toppling off her heels.

"Oh Hilary, what a transformation," said Sarah, discreetly steadying her. "I won't disturb you. Is this a Christmas celebration?"

"We're celebrating all sorts," explained Suzanne. "Christmas, a wedding, a trip of a lifetime, a new Hilary. Oh, and you know, just getting through another year," she tailed off.

"I'll get back to Tom."

"Give him my love. We'll get together in the new year. Have a lovely Christmas. If I'd known I was going to see you today, I'd have brought Luke's present. I'll drop it round."

"Thank you so much, Hilary." Sarah blew a kiss and went back to her table.

With the plates cleared, they settled down to the serious business of choosing dessert, the book and everything else forgotten for the moment.

Talk then turned to Liz's wedding.

"Oh no. I'll miss it," said Chahna.

"Not necessarily," replied Liz. "We haven't set a date yet and you know what it's like trying to book a venue – it's two years in advance for some."

"Do I detect a little reluctance?"

"No," replied Liz, not very convincingly. "But there's no rush and to be honest I'm fed up with talking weddings. It's the only topic of conversation in our house and Mum never stops. Funnily enough, I would love it if we were arranging Lisa's wedding, but I hate all the fuss. Oh, we'll get it sorted." She sloshed a little wine into her glass and passed the bottle around again, Suzanne taking the last drop.

"Let's have a toast to change."

"To change," they chorused.

"It's certainly all change around here."

They became thoughtful then, and Carol said, out of the blue, "What about *Secret Journeys?*"

"I like the sound of that."

"Yes."

"I think it might work."

"I'd better read it though. It might not fit. I'm only going on what you've said. The title is very important," added Carol.

"Here's pudding." The desserts were distributed and talk stopped while proper attention was paid to the delicious delicacies presented to them.

Later that night, Hilary lay in bed wondering what her mum would have thought of all that loud laughter and Liz's irreverence. But Liz wasn't being irreverent, just having fun with words. Liz was the one who really thought publication was worth pursuing. She had investigated what the next stage would be. She wasn't doing it for the money because she had no stake in it. Liz had been kind to her in the past in an offhand sort of way, but Hilary knew she hadn't really noticed her. All of a sudden, because of her mum's legacy, she had become interesting. But perhaps she wasn't being fair – she had always been in the background, never wanting to be noticed.

The others had shown an interest, but she wasn't sure it was their sort of book. What sort of book was it? If it was published, who would read it with its dated language and lack of plot? If it sold, the money would be nice, but the bungalow was paid for and she had enough for the bills. She had never been a big spender; her savings were substantial.

After seeing her mother go so suddenly, the need to squirrel away money seemed less important. It wasn't earning much just sitting in the bank, so she might as well do something else with it. If the book brought in some money, all to the good. Perhaps she could donate some to one of her mother's favourite charities. Her thoughts dwindled to images of the day, a smile coming to her lips before she fell into a deep sleep.

Her mother was reading to her, her voice soft and soothing. Hilary was lying naked, draped in a cover made of ostrich feathers, the fronds tickling her skin. She was five, then she was fifty. Her mother was stroking her brow. Hilary strained to hear the words she was reading but she couldn't distinguish them. Then she was surrounded by words, huge wooden words, plastic scrabble words, words carved into gravestones. The ostrich feathers had gone, wood splinters were sticking into her arm, the rough stone scraping her back. The soft voice had stopped, but her mother was pushing her hands into Hilary's stomach, stopping her from breathing. Hilary woke to find Hector with his favourite stick lying on top of her.

"GET OFF," she shouted, scrabbling to get him and the duvet off. "What on earth are you doing here?"

She was out of bed, pulling on her dressing gown. She realised that she had left the bedroom door open and, what with the unaccustomed late night, Hector had strayed from his usual routine.

"Bad dog," she said, but not very convincingly, and as she absentmindedly stroked him, he realised he wasn't in as much trouble as he had first thought.

Hilary tried to catch her dream. The feeling of total relaxation with her mother remained, but the rest was gone.

Chapter Twenty-Five

A Christmas Drink

"What have you got planned for Christmas? I shall certainly be down here Christmas lunchtime, escaping a houseful of women. You are open Christmas Day, aren't you?" David called over his shoulder, as he picked his drink off the bar and threaded his way to the table.

"Till two," Sheila threw after his departing back.

"I'll tell him," John said, picking up his pint from the bar. "He never waits for an answer."

John joined David at the table. "I'll be here with you Christmas morning for precisely the same reason – escaping the women and, in my case, the incessant wedding talk. I naively imagined Liz and I would say a few words in front of a registrar and have a family lunch. Pearl is the worst. Her plans would rival a royal wedding. How come you've got a houseful? There's only Suzanne, oh, and your mum, of course."

"Suzanne has invited that woman we met on holiday, the one whose husband died. She's nice enough, but you'd think she'd want to be with her own family – but no, she jumped at the chance. She'll be here till after the New Year. Arrives two days before Christmas Eve, day after tomorrow." David pulled a face and took a drink from his pint. "That's not all. She's also invited Hilary from opposite. They'll be able to compare notes – we'll talk about death the whole time. Mum likes nothing better than a good funeral. Suzanne is too kind for her own good and she's working right up to the last minute. It's her turn to cover Christmas Eve."

"She'll get it all done, though. She's amazing. You'll enjoy it."

"We'll see… Will you be joining us, Richard?"

"Joining you in what?" Richard put his pint down before unwinding his scarf and taking his coat off.

"Christmas morning here, before lunch and before we get swallowed up by hordes of women."

"Can't, sorry. We're off to be with Janet's parents. At least I can take her dad for a drink. I find it so depressing with her mum. I don't know how he does it. I don't know how Janet copes, come to that. But Claire's coming with us. She'll brighten the day. At least Janet's sister, Julia, won't be there. She's off to Mexico. She's no help at all and she drives Janet mad. Still, she's fun."

"Siobhan makes Christmas wonderful. It's all a bit forced without children, isn't it? Sitting round in paper hats, eating and drinking too much, sleeping in front of the telly."

"No danger of that in our house. Suzanne has quizzes and games planned after we've all been for a walk with that daft dog of Hilary's. Even more reason for me to have a drink first."

"Siobhan believes in Father Christmas. It's lovely," persisted John.

David grunted, finished his pint and got up to get another one.

"Half our lot believe and the others take the mickey out of them, but they all like to get their stockings on Christmas morning. There'd be hell to pay if Santa Claus missed one of them. Carol is just as bad – Father Christmas has to bring her a present as well. It'll be a squash as usual, but I love having them all to stay. Carol's cooking and baking. I don't know how she finds the time." Jonathan had joined them with his drink and taken his coat off to reveal a bright green jumper with a red-nosed reindeer emblazoned across the front. David looked at it askance as he came back with fresh drinks for John and himself.

"We've been to see Father Christmas," said Jonathan, by way of an explanation. "I don't know how they put up with it. Most of the children are revolting, except our grandchildren, of course."

John took his drink and before David could say anything about children or Christmas, he said, "How's the planning application going? Any objections yet?"

Talk turned to David's project and, in spite of Jonathan's jumper and an interruption by a group of carol singers, they managed to avoid all talk of Christmas for the rest of the evening.

"I'm off. See you Christmas Day or, if not, then New Year's Eve. That'll be different too. Jag and Chahna are off on Christmas Day, so they won't be there. Mum will be there and, of course, Esmee. All change."

"See you Christmas Day, about midday."

David left, battling through the crowds to the door.

"Do you think children will be allowed? I'll ask next time I'm at the bar. We could all come then."

"That'll cheer David up no end, a pub full of children. He's not usually such a misery."

"Oh, he'll be fine. A few drinks down him and he'll be the life and soul as usual. Anyway, I'm off too. Two more days at work and then it all starts. We're driving up Christmas Eve, so see you at New Year. Merry Christmas." Richard wrapped himself up again and pushed his way out, smiling and acknowledging friends and acquaintances as he struggled through the crowd.

David left his car at the pub and started to walk home. He'd drunk more than he'd intended. He'd only gone in for one. Oh well, the walk would do him good and keep him out of the house a bit longer. Suzanne was on an organisational express train. There were lists everywhere, everything he put down she moved, she was most unlike herself. It suddenly came to him that it might be Jag leaving for twelve months that was giving her the jitters. Jag had been there for her right from the start; she rarely needed to ask advice, but when she did, he was always supportive. She knew more than Jag about lots of things but it still must feel as though the rug was being pulled from under her feet. A year is a long time and she had mentioned last night that she wasn't sure whether she'd get on with the locum as she seemed too sure of herself. It was all just so unlike Suzanne.

David hoped that he was right and it was Jag going that was upsetting her. He could deal with that, be understanding, stay out of the way or just be there, whichever was needed at the time. He hoped there was nothing else. He hoped that was what was wrong with her.

He felt calmer for working things out. He was glad he'd walked now and regretted being such a grump in the pub. He didn't like feeling unsure. He liked to be in control or just know what was happening. Perhaps he'd ask her tonight, see if he could do anything to help. Probably not. But just acknowledging it might put her back on track. And if he was completely on the wrong tack, perhaps she'd give him a clue about what was troubling her. He wanted his Suzanne back.

Chapter Twenty-Six

Christmas Preparations

Hilary wept noisily as she surveyed the gifts that she had bought, without thinking, for her mother's Christmas stocking. For many years, they hadn't bought big presents for each other. If they needed or wanted anything, they bought it as the need or desire arose. But the tradition of Christmas stockings lived on, stockings filled with extravagant lotions and potions, pointless pretty trinkets and hardback books. As her mother had become less mobile and less able to get out, she had mastered the internet and continued to surprise Hilary with presents from Father Christmas.

On the bed next to her was a bottle of rose-scented body lotion, the glass bottle decorated with enamel rose buds, a string of blue glass beads – her mother loved coloured beads to brighten up her plain jumpers – and a large, heavy new biography of Queen Victoria.

What had she been thinking of?

The body lotion she had bought soon after her mother's death, on one of her rare forays into town during those dark days when she was still setting two places at the table and putting her head around her mother's bedroom door to ask if she needed anything before bed. She had no recollection of buying it, but the faded receipt told the story and she had hidden it with the Christmas decorations, just as she always had.

Hilary remembered buying the beads before her mother died, feeling embarrassed that she was buying a Christmas present in January – but the colour had been so perfect. She had carefully chosen a box to set the beads off and had hidden it with the decorations.

The book had been the most recent purchase. An email from Amazon highlighting her interest in similar books prompted the thought, 'Oh, Mum would love that' and two clicks later it was on its way. It had arrived as she was getting the Christmas decorations out.

"Stop crying," she told herself crossly, and scrubbed at her face with a tissue. She put the presents to one side and started pulling the Christmas tree out of its box. Bits of green plastic scattered on the floor; the branches were bent and twisted from their imprisonment in the long tatty box. She surveyed the tree after pulling out the branches and straightening the top. Its plastic stand was a little lopsided with the remnants of last year's red crepe bow clinging to one leg.

"It'll do for this year, then perhaps we'd better get a new one," she told Hector. He sniffed around the base but found nothing of interest. As far as he was concerned, she could get rid of it now.

She pulled it backwards through the door into the living room and stood it in front of the window. She straightened the branches again and sighed at the trail of the bright green 'pine needles'.

"Right, let's get this decorated." She returned to the bedroom and picked up the plastic box crammed with baubles, tinsel and lights, decorations they had collected over the years.

Not for Hilary the stylish white or silver favoured by Suzanne and Janet. She loved the bright colours and sparkle, the gaudiness, the childishness. She opened the box. The multicoloured lights were twisted around the branches first. The action made her think of her father. It had always been his job to untangle the lights and replace the bulbs that had gone. Like everything else, he had taken it very seriously and the real decoration of the tree couldn't start until the lights were done to his satisfaction.

He was there in her mind again when she took out the box of tiny wooden figures that had been bought on a holiday in Germany. She and her mother had chosen them, rejecting ones with less happy expressions or imperfectly painted costumes, taking their time, to the amusement of the shopkeeper and the frustration of her father. She could almost hear him harrumphing in the background as she just as painstakingly chose the right spot for them on the tree. To cheer him up, Hilary put the bright red glass baubles with the gold necks onto the tree next. Then she started on the decorations that she and her mother had bought each year since he died. Christmas teddies, dogs with happy smiling faces, fairies and cherubs, drums, parcels, bells and sprigs of holly. The branches were soon laden with gaudy decorations, each item evoking its own memory.

Finally, with an elastic band, she attached the fairy, resplendent in a pink Barbie ball gown, to the very top of the tree.

She stood back and smiled. She could feel her mother looking over her shoulder from what was now Hector's chair. She could feel her approval and, as she thought fondly of her mother, she knew what she would do with those presents that she had bought.

Sarah would love the body lotion and the vintage style of the bottle would enhance the bathroom she was trying to create. She certainly wouldn't be buying that expensive body lotion for herself. She was more likely to pinch a bit of Luke's baby lotion, if she thought about her skin at all.

Liz would love the beads. She'd probably wear them with lots of other strands of beads and pieces of jewellery, or Hilary could even imagine her looping them through her hair.

Carol (and probably Jonathan) would enjoy the book about Queen Victoria. As staunch Royalists, they devoured books, films and television programmes about the Royal family but such an expensive tome was not one they would buy for themselves.

I'll enjoy having a look around for presents for Janet and Suzanne and, if I'm quick, I can get something for Chahna before she leaves.

Thanks, Mum.

"New Year is going to be a bit different this year. I think I might do a buffet instead of a sit-down meal."

Suzanne and Betty were sorting through the boxes of white and silver decorations. The eight-foot Christmas tree stood in the corner of the square panelled hall, patiently awaiting their ministrations.

"I love these glass baubles. You have some beautiful pieces, such exquisite taste. I love all this white and silver, but the boys and Bill always wanted the bright colours and flashing lights. I remember once, years ago, decorating our tree all in white. I thought it looked beautiful, as if snow was glistening on the branches. Like a winter wonderland. Bill came in and asked when I was going to decorate the tree, James said it looked too posh for our front room and David asked me if I wanted him to get the decorations out of the loft. I felt crushed when, in the end, the only thing you could see of all my efforts was the silver star on the top."

"Philistines. I like the green and red of Christmas but it doesn't look right here. I didn't think I was being posh, just trying to fit in with what David already had. Anyway, let's get started. You twist that bower in and out of the bannisters and I'll get the lights on the tree, then we can decorate it together. It's lovely to have someone to do it with. David just leaves me to it. In fact, I sometimes wonder if he thinks it all happens by magic."

"I can help at New Year too. In fact, why don't you ask everyone to bring a dish? As long as you organise it and tell them what sort of things to bring – otherwise you are likely to end up with five quiches and two trifles."

"A variation on the five loaves and two fishes. It sometimes feels as though I am feeding the five thousand, the amount we all eat. That's a good idea. I love cooking but the last couple of years it's felt a bit more of a chore and I've just ended up doing the same things, really."

"Let's make a bit of a list when we've done this and then you can start getting in touch with people, see what they think. I'm sure they won't mind." Betty was enjoying being involved.

"Good idea," Suzanne replied, pulling the steps out of the cupboard under the stairs. She climbed to the top, trailing the silver lights after her, and started to loop them around the branches.

Together they started to put the ornaments onto the tree. Then, without a word, she went into the dining room and retrieved a chair, placing it so that Betty was next to the box of decorations. From there, she could sit and unwrap them from their tissue paper and pass them to Suzanne to attach them to the tree. Suzanne had seen Betty's fingers fumble with the fine white ribbon on the delicate glass baubles, the look of fear on her face as she almost dropped a crystal icicle and then the wince of pain as she stretched to reach the branches.

Surveying their handiwork a little later, Suzanne said, "Right, I'll get the vacuum and get up all the pine needles and sparkles. At least trees don't drop all their needles like they used to. I think they must spray them with glue or something."

"Shall I put the kettle on?"

Suzanne could easily and more quickly have made two coffees using her up-to-the-minute coffee machine, but she knew Betty was afraid of the machine with its noisy grinder, multitude of dials and lights, and the angry-sounding steam.

She still pinched herself about how quickly she and Betty had slotted in together. They still phoned before visiting and knocked on each other's doors. They treated each other and each other's space with respect. It worked. Betty felt useful and wasn't lonely. Suzanne knew that David was more relaxed, knowing that his mother was nearby and safe. For all his bluff and bluster, he was a worrier. As she vacuumed, she smiled to herself; she probably knew more about David now from his mother's stories.

Vacuuming done, she went through to the kitchen to find Betty, pen poised over the back of an envelope fished out of the recycling. Headings of starter, main, dessert and cheese had been written in her spidery hand. She started to get up to make the coffee but Suzanne gently pushed her back into her seat and made two mugs of instant coffee.

"Do you think we need to ask people first or is it easier just to tell people what we want?"

"Tell them. Everyone has enough to think about around Christmas without more decisions to make."

"Think I'd still like to do it as a sit-down meal. It might be easier, really, than us milling about with plates and glasses. David and I will provide all the drink. I think he's already ordered the Champagne, anyway," Suzanne continued.

Suzanne pulled her laptop towards her and started to compose an email to the group, removing Chahna and adding Esmee to her list of recipients.

Subject: New Year – All change

Dear All,

With all the changes this year, I thought we'd change the format of the New Year's Eve party. I hope you don't think that this is too short notice, but I wondered if you would all be willing to bring a dish – starter, main or dessert – to make up our meal.

Esmee, I did wonder if I could ask you to bring the cheese and biscuits? That might be a bit easier to carry than a casserole or trifle on the train.

We need:

One starter

One meat main/one fish main–I will do all the vegetables, once I know what the mains are.

A couple of desserts

Don't go making exotic dishes (unless you want to). Shop bought is fine.

We will be eleven as usual (although a different eleven).

I don't want to add to the pressure of Christmas. I just thought it would make a nice change. If it's a disaster, we'll go back to Plan A next year.

Love,

Suzanne

xx

Everyone must have been looking at their emails at that exact moment, because the replies soon came in and Betty's list was populated with delicious-sounding food. Suzanne had her menu planned.

Everyone thought it was a good idea. Liz summed their feelings up in her reply:

> Great. This way we can carry on enjoying the party without feeling that we are putting on Suzanne and David and without feeling the need to offer to have it at ours. L

Later that evening, Carol and Hilary contacted Suzanne, both with favours to ask. Suzanne found it easy to say yes to both. Carol's brother would be on his own, having recently separated from his wife. He would hopefully be with his daughters for Christmas, but faced a lonely New Year.

Suzanne replied:

> Perfect that will even up the numbers. The women side of the table was getting a bit top heavy. x

Then Hilary asked if she could bring Hector:

> I'm not sure how he'll be with the fireworks. I stayed in with him on Bonfire Night. He wanted to be near me the whole time and that was with the television on and the curtains drawn. I'll bring his bed – he'll sleep in the corner most of the time. x

Suzanne could see no reason to refuse. David might have something to say but she'd get round him. That reminded her, she had better add stilton to her list of things to get. She wasn't sure if there was such a thing as Dutch blue cheese and it was better to be prepared. David was a bit fussy when it came to cheese.

All sorted.

*

Carol put the phone down with a grimace. Her younger brother was worrying her. Once lively and fun, he was now flat and monosyllabic. She wished she could do more but they didn't have room to take him in and, anyway, he needed to carry on working. She was glad she could help over New Year. He could certainly stay for the few days after Christmas and then from New Year until he returned to work on the fifth.

She couldn't believe what her sister-in-law had done. She and Joy had never been close, physical distance and busy lives getting in the way, but she just wouldn't have believed that she'd leave Dan and set up home with another woman. But that was just what Joy had done. She'd always thought she was a bit intense, all those causes and committees, but she had brought the girls up well, lovely girls, a credit to both of them. Amazingly, the girls weren't taking sides. In fact, they seemed more balanced than she would have believed. What a situation!

However, according to Dan, the village *was* taking sides, making it even more difficult.

The other woman was on the parish council. Bizarrely, they'd met when Joy was protesting about plans for new houses on some land with some sort of special significance. Dan had agreed and even gone along to one of the meetings. Joy had stayed late at that meeting, and several other meetings. He had been proud of her, proud of her persistence; he'd had no idea what was going on. He had lost his wife, and planning permission for the houses had been passed.

Joy would stay in the village and Dan was currently living in a Travelodge near his office. He couldn't stay in the village. He would move away once the house was sold. He couldn't stand all the pitying glances and muttered asides from other men, as if he was deficient in some way.

Oh, Dan, thought Carol, remembering the little boy she had taken to the park, armed with fishing nets and jam jars, in search of sticklebacks.

Poor you.

At Dan's request, she had told their mum the bare bones of the story. Their mother didn't need the details. She'd never liked Joy, too loud, too strong for her little boy. Dan didn't need his mother going on about how he could have done better.

"Shall we put up the Christmas decorations at the weekend?" Jonathan startled her out of her reverie.

"Brilliant idea – it'll occupy you and the little ones. You've remembered we've got all three the whole weekend. You can do it while I go and see Mum. Shall I go to your dad too?"

"If you like. Let's get the stuff down from the loft and I'll pick up a tree tomorrow with the big van."

"Not as big as last year. We want to have it inside." They both laughed, remembering the six-foot tree that had ended up in their tiny front garden when they couldn't get it along the hall into the living room. "You are more of a child than the grandchildren when it comes to Christmas…"

"Let me, let me." Siobhan climbed onto the bar stool and tried to elbow John out of the way.

"Careful, pickle, you'll knock me over." John was spearing the Christmas cake with a metal cake tester. He handed the spike to Siobhan and allowed her to dot the cake with deep holes.

"Enough, enough, we don't want it to fall apart. We just have to put some brandy on it now."

He took the brandy bottle and poured some into a teaspoon.

"Yuck, that's horrid, ugh…" Siobhan pulled a face and tried to push her stool away from the counter.

"It's like medicine for the cake. It soaks in and then the cake smells lovely."

She watched from a safe distance as he spooned the amber liquid over the cake. It sank in, leaving the surface glistening, the vapour of the brandy combining with the sweet smell of the fruit.

"I don't like medicine, it always tastes yuck, but he's drinking it like a good cake."

"Now we wrap him up again in foil and put him back in the tin to sleep till next week and then we can put his coat of marzipan and icing on. I'm sure Nanny will let you help with that."

"Will you, Nanny?" She turned to Liz, who was stirring a pudding.

"Of course, poppet. Come and help me stir this pudding, then we can put it on to cook."

Siobhan clambered off the stool and dragged it over to the sink where Liz was working on the draining board. John seemed to need the whole work surface for the operation with the cake.

"Mmmmm, smells like something out of a Dickens story in here. Proper Christmas." Lisa put her head around the door. "Have you been good, young lady?"

"We stabbed the cake and gave it some yucky medicine to make it better. Now I'm making a pudding for Nanny."

"She's been as good as gold. How was work?"

"Oh, you know…"

"I'll put the kettle on," said John, putting the cake tin back on top of the kitchen cupboard.

"Come on, Siobhan, let's get this in the bowl, then we have to tie a hat on and put it in the steamer."

Siobhan was peering through the holes in the bottom of the steamer. She put it down for Liz to put the pudding in and soon it was steaming quietly on the hob.

Liz looked at Lisa, who was looking tired and pale. She felt guilty for upsetting her earlier. At least Lisa seemed to have stopped sulking now. She'd got upset yesterday when Liz had refused to look after Siobhan on New Year's Eve.

"But you always go out," Lisa had whined like a child.

Liz had had to remind her that she and John had hardly gone out when Lisa and Edward were children and that she hardly ever refused to take care of Siobhan.

Liz had to stand firm against several rounds of "But Mum…"

Then when Lisa had dropped Siobhan off on her way to work this morning, she had looked so forlorn and tired Liz had almost relented, but a warning look from John, as if he had read her mind, stopped her.

They had talked about it over coffee while Siobhan was watching *Peppa Pig.*

"The big sulk yesterday really annoyed me," John said. "You do enough."

"I know, but I do wonder if it's more than just a New Year party. Perhaps she's got a date? She could do with cheering up. I certainly wasn't going to give in to that sulk but we'll see how she is later. I could ask Suzanne if Siobhan could sleep upstairs at theirs and we could take her buggy to bring her back. She still just about fits in."

"You've been thinking about it, haven't you?"

"Well…"

"Perhaps check with Suzanne before putting it to Lisa though – we don't want to get her hopes up. David isn't that keen on children. It would be nice," he continued, "if she found someone, but just to go out with friends would do her good. She's been a bit low lately. I don't suppose I helped by disappearing like that."

"We're past that now," said Liz briskly, but she touched his arm as she went past. "I'll go and phone Suzanne now. Can you go and see what madam's doing? I can't hear the video."

Suzanne, of course, said yes to the little visitor and arrangements were made. She'd leave it till the last minute to tell David, although hopefully it shouldn't affect the evening.

Lisa was over the moon and hugged Liz and then John and then had to hug Siobhan as she complained about being left out.

"Will I sleep in a big bed? Can I take Teddy and Sukey? Will I have my tea there?"

Janet hadn't wanted to put the Christmas decorations up. After all, they were going to be away for most of the holiday and it was such a hassle getting them down from the loft and putting them up, only to take them all down again a fortnight later. She couldn't really be bothered with any of it. She'd ordered all the food they needed to take to her parents. All she had to do was remember to collect it from the shop. It was the first Christmas since she and Richard had been together that she hadn't made a cake and Christmas pudding. She couldn't be bothered with mince pies; she didn't like bought ones, but they'd have to do. She ordered ready-prepared vegetables; she wouldn't even have to peel a parsnip. This way even did away with the washing up – all the containers went straight in the bin. Christmas had never felt a chore before. There was no joy in choosing a present for someone who didn't know what the occasion was and who, on the day, probably wouldn't recognise the gift-giver. She'd tried to find nice things for Richard, Claire, her dad and others, but everything seemed a bit tacky, a bit forced. Still, she'd done her shopping and everything was wrapped and ready to go.

She'd got the decorations out after Richard had pointed out gently, at breakfast, that burglars looked for houses with no decorations or lights, assuming (usually correctly) that the occupants were away. She couldn't cope with a burglary on top of everything else. Richard enthused about the tree and the other decorations when he got home, but she knew they looked a bit lacklustre.

Oh well, it would soon be over…

Jag and Chahna's house was crammed with Christmas lights and baubles. The girls loved it all and had decorated every corner when they arrived home from university.

Jag and Chahna left them to it. Their cases were packed, paperwork all sorted. They were ready for an adventure.

Chapter Twenty-Seven

Christmas Morning

"The dog was a real success," Claire said to her mum as they sorted through the trays of turkey, stuffing, pigs in blankets and vegetables, trying to work out the timings, so that it would all be ready at the same time.

"I needn't have spent all that time choosing the one with the cutest face. She's as happy staring at his bottom as his face."

"But," persisted Claire, "she loves the feel of him. She's cuddled him all morning and I couldn't believe that when she saw him, she said, 'Hector'."

"Neither could I. It's awful that she can't remember our names or the name of the man she's been married to for nearly sixty years, but she related that toy to a dog she's met once." Janet sounded unnaturally bitter.

"But mum, she loves him – that's the main thing. She smiled. There was almost a light in her eyes. We have to be thankful for small mercies."

"I know," said Janet, touching Claire's arm. "I'm sorry I'm such a misery. I just wish it was like it used to be with Mum bossing me about."

The doorbell went.

"They can't be back already. Have they forgotten their key? Has there been an accident?" Janet sounded a little panicky. Richard had taken George to the pub.

"No, Mum, it's Julia," said Claire, looking up the hall and seeing her aunt's outline distorted by the bevelled glass at the side of the front door.

"She's supposed to be in Mexico," Janet wailed, wondering if there would be enough food for them all. Trust Julia just to turn up unannounced. Considering she worked in IT, she was hopeless at using her phone or communicating in any way. They were all supposed to work around her. Janet pushed these unchristian thoughts aside and went up the hall to give her rather damp sister a hug.

"Have you walked?" she asked, surprised. Julia went everywhere by taxi.

"Only from the station. The person in front of me took the last cab and I couldn't be bothered to wait in the rain."

"What are you doing here? I thought you were in Mexico for Christmas."

"No, we're not going until Wednesday now. We'll be there for New Year. Someone made a cock up with the booking." From the look on her face, that someone was going to have to work hard for forgiveness. "So I thought I'd better come here. I'd never have heard the end of it if I'd been in the country for Christmas and not visited the folks. Where are they?"

"Grandma's in the living room and Richard has taken Grandad to the pub," answered Claire, correctly guessing that her mum was trying to digest Julia's last statement, remembering many Christmases with her grandparents when her mum had had to explain or excuse Julia's absence.

Julia put her head around the living-room door, but seeing her mother was asleep, she pulled the door to and said, "Let's have a sherry while it's all quiet. Looks like dinner is all prepared. There'd better be enough for me," she added, digging Janet in the ribs.

Claire leapt to her mother's rescue again. "There's plenty – I'll go and get the sherry." She returned from the dining room with the bottle of sherry and three of her grandma's sherry glasses.

"You always over-cater, don't you… Just in case."

252

"Just as well I do," replied Janet, a little tersely. "Otherwise some people would go hungry."

"Temper, temper," said Julia, good-naturedly, taking a glass of sherry and opening tins until she found the mince pies. "Mmmmm, homemade, perfect." Janet didn't bother to correct her.

George and Richard sat in companionable silence on the edge of the noisy jollity of the Christmas drinkers in The Dancing Bear, sipping their beer, lost in thought. George was comfortable to be in male company in the absence of any demand, and Richard was happy to have found a way to be helpful and stay out of the way at the same time.

Like synchronised swimmers, they simultaneously put their glasses among the sticky rings on the dark wood table. A glance between them was correctly interpreted by Richard, and, picking up the glasses, he fought his way from the safety of their window seat to the scrum at the bar. Sometime later he returned with two halves and nudged George awake as he sat down.

They resumed their quiet contemplation of other people's Christmases.

The pub was packed with regulars being extra jolly. Ben was beaming for once, the lights on his Christmas jumper dipping in the beer on the counter as he stretched across to pass drinks. There were lots of people who only came out on high days and holidays, looking slightly uncomfortable, as if they didn't know how to behave, like the crowds who had packed the church for Midnight Mass.

David was back on form, talking to John and Jonathan, shouting over the melee. They held their drinks above their heads as people tried to get past.

"I got it wrong. Esmee is coming two days before New Year, so it's just Hilary and Mum joining us for lunch. They're busy in the kitchen now."

"Or starting on the sherry."

"Or both."

David couldn't believe how unreasonably relieved he had felt to find that Esmee wasn't joining them for Christmas. He couldn't explain it, so he just accepted the feeling. Hilary was OK, and she always wanted to help, which let him off the hook. He wondered if it would be different from the last few years since Dad had died and Mum had started to come to them for Christmas Day. It had always been a bit strained, Mum keen to be taken home as soon as they put their pudding spoons down, not wanting to be in the way, and Suzanne leaving him to do a lot of the talking, reminiscing about Christmases past. They could never have pre-dinner drinks in the pub because one of them had to be able to take her home. Betty would never stay and always said that she would be happy to have a quiet Christmas on her own, but Suzanne wouldn't let him agree to that.

David was pulled back to the moment as a sudden break in the crowd revealed three people leaving a table by the window. Gesturing to the others, he pushed his way through to secure the seats, saying Happy Christmas to the family gathering scarves and hats. A sulky teenager raised her eyebrows to the ceiling as her father responded with the usual 'Jump in my grave as quick?' quip, and then, with another round of Happy Christmas, they were gone.

"That's better," said John, as he eased into the chair.

They settled down to enjoy the short time remaining before they were expected back for the celebrations.

The Christmas dinner was perfect and now Suzanne was walking carefully through from the kitchen with the pudding surrounded by a blue flame, Hilary fussing around the table with brandy butter, a jug of custard and a bowl of cream.

David looked across at his mother, her face smiling, her shiny purple hat rakishly askew. Suzanne had done them proud and, for once, everyone was relaxed. The table looked stylish, with silver-sprayed holly and ivy weaving around the base of the candelabra, soft Christmas music playing in the background. Even the crackers had revealed useful presents and hats that fit (Suzanne still hadn't told

David how much they cost). It was like something out of a picture book.

The flames died as Suzanne put the pudding down, and with it the picture-book image. He took a sip of the dessert wine that Hilary had brought and tried not to let the distaste show on his face as the sickly sweet wine went stickily down his throat.

"Mmmm, lovely," said Betty, holding her glass up to Hilary, who was adding custard to the pudding already smothered in melting brandy butter and cream.

Hilary lifted her glass and toasted them all, saying, "Thank you for a wonderful lunch. I'm so glad you persuaded me not to spend it on my own. Have you seen what's on television? Nothing, nothing at all. Whatever happened to *Morecambe and Wise* and *The Wizard of Oz*? Hector and I would have had a miserable time."

Things were not so perfect in Carol and Jonathan's house. The grandchildren were squabbling over what to watch, their parents trying to restore order. Although it sounded as though there were thirty children in the house, only two of their children and four of their grandchildren had joined them this year. The living room was strewn with wrapping paper, sweets, presents, games and DVDs. Their daughter Lucy was going round picking things up, holding them aloft.

"Whose is this?"

"Who bought it for you?"

"Why didn't you put the label with it as I told you?"

Dan was helping Carol and Jonathan to clear the table. "She sounds like our mum. Do they still have to sit down and write thank you letters?"

"We try to get them to, but it's mostly texts now. Shame really. You can't keep those in a keepsake box. Mum still has all of ours."

Dan smiled. "Thank you for letting me come at the last minute. At least all your lot took my mind off things for a while. Will they be staying?"

"No," said Jonathan and Carol together.

"They'll go after tea, then they have to descend on in-laws for Boxing Day. You can stay though," added Carol.

"I'll see. Can I wash up?"

"You always hated drying," said Carol, playfully cuffing his ear.

"Is it OK if I leave you two to it?" Jonathan left to broker peace in the living room so that he could sit down and have a bit of a nap.

Dan had his hands in the hot soapy water. "I think the biggest loser is the village. All those new houses behind the church will completely change the character. She was bewitched by *that* woman. We were bored and boring and Joy wanted a big adventure. It started with a fight against developers and ended... I feel such a fool for not seeing what was coming and feel betrayed by all my friends – well most of them. Some were just weak and swept along. I don't blame them. They *have* to stay in the village."

Carol took the clean plates from the drainer and dried them, putting them back in the rack above the dresser. She didn't want to stop Dan's flow by asking questions; at least he was talking now. She had been so worried about him. He turned now and handed her the big vegetable dish that had been their grandmother's.

"The girls have been so good, so grown up. I think it would have been different if they had still been at home. What a nightmare if they'd still been at school. Prejudice is alive and well in rural England but it's a prejudice against the ordinary. Everyone is looking for excitement, trying to be different, but by trying to be different, they all end up the same. They certainly aren't the only gays in the village!"

He changed the water in the bowl. "Just when we thought, or I thought we thought, that we could start to do things together, just the two of us, she goes and finds another partner. Devastated doesn't describe how I felt. Humiliated. Wrong footed. Stupid. Blind. My only consolation, and it's no consolation really, was that the girls didn't know either. I can take all the criticism, all the jeers and jokes. What I can't take is all the pity – the pitying glances from people who I thought were friends, as if they think I am deficient in some way. And people avoid you as if it's catching."

"I think it's more that they haven't a clue what to say, like after a death," put in Carol, although she didn't think he heard her.

"For all our forward thinking and openness, when something like this happens, our own and others' reactions are like something out of a Victorian melodrama."

Carol took a handful of dripping cutlery and, getting another cloth out of the drawer, started to dry it.

"I'm really sorry I had to lie to you at your party. I couldn't tell you the real reason she wasn't there."

"It's OK, I understand. I thought you must have had a row or something but never imagined anything like this. I still can't really believe it."

"I made the girls promise not to say anything to anyone there. They were happy to agree. I think then they were hoping, like me, that it would all blow over. It's been quite an adjustment for them. So we just all agreed to say that she was poorly."

The washing up continued in silence for a few minutes. Jonathan came through with a few more glasses and plates that he had found while trying to clear a space to sit down. Seeing they were in the middle of something, he discreetly shut the kitchen door.

"The trouble is, she's still the same person with the same life. I went around to get some of my things – yes, Joy's in the house," he added, as if Carol had asked a question. "We'll sort it out later. We'll have to sell and divide it up, I think, unless she can buy me out. Anyway, I went around to get some stuff and there was Joy, doing the ironing in front of *Coronation Street*. I could see *her* in the kitchen, mashing swede and potato, the sausages sizzling in the pan. It could have been us on any Wednesday night in the last twenty-five years. I couldn't have been more surprised if they'd been cavorting naked on a bear-skin rug in front of the fire."

Carol started giggling and, in spite of himself, Dan laughed too. It was just like when they had been children and they had frequently set each other off into fits of giggles, laughter spreading from one to the other like a virus, resulting in black looks from their mother when it happened at the table or in public.

Soon they were leaning over the draining board, the tension of the last few weeks bursting through Dan into loud guffaws of laughter that brought the rest of the family to the kitchen door to see what was happening.

Carol flapped them away with the damp kitchen towel, and leaned against the door, exhausted. "Oh Dan, I'm so sorry. I'm not laughing at you, but the picture you painted just touched my funny bone."

Looking at each other, they were off again, leaning into each other until tears rained down their cheeks.

"I'll never be able to watch *Coronation Street* again without that bear-skin rug getting mixed up in it," spluttered Carol.

The washing up that wouldn't fit in the dishwasher was piled up on the work surface. Liz looked at it and then got another bottle of wine out of the fridge. Lisa had taken a very excited and tired Siobhan home, and John was just giving Pearl a lift back to her flat. Peace reigned.

Liz sat down, filled her glass and stared at the muted television. A gaudy cartoon was playing, characters with impossibly big eyes gadding about. She left it and, leaning her head back against the chair, shut her eyes.

The pictures that came into her mind made her eyes spring open, their horrified look mirroring the cartoon characters. She had seen a Christmas without John, like a reverse version of *A Christmas Carol*. She took a large gulp of wine and, taking the TV remote control, turned to the pretend normality of *Call the Midwife*.

The three adjacent seats taken by Jag, Chahna and his mother were now at 32,000 feet above the Black Sea. They were on their way to their adventurous year in India.

If my mother tells anyone else on this plane that I am a doctor, I will have to gag her, thought Jag as, for the hundredth time, his mother told another unsuspecting stranger about her brilliant doctor son.

I hope I am as proud of my children as Mother is, when I am older, Chahna thought sleepily.

Finishing her story to the man stretching his legs in the aisle, Harini closed her eyes and wondered if the village just outside Mumbai where she was born had changed. She fell asleep dreaming of all those people who she could proudly tell about her son, the doctor.

Chapter Twenty-Eight

New Year's Eve

"I've got a nappy on just in case," announced Siobhan as she came through the door.

Liz and John followed.

"We've left the car on your drive – is that OK? We'll get it tomorrow sometime. It's not in the way, is it?"

Hilary had opened the door, leaving Suzanne trying to sort out things in the kitchen. She and Liz exchanged a kiss and a smile, looking down at Siobhan. She kissed John and directed him to the kitchen with their contribution to the dinner.

Hilary crouched down in front of Siobhan as she struggled to get her coat off without letting go of her book or her teddy.

"I love your pyjamas," she said, as the lurid pink Peppa Pig outfit was revealed. "Who's that?"

"Teddy," replied Siobhan scathingly, as if anyone should know that.

Free of her coat at last, she put her arms out to Hector, who had chosen that moment to skid into the hall. Dropping Teddy and her book in her excitement, she greeted Hector effusively. Unfortunately, he was more interested in Teddy, who looked startled as he was grabbed around the waist and whisked off into the corner. Siobhan's face crumpled, but before she could emit a single sound, Liz had picked her up and Hilary had retrieved Teddy.

Suzanne looked a little flustered as she came out of the kitchen, hearing the commotion. She was beginning to regret this new plan already. How did people manage with families? Her kitchen was no longer her own, festooned as it was with dishes, platters and unfamiliar tea towels. She'd been given advice from all sides about cooking temperatures, timings and finishing touches needed. Now all this chaos in the hall. Dogs and children – what had she been thinking of? Why did she always say yes?

Liz greeted her warmly, and Hilary looked apologetic, holding onto Hector's collar. She had only come out to open the door to help out. Now all was mayhem in this perfect house. At least the Christmas tree was still standing.

"Bed, young lady," said Liz.

"Can I sleep with Hector?"

"No. He has own bed next to the washing machine."

"Can I see it?"

"I'll show you," said Hilary, taking her hand, "while Nanny takes your things upstairs."

Siobhan, not liking anyone to be left out, put her other hand into Suzanne's and said, "Will you read me a story...please?"

"Suzanne's too busy, but I can," said David, surprising everyone with his offer and his presence. He wasn't usually a quiet observer. "I'm a very good BFG. That's a big girl's book. Do you like it?" he added, seeing the book she had brought.

"She loves it. It was Lisa's," answered Liz. "We thought it would be too old for her but she loves the sounds of the words and I think she thinks she's Sophie. She got thoroughly involved when we took her to a local stage show, and only a bit frightened." She lovingly tousled Siobhan's hair.

"Right then, you go and get into bed. I'll be up when I've made sure everyone is all right down here."

"I'm seeing Hector's bed first," Siobhan reminded him.

"Off you go then." He turned back towards the living room, not seeing the amazed glances pass between Suzanne, Liz and Hilary.

Janet and Richard had crept in during this exchange and were taking their coats off.

Seeing the disbelief on the others' faces, Janet said, "David used to love reading to Claire when she was a little girl. *The BFG* was one of his favourites."

"I never realised. However long you live with someone, there's always something new to learn." Suzanne shepherded everyone into the living room and went back to the kitchen to try to restore order.

Everything was as organised in the kitchen as it could be. Suzanne took off her apron, hung up the tea towel and, picking up her glass of wine, went to join the others in the living room. She perched on the arm of the sofa next to Hilary, who was comparing notes with Betty on the difficulties of clearing possessions that evoked so many memories.

"Suzanne really got me going. I was terrible, couldn't get started, just kept shutting the door on all Mum's things."

"I was the same when Bill died," admitted Betty. "But then, when it came to clearing the house to sell, it seemed really easy just to get rid of everything."

"It made a great excuse for some lovely shopping trips though, didn't it?" said Hilary.

"It did and it really worried David when he realised how proficient I was with online shopping. I think he thought he could see his inheritance trickling through my fingers. He needn't have worried. I still write down everything I spend and balance the books at the end of the month. I don't have a credit card. I have an old lady's fear of debt."

"I don't like debt," put in Hilary, "but I couldn't manage without a credit card. I try and pay it off every month and, if I can't, I put the brakes on my spending until I can. I'm definitely my mother's daughter."

Suzanne kept quiet, knowing that she and David used their credit cards freely. She felt his mother wouldn't approve and what she didn't know couldn't hurt her. Taking the conversation back to what was, for her, a safer topic, she said, "When we went into your mum's room that day, bizarrely, it took me back to my own childhood. It was your mum's candlewick bedspread. It brought back memories for me of my own as a child – bubble-gum pink, with a lithe netball player reaching up to score. I loved it but, whenever I was worried about something, I used to pull out the threads, creating bald patches, and then I'd chew them into a soft, comforting ball. Ugh, what a revolting child."

"That's made me think of feeding the ducks with Mum and Dad," said Hilary, "hiding from the greedy geese behind adult legs, chewing the hard, stale bread. The ducks didn't get much to eat. Ooh, I can feel it in my mouth now."

"Bread doesn't go stale like it used to, does it?" piped up Betty from her chair. "It goes mouldy and horrid – or at least the sliced spongy stuff the supermarkets call bread does."

"David used to put everything in his mouth," she continued, pulling a disapproving face. "We had a dog when he was a toddler and I soon learnt that David had to be in his high chair before I fed the dog, otherwise he'd race the dog and they'd both be tucking into the dog bowl on the floor."

She jumped as David came up behind her chair, saying, "I'm not giving you any more to drink, Mum. Who knows what you'll come out with next?" He topped up Suzanne's and Hilary's glasses.

"You're not too old to be sent to bed without supper," Betty laughed, jokingly cowering from him. "Or perhaps you are..."

He filled her glass, then turned and went to see to the other guests.

Betty continued conspiratorially, "When he was little, he had to be tucked in bed so tight. He was frightened that if he wasn't, something would take him away in the night. All his toys had to be in order, facing the right way. Bedtime was a right performance." She looked across at him, fondly remembering.

"I used to love to be tucked in too – it felt so safe. Duvets aren't the same at all," said Hilary.

"I had no idea. How long have I lived with him? Although why he would tell me something like that, I don't know. I've learnt so much since you moved in." Suzanne smiled at Betty. "That does explain why he is so fanatical about tidiness in his study, though, and why I have never yet managed to load the dishwasher to his satisfaction."

"Don't talk to me about men and dishwashers," said Liz, sitting down next to Betty, slopping her drink down her dress and ineffectually brushing it off. "John is the worst. In one of my crazy moments when he had left me, I even loaded it completely haphazardly hoping that he would turn up to tell me off and put it right. He didn't. But..." She started to look sad and tearful.

"No time to be maudlin tonight." David topped her glass back up. "Is Siobhan ready for me?"

"Definitely. She told me not to send you up too soon. She doesn't want to go to sleep yet – she wants to make the most of the great big bed with its cover like a shiny sweet wrapper. She's looking like a little princess up there. Bless her."

She turned to Suzanne. "Don't you regret not having children?"

David winced slightly at the tactless question.

"I used to," Suzanne replied honestly. "But over the years, I've realised that I'm too selfish for children. I couldn't give them everything they need. I couldn't give up my life for them, like my mother did and your mother. Even mothers who work have to give up such a big part of themselves, and I couldn't do that."

"Attention, that's what they need. Now it's the grandparents giving up their lives for the little ones."

David missed the next words as he climbed the stairs. A lump came into his throat as he looked into the spare bedroom and saw Siobhan, her pink pyjamas clashing with the shiny gold stuff of the throw that she had pulled to the top of the bed. She was earnestly telling Teddy something, showing him how the light shone on the shiny folds. He couldn't catch the words.

He wished he'd had children, but it had never happened. He assumed he couldn't. He had never been careful. Previous girlfriends had gone on to have families. When he met Suzanne, children had been mentioned and talked about as a possibility not to be discounted, but when none came, the issue was never mentioned between them. It was too late for Suzanne now and, although not impossible, too late for him too. Who wanted to be a dad in their fifties and sixties?

He had been so jealous of his brother, with the child that he wasn't bothered about. But he enjoyed being Claire's uncle, at a proper distance and without the responsibility. He had taken it very seriously when Janet had asked him to be a godparent and he would gladly have become guardian to Claire had that unlikely event ever arisen. For all sorts of reasons, he was glad that it hadn't, not least for the complications it would have caused between him and James. He knew he would never have done such a good job as Janet and Richard. It wasn't in him to make all those sacrifices – especially, like Richard, for a child that wasn't his own. You would never know. It was easy to be generous on his own terms, but as far as David could see, children took everything from you and then asked for more. Or at least that's how it appeared from the outside.

He moved from the doorway and, picking up the slightly tattered copy of *The BFG* from the dressing table, he sat on the chair beside the bed.

Siobhan shuffled across the bed and insistently patted the mattress next to her.

"Here," she said. "I want to see the words."

Self-consciously, David pushed his shoes off and sat on the edge of the bed.

"Legs up," she ordered.

He rested back on the pillows, his legs out in front of him, and she slotted her little body into the crook of his arm so that they both had the same view of the book. She wriggled impatiently and turned to the first page. He began to read.

Liz crept upstairs and peeked in to see Siobhan's eyes drooping. David looked completely relaxed and calm with Siobhan snuggled under his arm.

Liz felt herself relaxing, listening to his soft voice. It bore no resemblance to his usual harsh, loud tones. She crept down again without

265

a word and winked at Betty as she re-entered the room before picking up her glass and sitting down next to John, who was regaling Richard and Janet with details of the forthcoming wedding.

At that moment, Esmee appeared, looking a little nervous and afraid. Suzanne leapt to her side. "Did you manage to get hold of them? Esmee's been having some difficulty getting in touch with her sons," she explained to the others. Putting her arm around Esmee's shoulder she drew her into the circle and introduced her.

"Lovely to meet you."

"We've heard lots about you."

"Sorry for your loss."

"I'm very pleased meeting you all. I feel I know you. I am sorry for being late." Esmee was swept in amongst them.

After a few minutes, David reappeared and started topping up glasses again. "You've emerged, Esmee. Everything OK at home?" He kissed her on the cheek.

Suzanne took the opportunity to go to the kitchen to organise the food. She finally felt relaxed. Everything was going well. David came up behind her on the way to get another bottle and, putting his arms around her waist, he snuggled his face into her neck. "I do love you, you know," he said. Suzanne leaned back into his arms, turned, kissed him and then pushed him away.

"Duty calls. Their glasses won't fill themselves and I've somehow got to get all this hot and on the table to everyone's satisfaction."

"It will be perfect. You are lovely, you know."

"I know, I know. Open the bottle, you sloppy thing."

Hilary came in at that moment. "Can I help – take things through, garnishing, whatever?"

"Thank you, Hilary. Can you check what temperature we need for Liz's dish? Mmm, it does look lovely."

"This is my brother, Dan,' said Carol to Hilary as she came past.

"Nice to meet you. Would you like a crisp or some nuts?" She held the bowls out to him. "Are you staying in Barwell long?"

Dan flapped his hand in front of his mouth as he tried to swallow the peanuts without choking.

"We don't know yet," said Carol. "As long as he wants to."

"Sorry," said Dan, as he finally managed to swallow. "Yes, I'm not sure what's going to happen yet. It's all a bit up in the air."

Carol moved away and Dan, left with Hilary, still proffering her bowls of nuts and crisps, said, "Do you live nearby?"

"Yes, just opposite – the bungalow, the drive directly opposite. I've always lived there. Don't you live near Leeds? I seem to remember Carol saying that your daughters went to university in Leeds to be near home…"

"I did. I've moved out."

"Oh."

"My wife and I have split up."

"Oh, I'm sorry."

"Yes, so am I." Dan looked around as if for an escape route and just at that moment David came over and asked him to help get some more drink out of the garage.

"Sorry, Hilary, I've got to steal Dan for a mo."

Dan breathed a sigh of relief as he followed David.

Hilary was just going to continue her rounds when Suzanne appeared at her elbow and took the dishes from her. "Come on, Hilary, you're not staff. You've done enough. You're here to enjoy yourself. Come and talk to Esmee and the others. Where's your glass?"

With a replenished glass, Hilary was steered towards Esmee. They smiled at each other, both a little nervous and Hilary sat for a few moments sipping her drink, wondering if perhaps there was something that she could be doing in the kitchen. Esmee broke the ice by saying, "I love your dog." There was no stopping Hilary on that subject and when Suzanne glanced across a few minutes later they were chatting like old friends.

Across the living room Carol and Liz were sitting on the settee with Betty. Carol and Liz were comparing notes about grandchildren; Betty was lost in her own thoughts.

She was sorry that she only had one grandchild, but Claire had turned into such a lovely young woman, so caring and calm, nothing like her father. Even Betty had to admit that James was selfish and thoughtless. She loved him – he was her son – but she didn't like the way he treated others. David was full of bluster, but he was generous to a fault and always put others first. She couldn't think where James had got it from. Her late husband had been so kind and gentle. Perhaps he had been too gentle and perhaps she had been too indulgent towards her younger son. His birth had been so difficult that she had been advised against further pregnancies. So, knowing that he was her last, she had spoilt him. David had been such a self-sufficient little boy with his funny fears and routines that, she admitted to herself now, she had given more of her time and energy to James. He had been more fun, more responsive. At least he seemed settled now in Australia. It was probably more suited to his unpredictable ways.

She couldn't believe how settled she herself felt now and how well she was getting on with Suzanne. She loved living in the flat, with its clean lines and new furniture devoid of all but a few ornaments. She was excited about the prospect of redeveloping the site of the old family home. She'd had no idea how imaginative David was. Who would have thought that all this could open up for her in her eighties?

She had been devastated when Bill had died. It had all seemed to happen so quickly; his last months went by in a blur of confusion and pain. David had been so good, considering how he hated illness, but he was so practical and always seemed to have answers for every problem that arose. Betty now wondered how much of that knowledge had come via Suzanne.

James had phoned, every day, offering sympathy, but he was never there. He didn't even manage to get back for the funeral. He just arranged some completely inappropriate flowers that Bill would have hated. She loved to hear from him – he'd always be her baby, but…

She jumped as David tapped his glass to quieten the chatter to announce that dinner was ready. No-one seemed to have noticed that she had been in her own little world as they had talked. Richard came and helped her to her feet and everyone made their way to the dining room.

The sideboard was loaded with colourful, wonderful-smelling steaming dishes, the table laden with bowls of vegetables and salads.

Suzanne brought the last dish through from the kitchen and placed it on a trivet in the centre of the sideboard.

"I know it was supposed to be a buffet, but I think it would be easier if I served everyone from here and David can be waitress – I'll find him a pinny and lacy cap."

Esmee looked a little bemused as everyone laughed, failing to understand the joke.

Richard, sitting down next to her, gave a whispered explanation.

"A toast to our hosts," said Jonathan, raising his glass. Everyone joined him in a toast and Suzanne started to serve the food.

Glasses were filled with wine, plates were piled high with food, and the noise of conversation and the rattle of cutlery against plates rose and fell. Compliments about the food flew around the room. No-one saw a little pink-clad person, followed by a small brown dog, creep in and slink under the table.

"That's my foot," said Carol crossly to Jonathan, as a weight leant on the corn on her middle toe.

"What?"

"You're on my foot."

"I can't be. There's a table leg between us."

Carol looked across at David opposite and, realising it couldn't be him, lifted the table cloth. A wet nose brushed her hand and four bright, brown eyes stared at her, a cheeky grin next to a soft brown muzzle.

"What are you doing there?" spluttered John, seeing what Carol had revealed.

"We came to see. I'm being very quiet."

"How did you get in here? I didn't see you come in."

"We came through the legs. Legs can't see."

"She's got a point there," said Richard, trying not to laugh.

"But you were asleep," said David, lifting the cloth at the other side of the table.

"Hector came up and got me. He jumped on the bed."

"*What?*" Hilary leapt up. Her silver sequined dress shimmered indignantly as she ran after Hector, who was making his escape to the kitchen, realising he had misjudged the situation. By the time Hilary caught up with him to remonstrate, he was curled up in his basket, perfectly still apart from the tip of his tail, which beat a cheerful tattoo on the side of his bed.

"Bad dog." He looked suitably chastened. "How could you? We'll have to go home." She was almost in tears.

"Of course, you won't. Don't be ridiculous. Everyone thinks it's hilarious. Come on back to the table." Suzanne gently guided her back to her seat.

Siobhan was still holding court under the table.

"Enough now, madam. Let's get you back to bed. If you are lucky, you'll go to sleep in the toffee-wrapper bed and wake up in your bed at ours." John was trying to entice her.

"*Now*," said Liz, standing no more nonsense, aware of everyone's cooling dinners.

They all unsuccessfully tried to keep a straight face as Siobhan crawled out between Esmee and Richard's chairs.

"What's your name?" she asked.

"Esmee."

"Esmee's from Holland," explained Richard.

"Do you live in a windmill?"

"Siobhan," growled Liz threateningly. "Bed."

Siobhan grabbed Teddy, who had somehow ended up under the sideboard, and scampered up the stairs, leaving silence followed by a burst of laughter before everyone got back to the serious business of eating.

Liz slipped back into her seat a minute or two later, after giving John whispered instructions to check on the little monkey in five minutes.

"She's a delight. I miss the nonsense – or is it sense? – they come out with at that age. Ours are getting too grown up and sensible," said Jonathan wistfully.

David got awkwardly to his feet, jamming his chair against the sideboard. Suzanne's face became anxious at the thought of scratches on the wood, but she didn't say anything, as, dropping his napkin on the floor, David tapped the side of his glass. As silence fell, he said, "Let's have a toast."

Pushing back their chairs, everyone tried to get up. With a lot of scraping, shuffling and groaning, they all got to their feet and picked up their glasses.

"To new friends," he said, raising his glass to Esmee and Dan.

He turned towards his mother. "To new neighbours."

"To new beginnings," he said to Liz and John.

To Hilary, who blushed scarlet, he said, "To reincarnations."

"And, finally, to everything that reassuringly remains the same." Carol and Jonathan smiled, and touched glasses, taking that toast for themselves but realising that it was probably aimed more at Suzanne.

"To us," they all replied.

"To change."

"To everything the same."

"To us."

They touched glasses across the table, drank a toast and then shuffled back into their seats. Esmee looked a little bemused, but smiled through the whole process. It was so lovely to be among these people. She turned to Jonathan to continue their conversation about the Wendy house he had built for the grandchildren. The noise of chatter and cutlery rose again. Suzanne and Hilary cleared empty dishes from the centre of the table, declining Esmee's offer of ''elp'.

The next course was laid out to exclamations of praise. Hilary took her seat next to David.

As she put her napkin back across her lap, a rare moment of silence fell, which David inadvertently filled with "And now for the $64,000 question. What are you going to do about the manuscript?"

All eyes fell on Hilary. They waited as she straightened her knife and fork.

"Nothing."

"What?"

"*Nothing?*"

"You can't hide it away again."

"Think of the money."

The incredulous exclamations battered her from all sides. Holding up her hand to deflect them and quieten the clamour, she continued, "I couldn't publish it. I couldn't cope with the embarrassment. And think of Mum's acquaintances and friends around here. What on earth would they do? It would kill some of them. They are more prudish than the pope. Unless it could be done anonymously, a pseudonym perhaps, in another country... But with the internet, if it was any sort of success, it would lead back here. I couldn't cope with it. Even if it was only a minor, local success, that free magazine would pick it up – they are always looking for something to fill their pages. They'd have a field day and I'd die of embarrassment. I think I'd feel the same whatever the book was about. I can't cope with it at the moment. I'm getting used to the fact that Mum was someone I really didn't know. A very clever talented woman, who had more secrets than I don't know what, but I want to keep her to myself for at least a little while longer. Perhaps I could leave something in my will to make sure it got published after I died. It would be safe then. No-one could get hurt and I'm sure I could think of a charity that could benefit – Marie Stopes or something." She stopped and looked embarrassed for having held court for so long. She fiddled self-consciously with her knife and fork.

"I can see what you mean, Hilary," said Richard. "If it was published and successful, which of course is not a given, it would mean that you would still be living life through your mum. I think it's about time you had a bit of your own life without her influence."

"You are right, Richard. Hilary deserves a bit of freedom," agreed Janet.

"I'm trying to work out what Mum would have wanted," said Hilary, "and it's so hard. Surely if she had wanted it published, she would have just done it. She wasn't exactly backward in coming forward."

"She obviously left it until after your dad died. Perhaps she had forgotten all about it." David picked up the wine bottle and refilled their glasses.

"I don't know. I feel a bit helpless because the trouble is she would have known what to do straight away. She would certainly have told me what to do. I thought I was independent before she died. I had no idea!"

"You'll know what to do when the time is right. There is no rush. I suppose we all want a bit of excitement, but you do what you think is right. You have changed so much in the last few months, reinvented yourself. You wouldn't say boo to a goose and if we'd had this conversation last year, you'd have just done as we all suggested – you would have just been swept along without thinking. I admire you for standing your ground." Suzanne held her glass up to Hilary and smiled.

"For the moment, it's like having a lottery ticket and not checking the numbers," said Liz. "You're a winner until you find out that you're not. *We* all think that the book is great, but what if you can't find a publisher. What if it's published and it flops? What if it was written about a real person and they come forward and sue?"

"That's right, Liz. Look on the bright side. It's already given me more than money ever could. It sounds a bit melodramatic, but it's given me permission to live a little. Mum had her life and her adventures when she was young and then she knuckled down to the mundane and a life of sameness. I've done that bit – now it's my turn to live. Oh no, don't worry, I'm not going to go mad, but Hector and I are going to have some fun. He was my first rebellion. I'm going to change the house. I've already had a go at me. You've all said Mum wouldn't recognise me – I think she would. I think this is how she would have liked me to have been. I think I was always a disappointment to her. I was useful, but she often said that I had no spark, too much like Dad. Dad and I both bowed down to her wishes and let her have her own way and let her control us. I need to have my own bit of freedom. I'm going to have a life."

To her surprise, David clapped his hands. "Well done, Hilary. Go get 'em."

"What a speech."

"Oh, er, I'm sorry. You should have stopped me going on."

"Oh Hilary, you look so different, but don't change too much," said Suzanne affectionately.

Everyone started to talk together and Hilary turned to David and said, "Are you sure I'm doing the right thing?"

"Definitely."

"I worry that I may need the money it could bring in, but I genuinely think that no amount of money could compensate for the trouble it would bring."

"You stick to your guns and enjoy yourself. I can't wait to get going on your bungalow."

"You always worry too much Hilary. I'm a great believer in fate," added Liz from across the table, wiping her lips on her napkin. "You'll know what to do when the time is right. I'm like David though, I tend to dive in and do things straight away and then I have to let fate – or John – sort it all out."

"I'm very jealous that you are going to make all these changes, letting David loose on your bungalow," said Janet. "But I'm more interested in where you got your hair done. I love it. You are very brave."

Talk turned to things David had no interest in, so he pushed back his chair, picked up the bottle and got up to refill glasses and help Suzanne.

Liz came down from checking on Siobhan, now sleeping peacefully, the toffee-wrapper throw pulled up onto her pillow.

Hector was chewing the last of the bones from the sticky-rib starter.

They were all full to bursting but still picking at the cheeses left on the table and, although a groan went up when Suzanne appeared with a massive box of chocolates, no-one was able to refuse.

"We should dance," said Liz, making no move to get up. "Work a bit of it off. You must have a dance playlist on this fancy system of yours."

'Frosty the Snowman' was playing for the second time, the Phil Spector Christmas album interspersed with carols from King's College and a smattering of Slade. More left-overs from Christmas.

David took his mobile out of his pocket. "Motown or seventies music?" he asked.

A chorus of "Motown" seemed to galvanise them into action. They moved through to the living room, picking up their glasses from the table, Liz topping hers up as she passed the bottle, Carol collecting a chocolate as she passed the box – my last, she promised herself. Jonathan and David were manoeuvring the coffee table out of the way, and Richard rolled up the pale expensive-looking rug as he saw Liz shimmying through with a glass of red in her hand. The dancing started.

Suzanne took the opportunity to slip into the kitchen and try to find her way through the chaos. Janet joined her, wishing she could feel jollier. She usually loved these dos. She loved dancing, but tonight she wasn't in the mood. She picked out a dry tea towel and started drying as Suzanne washed.

"Sorry to hear your Christmas was a bit stressful."

"Oh, it was OK. Julia annoyed me but, actually, the fact that she takes nothing seriously helped in an odd sort of way – and Dad certainly appreciated her being there. He thought she had made a special effort and I certainly wasn't going to disabuse him of that belief. He's got enough on his plate without having to know how selfish his daughter is."

"He must know though."

"They've always been a bit blind to her faults. It was me who couldn't do anything right for years. She was the golden girl and she's never lost that veneer. Life's not fair. Oh, I'm sorry. I wish I could stop being such a misery. I couldn't even be bothered to dance. I thought I'd just come and do a bit of clearing up on my own."

"But I'd had the same idea," Suzanne interrupted, putting the last of the dishes on the drainer. "It's been a bit of a rollercoaster this year, hasn't it? And then Jag deciding to go off for a year knocked me sideways. I don't know why really. I've worked there long enough to know what I'm doing. I had such a wobble poor David thought I'd got some incurable disease or something, but being David he just came out with it one night when he came in from the pub and, bless him, he was so relieved that I was just worried about Jag going. It sort of put it into perspective for me too. What a year! Still, another three quarters of an hour and it will be over. Come on, everything else can go in the dishwasher. I feel a bit better now that it looks a bit tidier. I'll just put all these tea towels in the washing machine and we'll go and join the others. Where's your drink?"

*

Mary Wells was singing her heart out when they got back to the living room to see all their friends dancing away with varying degrees of style and rhythm.

Liz and John were in what could only be described as a clinch, Liz held firmly in John's arms to stop her swaying. Carol was serenading Jonathan. What took Janet and Suzanne by surprise was the extravagant moves Hilary and Esmee were making as they sang "My Guy" into imaginary microphones clutched to their chests for a rather bemused audience of Richard and David.

They lost no time in reclaiming their men. Janet let the music and the rhythm take her and was soon belting out the words, leaving Richard in no doubt about her feelings, but no less self-conscious about his lack of skill on the dance floor. David was throwing himself about now that he was on safer ground with Suzanne. Dan was looking a bit lost and quiet, but Betty, fired up by the wine and general frivolity, got him to pull her out of her chair and was soon moving with the music.

"It's quarter to. We need to get the champagne poured. Let's hope the display is as good as last year. Come on through." Suzanne chivvied them along, securing a comfy seat for Betty and putting a glass into her hand before seeing to the rest of them.

"Where's Hilary?"

"Getting Hector. She doesn't want him worried by the fireworks." John came in with a sleepy Siobhan in his arms.

"I went to the loo and a little voice called out to me," he said, before Liz could tell either of them off. "I thought she could watch the fireworks."

The grandfather clock started to chime at exactly the same time as Big Ben on Radio 2 and they noisily raised their glasses to say goodbye to the old year and welcome the new. They sang a muddled verse of Auld Lang Syne as the first fireworks shot into the sky with screeches and bangs.

Hector stood shivering ignominiously behind all the legs, his nose nuzzling for comfort in Hilary's palm. How he wished those horrible high-pitched whooshes would stop.

Snuggling into John's neck, Siobhan opened her eyes wide as a bright red flare shot into the air, a million silver shards flying out of the top of it. "Look Nanny, someone's opened up the sky."

As Siobhan spoke, they all laughed and looked at her, a little ray of hope for the future.

Acknowledgements

I wish to thank the tutors at the Arvon Foundation who gave me the skills to create and the courage to delete. Also, Jan Birley from Writers' Retreat UK who helped me to believe in myself.

I am indebted to my husband, Stuart Lloyd-Beavis, and mother-in-law, Margaret Beavis, for their support and encouragement. To Claire Morris, Usha James and Keith Munro for reading the manuscript at various stages and helping me to move forward. To my sister, Janice Morris, for her unstinting patience and her ability to boost my flagging confidence.

Finally, I wish to thank Alice van Raalte at SilverWood Books for gently guiding me through the publishing process.

Lightning Source UK Ltd.
Milton Keynes UK
UKHW010727220121
377506UK00001B/21

JACQUELINE JAMES is a retired GP now living in Cambridge. Born in Solihull she went to Sheffield University Medical school, qualifying in 1980 and, after a stint in hospitals, became a GP and family planning doctor in 1986, first in inner city Sheffield and then in rural Cambridgeshire. She retired in 2016 in order to spend more time writing. This is her first novel.